Flashpoint

The Speculative Elements
Volume 4

A Cape Breton Anthology

Edited by:

Sherry D. Ramsey | Julie A. Serroul | Nancy S.M. Waldman

Third Person Press
Cape Breton, NS

First Published in 2014

Third Person Press
Email: thirdpersonpress@gmail.com
Web: www.thirdpersonpress.com
Cape Breton, Nova Scotia, Canada

Flashpoint: The Speculative Elements, v. 4
Print ISBN: 978-0-9936325-0-1
Ebook ISBN: 978-0-9936325-1-8

To our wonderful husbands, Terry, Barry and Greg.

For supporting us in this crazy game we play. For not committing us when we not only talk to our characters, but also insist that they answer back. For understanding that our far-away stares are not inattentiveness, but the birth of new story ideas. For thinking we are the most brilliant writer on any planet, no matter what that stupid editor said. And for their patience in this, our other labour of love: Third Person Press.

*The Speculative Elements Series
from Third Person Press*

Undercurrents

Airborne

Unearthed

Also from Third Person Press

To Unimagined Shores,
the Collected Stories of Sherry D. Ramsey

Grey Area:
Thirteen Ghost Stories

Contents

Introduction *by D.C. Troicuk*   7

A Year and a Day *by Stephanie Snow*   11

Epilogue *by Jenn Tubrett*   19

Battle Scars *by Patrick M. Charron*   31

Invasive Species *by Peter Andrew Smith*   51

B.R.A.N.E., Inc. *by Sherry D. Ramsey*   65

The Fire-Eater *by Donald Tyson*   93

And Again *by Bruce V. Miller*   105

Fever *by Kerry Anne Fudge*   113

Hair Trigger *by Katrina Nicholson*   137

Burning Fear *by Steven Fraser MacLean*   163

Spark *by Julie A. Serroul*   171

Flame Out *by Sue McKay Miller*   199

Keeza's Retribution *by Bridget Sprouls*   215

Loving After Dark *by Larry A. Gibbons*   225

Hearth's Glow *by Nancy S.M. Waldman*   239

Introduction

It seems whenever I mention that I write speculative fiction (spec-fic), the question pops up: what is that? I keep it simple: spec-fic is a genre that incorporates any element of unreality. If further pressed (I never have been) I would add that these elements may be as wild as a "trip" on some hallucinogenic drug, or as subtle as a feather wafting, inconspicuously out of place, on a light summer breeze.

I cut my speculative fiction teeth reading in the science fiction sub-genre—space adventures and aliens, and the wonders of future tech, which are now either laughably out of date or amazingly, often frighteningly, close to fruition. It wasn't until I discovered Ray Bradbury (*Fahrenheit 451*) and Robert A. Heinlein (*Orphans of the Sky*) that I thought, *this* is what I want to write. The possibilities of societies and governments and relationships— in addition to all the alternative realities that a writer's mind may conceive. And although my work has diverted away from these realms, I thoroughly enjoy diving back in whenever I have the chance.

When you think about it, the origins of spec-fic go as far back as story-telling itself. Primitive man devised tales of nature gods to explain aspects of their world. Likewise, a long list of Egyptian gods and Greek gods and Roman gods populate the stories of their respective cultures. In more modern times, we circulate creepy urban legends, pass on accounts of Sasquatch and the Loch Ness monster and the Wendigo that stalks the woods and devours human flesh. What are Grimms' Fairy Tales, Aesop's Fables, 1001 Arabian Nights, if not spec-fic? Or Dr. Seuss, or Dennis Lee. Or classics from Mary Shelley and Jules Verne and George Orwell.

As spec-fic writers, we are not totally without limits. We have one single constraint, an important one: the world we draw must be real, in its own context, for the reader. Reading the fifteen stories in this volume, I've been pulled into fifteen different realities. I doubt two of them could exist together. But that is the joy of reading – and of writing – spec-fic. We put our logic on hold and let something awesome fill our minds with possibilities that we have not—perhaps no one has—ever considered.

Sometimes the theme is a familiar one, though the tales told are as unique as the individual writer. Sue McKay Miller borrows on myth for her story "Flame Out," where Greek gods involve a modern couple in their age-old squabble over the gift of fire. Stephanie Snow, in her story "A Year and a Day," draws on the folktale of a soul sold in exchange for favour.

Some stories raise the little hairs on the back of your neck. In "Loving After Dark" by Larry A. Gibbons, the depths of grief and loss lead a man into "the dark behind the dark," where spec-fic often goes. As does Donald Tyson's tale "The Fire-Eater," where one little boy learns what a dollar can buy at the carnival.

On the action/adventure side, Patrick M. Charron's "Battle Scars" tells of warring peoples and heroic sacrifice, while Katrina Nicholson's heroine had me on the edge of my seat in "Hair Trigger," a story of Cave Divers who scout the moon's ice mines for nuclear bombs that must be disarmed. (Tick. Tick. Tick.) Another unlikely heroine in "Hearth's Glow," by Nancy S.M. Waldman, works to evacuate a starship's population before the coredrive meltdown.

There are lessons to be learned in these pages. For example, in "Keeza's Retribution" by Bridget Sprouls: when disaster hits, look to the eccentric neighbour, but first consider how you have treated her. "Fever" by Kerry Anne Fudge warns us: when humans play with witches and vampires, the game of Truth or Dare can have dangerous consequences. (I'll have to remember that one!)

Aliens and terrestrial "others" may have their own agendas, but that doesn't make them monsters. In "Spark," Julie A. Serroul's pair of impulsive Blikkets are pursued to Earth by a well-intentioned, tentacled commander. And the "Invasive Species" of Peter Andrew Smith are familiar faces in our Cape Breton forests. Well, sort of.

Folklore tells of elves and faeries, sirens and silkies, banshees and trolls and all manner of supernatural beings. I seriously doubt you'll ever encounter a brownie when you stick your hand into a photocopier to pull out a jammed sheet, but after reading "B.R.A.N.E., Inc." by Sherry D. Ramsey, you may never look at the photocopier guy in the same way again.

Bruce V. Miller's selection, "And Again," is an example of that subtle feather wafting down, reminiscent of waking from a mildly disturbing dream, lying in bed and replaying it until you can resolve it. If you can.

And, of course, no spec-fic collection would be complete without an end-of-the-world story. Jenn Tubrett brings us "Epilogue," the android that seeks to carry on with its mission of being "useful" after the Earth's surface becomes habitable again.

"Burning Fear" by Steven Fraser MacLean raises the question I've been asking in writing this: where does real life leave off, and spec-fic begin? Somewhere in the world there may very well be a psychiatrist like Dr. Stanton. If there is, I see a reality show in the near future.

One more thing: always remember—the brownies are on our side.

D.C. Troicuk
October 2014

D. C. Troicuk's short fiction has appeared in *The Antigonish Review*, *The Nashwaak Review*, *The Gaspereau Review*, *Pottersfield Portfolio* as well as several anthologies. Her first book, *Loose Pearls and Other Stories*, was released in 2010 to favourable reviews. Publication of her first novel *The Value of the Land* is scheduled for late autumn 2014. She is a past contributor to The Speculative Elements series from Third Person Press.

Stephanie Snow

A Year and a Day

I heard the voice as I approached the grave, but I ignored it for now. There would be time for it soon.

Instead, I pushed through the dry, withered grass at the edge of the woods to kneel down by the grave marker. The blaze of the flowers I had brought—red and orange, his favourite—looked surreal in the dead landscape. This year's drought, the worst in a decade of them, had stunted the growth for hundreds of miles around our little farm, but a mat of yellowing grasses still struggled to cover Dennis' name and dates. I didn't need to see them, since I knew both as well as my own, but I started to clear it anyway.

The voice wouldn't leave me alone. It had grown bolder in the last few months. *One more day, Helen,* it whispered, coiling around me like smoke. It could have been nothing more than the wind through the dead grass, but I knew better. I had made that mistake once before. *One more day, and this is how you choose to spend it?*

Ignoring it as best I could, I pulled up clumps of dry grass and weeds, piling them to one side with the remains of the flowers I had brought every week for almost a year. I never bothered to get rid of them once I moved them from the grave, and now a stack of dried flowers and grass crouched behind the marker, rattling in the breeze.

The air stirred at my side, against the hot flow of the wind. *You should be preparing yourself,* it said, its tone the mockery of solicitude I remembered from the night of the accident. *Your time grows short and the transition will be…difficult.*

Not nearly as difficult as the last year, I thought. As far as I knew, it couldn't hear my thoughts. But I knew it wouldn't go away, either.

"It'll be what it is," I said, not taking my eyes off the grave marker. I had carved it myself, out of a plank of oak that Dennis had set aside for his new desk. I wasn't nearly as skilled at woodworking as he had been, but it would have been impossible not to pick up a few things after being married to him for ten years. I didn't think I'd done too bad a job.

All things considered.

Regrets? The voice was closer now, stronger. It had been intensifying ever since we struck our deal; now it seemed like anyone could have heard it. Not that I'd ever tested this theory. *Do you regret your choice now, Helen?*

It liked to say my name. Maybe because I'd had to give it when I made the deal. "I have a lot of regrets."

Humans usually do. The air moved around me, caressing insistently, tugging at the edges of Dennis' oversized denim jacket. It was far too warm for the coat—for any coat, really—but I ignored the sweat rolling down my back and continued pulling weeds. *There are no regrets here, with me.*

"Is that so?" I had cleared the grass from the dates, and felt again that sorrowing shock of wonder that Dennis had been dead nearly a year. "Sounds boring."

A pause. *What?*

I smiled; the movement felt odd, as if I had forgotten how to do it. "No regrets means no mistakes," I said, piling more dead grass. "And the only way that happens is if no one ever chooses to do anything." Now I paused, looking at the empty air between me and the trees. *Almost* empty, I should say; there were disturbances in the air which could have been mistaken for heat shimmers. "But that's how your people work, isn't it?"

Another pause. I could sense its confusion. I had barely talked to it for a year, preferring to spend my time at the grave thinking about happier times. *What?*

"You *can't* choose." I knew I shouldn't antagonize it, not now, but I've always had a spiteful streak. "You don't have the necessary free will."

Coldness, unknown in this baking summer, rippled through the air. *I have everything I desire.*

~ *Flashpoint* ~

I nodded amiably, a debater conceding that their opponent had made a worthy, if short-sighted, point. "Agreed. That's how you work, too." The pile of grass stirred a little in the breeze, a few pieces drifting away toward the woods. "I've been doing the research. For years, actually. I'm a folklorist. Did I ever mention that?"

Humans know nothing about me. About us.

"Oh, that's not true. I have books and books at home about your kind." I looked over my shoulder, back toward the empty house. I hadn't cared for the property as much as I should have the last year—overgrown grass and bushes abounded—but the neat farmhouse stood alone on this piece of land. The quiet had been one of the reasons we'd bought the place. That, and the closeness of the woods. Dennis and I had both enjoyed hiking.

"The deal isn't new. And you've been active around here for centuries. Maybe longer, but that's as far back as the news archives went." The breeze had pushed my hair into my face, and I ran my dirty hands back through it. "And it's always the same: people get lost. Like we did. I thought it was odd at the time." A glance at the trees, dark on the edge of the land. "After all, the woods aren't *that* big."

I am skilled. I could hear its smugness, and wished it had a face I could hit. *No one can find the path through unless I let them.*

"I certainly didn't. Not even after three days." The bright sunlight vanished around me, replaced by the cold and the dark of the trees on that third night. Hungry, exhausted, frightened... we must have been easy prey. "But that was the idea, right? Make us desperate."

I'd seen you before, it hissed, the cool breeze rustling through my hair like invisible hands. *Always walking in my woods. Always with that man.*

I stood suddenly, as much to get away from that touch as anything, and picked up the armload of dead grass and greying flowers. "We still would have been fine if Dennis hadn't fallen on that third night." The snap of bones in the dark, blood black against the tree roots. "We would have found our way."

You did find a way. It was laughing at me. *Once you agreed to my terms, I showed you one.*

"Let me know if I've remembered the terms correctly." I started to walk toward the woods, wiping sweat from my face awkwardly with one shoulder since my hands were full. The weight of the coat and its contents dragged at my shoulders. "My life for his. Dennis would live. And I'd get a year and a day grace period before..." I had to clear my throat. "Before I had to leave. And nothing would harm me in that time."

I wouldn't want anyone else taking what was mine. The grasses rustled, and I tightened my grip on them. *Not even you. Just in case you attempted...another escape.*

"Well, I never," I said as if I hadn't thought of it every night for months, before my grief hardened into something else. "No one can say I didn't hold up my end."

As did I. A contract like that cannot be broken, even by me. The man lived. He would still live, if not for you.

That just reminded me of the last words Dennis' mother had shouted at me, tears streaming down her face at the funeral home. "Living is broadly defined, then. He was comatose and brain dead." I remembered the doctors and their plastic sympathy when they told me, and the decision I made. "A blow to the head from his fall, as it turned out. A fall that *you* engineered."

Nevertheless, he lived. I did not break the contract.

"In word, no. In spirit...well, a couple of good lawyers would have a field day with it, but somehow I didn't think I could find one to take the case." I was within the shadow of the trees now, their coolness welcome after the heat of the day. "At least I never found any mention of fairy lawyers."

Do not call us that, it hissed. Here under the trees, the voice was louder, and the leaves rustled from its anger. *That is not our name.*

"I'm just talking." Leaves crunched underfoot. The drought had taken many of them already, as if fall had come early, and the air smelled like a desert tomb. "You like to talk all the time."

This is my place. I can do what I like here, Helen. As you'll soon discover.

"*Not yet,*" I snapped, my temper fraying. "One more day, remember?"

Oh yes. One more day. And you spend it here, with the remains of the stupid man who led you into this situation. You sacrificed yourself to me for him, and he's not even here, it said. *I was hoping you would run. Then we could have roused the Hunt, and had a chase.*

"Why should I run?" Pushing through one last clump of bushes, I reached the clearing. "This is where I need to be."

The clearing looked a little different now than it had that

night a year ago. Then it had seemed like shelter, and when the voice had spoken, I'd thought it a miraculous place. Now I saw it for what it was: a trap.

The trees here were large, much larger than they should have been, this close to the border of a small wood. These leafy giants belonged in the heart of the deep forest. Maybe that's what this place had been, once upon a time, before humans hacked away at the edges, making homes and fields and roads. Now it was a small remnant, clinging to the border of town, but power still lingered here. I could feel it.

I came to a halt before the largest of the trees. It radiated strength even now, when all around it withered under the punishing blows of the sun, but it still looked a little tired. Its leaves drooped slightly, conserving their strength, waiting for rain that refused to come.

The air stirred, pushing the dead leaves of the clearing into a swirling column. If I squinted and kept it in the corner of my eye, it almost looked like a human shape, standing in the middle of the empty space. *You have come to offer yourself early?* It sounded amused at the idea. *Perhaps in the hopes of mercy?*

I laughed at that, a sound I'd forgotten almost as much as the smile. "Hell, no. If you can't break that contract, I'm damn sure I wouldn't be able to." I dropped the heap of grass and flowers at my feet, between a couple of twisted roots. Drifts of leaves had been pushed against the base by the wind. "Besides, I intend to enjoy my last day of freedom."

By talking with me? The leaf-figure moved toward me on the breeze. Folded leaves and shadows lent it a face. *You will be doing that soon anyway, once you make the crossing to the Court. I have many, many things I wish to know from you.*

I shrugged and sat at the foot of the tree. "It doesn't matter." Looking up, I studied the ancient tree, watching the sunlight shift through the brown-edged leaves. It didn't look like any type of tree I'd seen before. "This is yours, isn't it? Wasn't it an oak before?"

It shrugged as well, an oddly human gesture. *It appeared so. But there is no longer any reason to maintain the illusion with you.*

"And illusion takes power, right? There's always a cost." I dropped my head to look at it. A crown of gold-tinged leaves circled its head, I noticed now. "You talk about how powerful you are, but the power has to come from somewhere. And yours

~ Flashpoint ~

comes from here." I patted the bark. "It must be hard in this kind of weather. The drought must sap your energy." There was no reply, but I could sense its confusion, as if a sheep had quizzed the butcher about his financial practices. "Like it did back in the eighties. And during the Dust Bowl."

What?

"I found the missing persons reports in the records. The pattern wasn't hard to figure out." I looked at the tree again. It really *was* beautiful, something I could appreciate in a way that I hadn't been able to until now. "When you can't live on this...you live on us."

A ripple ran through the leaf-figure. I wondered if that was how it showed uncertainty, or if I was ascribing far too human an emotion to it.

You know nothing.

"I know a little," I disagreed mildly, shrugging off my coat. I heard the swish and clink of the things inside, and wondered if that leaf-body had ears that worked. "I know this is your place. You told me so."

It moved so fast I barely saw it shift before it was in front of me. I got the impression it wanted to hit me, but it didn't. Or couldn't. *Of course it is, foolish woman, foolish mortal. And here I am all-powerful.*

"Not quite. There's one thing stronger than you here: the contract." Fishing in the pocket of my jeans, I glanced up at the figure, which still hovered over me. "You're just as shackled by it as I am. More, actually, because unlike you, I still have choices." My fingers closed on what I'd been searching for, but I kept my hand in my pocket. "So, I'm choosing."

It laughed, the leaves shaking. *Your only choice is whether to come to me willingly, or be dragged to the Court screaming.*

"No," I said, standing. "I have one more."

In one motion, pulled out the bundle of safety matches and flicked one with my nail. I'd practiced this at home for the last week, making sure I could do it when I needed to. It flared to life, a hot spark in my hand, and started to spread to the others. "My choice," I said, and dropped the burning bundle into the pile of dead grass and leaves at the base of the tree.

It snarled, a much less human sound than before, and lunged for me. I made no move to defend myself, laughing again when it passed through me like a breeze, throwing itself on the fire. "I guess that 'no harm' clause really *does* work, then."

~ Flashpoint ~

No! The leaves burned like tissue, going up in puffs and flares. *This won't work, stupid woman! Not with dead leaves and grass and—*

Behind me, I felt the blast of heat as the flames reached my coat and the fire starters and lighter fluid concealed inside. Normally, I would have had to step back, but now the heat didn't seem to touch me, either. I supposed there were some useful parts of that contract. "You were saying?"

It screamed now, screamed as I had when Dennis fell in the woods that night: high and hysterical and filled with loss. The sound made me smile again. I was starting to get used to it.

The fire raced up the trunk of the tree, but the leaf-figure, still burning, staggered upright. *All you've done is anger me, Helen,* it hissed, every word a promise of pain. *This will not end our deal. And this will certainly not kill me.*

"No, I didn't think it would." Turning, I looked up. Leaves sparked and flared far above, already spreading the fire to other, less powerful trees. "But I'm betting it will weaken you. Maybe enough so that, during the next drought, you won't be able to take someone when you need them." Smoke and sparks drifted, filling the surrounding woods. "And you're going to find it damn hard to lead people astray without cover."

You will suffer for this! The leaf body was falling to pieces, the golden crown blackened and crumbling. *The contract still stands, foolish woman, and I swear you will pay for this!*

"I imagine so." Putting my hands in my pockets, I watched the blue-orange flames race skyward. The intense heat, fanned by the breeze, blackened the sky. "But you won't catch anyone else the way you caught me."

I started out of the woods, back to Dennis' grave. In the echoes of my memory, I could imagine him laughing, and the thought warmed me like the fire at my back.

I turned once more, watching the leaves crumble to ash, and smiled at the figure standing in the middle of the flames. "See you tomorrow."

~ Flashpoint ~

Stephanie Snow will one day be on your money as the Master of the Robot Army, but until then she writes, blogs, and runs amok in Nova Scotia, Canada. She recently learned how to use a sword, which probably won't turn out well for anyone. For updates on current weaponry and caffeine levels, follow her on Twitter @StephanieSnow or check www.bareknucklewriter.com.

Epilogue

Part One: Dawn

It had been so long since she'd breathed real air that Dawn had forgotten how it was supposed to smell and taste. She was quite certain that that sulfuric-plastic scent wasn't there before the fall, but wouldn't quote herself on that. The sun burned her eyes and the light wind made her skin tingle. It felt natural and yet it wasn't. A piece of her wanted to run until she couldn't anymore, then to lie on the sun-warmed ground and watch what was left of the day pass by.

Now was not the time though. She didn't want to be up here more than a few minutes. The Ascent was tonight and she would much rather enjoy this freedom—celebrating under the night sky—alongside the people she had struggled with for the last fifteen years. Epilogue had told them that there wouldn't be any stars, but Dawn doubted that the thing even knew what stars were supposed to be. She could see the sun just fine, even if it was like looking at it through a dusty pair of glasses. *No, don't look around, wait for tonight,* she told herself.

The reason for her early arrival to the outside world was to speak to Epilogue. Her husband, the "great and wise" (once upon a time she meant those words) Dr. Victor Knight, was supposed to do it. But he had balked from the task every day this week, and whenever she tried to urge him along, he looked at her like a child about to put down a puppy. If he thought she would let him delay this any longer then he had gone completely delusional like so many others during their decade and a half under ground. They had agreed, finally agreed: on the night of the Ascent, he would shut Epilogue down.

Dawn had named the machine. She was a newlywed when

the world fell. Her husband was one of the most renowned scientists in the world, so they were selected as two of the four thousand people for the underground shelter. The end had come on so fast that the day they closed the door to a world that turned into an inferno around them, the population was only 73. Her husband had worked on the thing incessantly for five months. They lived in a skyless metal village, so nearly empty that being alone would have been less lonely. Everyone else she knew and loved was dead and the one person she had left locked himself in a back-room lab since the day they went underground. When Victor turned it on—this eerie creation so human-looking that no man should have rightly made it—he asked Dawn what they should call it.

"Epilogue," she told him.

His bushy black brows bunched behind his glasses. "Epilogue?"

She shrugged. "Well, that's what it is, isn't it?"

He smiled. As always, her unhappiness was lost on him. He clearly thought it was a very clever name.

Epilogue had served its purpose. Dawn would never deny that. With this machine, Vic had saved what was left of the human race. Without Epilogue they might have lasted another three years under ground, possibly four if they really starved themselves. But because of her husband, this little corner of the world became livable. He had programmed the machine simply to be helpful and take instruction. After five years of tests the water showed clean, so he programmed it to dig a well and turn the soil. At seven years, there was promise in the soil above, so he had it plant small gardens. After two useless crops, the third had edible carrots and potatoes. At twelve years, the air above ground was on that 'fine line' that environmental surveyors used to argue over in court as witnesses for both sides of the dispute. Vic sent Epilogue above ground with four cows and four chickens. After observing those animals and their many offspring for three years, he made the announcement that all 73 people had been waiting for (and yes, coincidentally, between births and deaths, there were still exactly 73 people in the underground village). It was time to go above ground.

The transition progressed slowly. Epilogue spent three months surveying the land around them. They knew where to go

~ Flashpoint ~

for what they would need to build their city and knew where all the hazardous zones were. Vic predicted it would take them two years before they could close the doors to the underground city and say goodbye to this world forever. But from here on out, it would serve as shelter in bad weather only.

Since he had preached about how they needed to do this as a community, build it from scratch as their ancestors had, she had gotten him to agree—and announce to everyone—that Epilogue wouldn't be helping with the building. This was a new world; they had to build it themselves. Then she started her quiet campaign to have Epilogue shut down.

"What do you mean, 'shut down'?" Vic had asked her, one night a few weeks ago.

It had been late when she woke up without him. She went to his lab to find him working on the machine. Epilogue was powered off, he had a side panel open on its hip and he gently tapped at the gears that moved its leg.

Seeing that he was frustrated, she took the opportunity. With a little 'you poor thing' smile and a ruffle of his hair, she said, "You'll be glad when it's finally shut down."

Dawn tried not to laugh at the expression on his face when he asked what she meant. This was not because she was mean spirited, but because it amused her that Victor—with the most brilliant mind to ever build thoughts—had never realized how contradictory Epilogue was to the plan they had all conceived.

"Victor, the idea is to embrace the old ways. Epilogue is an android, for crying out loud."

He just stared at her, unblinking, unsmiling.

She placed her hand on his arm and spoke softly. "Epilogue is a brilliant invention and it served a purpose. When we needed it. That time will soon be past." She rubbed his shoulders and he didn't tense at her touch, so she knew her gentle approach was working. "How many late nights have you spent in here doing repairs? Where will that energy come from when we're spending our days building and planting? And the power required to charge it is going to be hard to come by once we close off the underground city. What little we'll have once we are up and running shouldn't be spent to charge a machine we don't need anymore. Darling, it's just not practical."

That was the basis of Dawn's argument. They didn't need

Epilogue.

Victor hadn't built the machine to be smart. He had built it to be helpful and take instructions. A grievous oversight, in her opinion. It wasn't until Vic had spotted the indicators in Epilogue's reports that they realized it had been trying to feed a dead cow for over a week. When tasked with building the first barn, she had been told to make it large enough to fit the cows, so she made it exactly that size. It fit the first four cows with just inches between them and nothing else.

Now that they could go above ground themselves, they didn't need a machine to perform daily tasks, especially not if that machine required constant instruction and attention. It would be more work, and they already had enough of that ahead of them. What more reason did she need to want it shut down?

Jealousy, don't forget jealousy. The thought came from a hateful part of her mind. The part that refused to muzzle the feelings she didn't want to admit. The feeling had only bubbled to consciousness after Dawn saw the photograph tucked away in the back of Victor's desk drawer three years ago. She shut the emotion down as lunacy back then and had continued to do so since. She wasn't jealous of a machine. That didn't even make sense. *So what if Epilogue hasn't aged since we went underground? Hasn't gotten that grey tint that the rest of us have?* Neither had her oven and she wasn't jealous of that.

"Dawn!" Epilogue called with an excited wave as it ran toward her, its brown skirt flapping out behind it. It grasped both of her hands in a grip that was almost painful. "You're up! I can't believe it!" It started to tug her toward the barns. "Oh, this is so exciting! Come see, come see." It changed its mind and spun Dawn in a different direction. "Oh, let's start with the gardens, you won't believe—"

"Epilogue, stop!" Dawn said, exasperated, pulling her hands back. "I need to speak with you."

Epilogue's smile only grew wider. "And I need to listen."

Dawn groaned but Epilogue just kept its grin trained on her. Perhaps the thing that irritated Dawn most about this machine was that it didn't have the mental capacity to realize that Dawn hated it. "The Ascent is tonight."

Epilogue grabbed Dawn's hand again and started jumping. "I know! I can't wait. I've been preparing all day! Do you need something else? Something that wasn't on the list that Doctor Knight gave me?"

"No. But I need you to understand something," she said firmly.

Epilogue looked a back at her, its smile smaller, matching Dawn in gravity. "Then of course I will."

Dawn groaned again and dropped its hand. It was time to just say it. She couldn't use the words 'I'm having you shut down,' as much as she wanted to. This machine could lift a truck and, even though Vic said it wasn't capable of anger, Dawn wouldn't risk really pissing it off. "I need you to understand that once we are living above ground, we can tend our own gardens and livestock. We can test our own air and water. You will no longer be useful to us."

For the first time ever there was no hint of a smile on the machine's pretty face and Dawn felt her own smile spread so wide that it hurt her ears."I won't," Epilogue agreed. "Of course I won't."

"And running you without any need of you, just won't be practical."

"It won't," Epilogue agreed. "Of course it won't."

This was going so well that Dawn actually reached out and rested her hand on the machine's cheek. "You understand what that means, don't you?"

Epilogue nodded. It looked a bit sad. Its blue eyes remained wide but its red pupils were cast down to the ground.

"Thank you Epilogue, for everything." Her tone was chipper and dismissive, meant to mock the machine, but it was not as if it could tell.

Dawn made her way toward the elevator that would take her back underground. For the first time since they had begun planning the Ascent, back when Epilogue brought in the results of usable water, Dawn actually felt like she could come out from underground. She felt like the world could exist again.

~ Flashpoint ~

Part Two: Doctor Knight

The celebration was winding down. The majority of the people had turned in for the night, including his wife. They had set up a village of tents because the weather had held up so nicely, and they were all sleeping above ground for the first time in 5,523 days. Dawn had given Dr. Knight that steely gaze as she paused before getting into their tent with their two daughters. It was time. As if he didn't know. He cast a glance at Epilogue. She hadn't left his side all night and he had specifically not given her any task because he knew that would keep her by his side. Dawn liked to use this logic to bash him, but this really was like putting down a pet.

His design was perfect.

The android formula had been misused and, therefore, catastrophic in the 2100s. By the time he was a working scientist, it was forbidden completely. He had designed her in secret, years before the end of the world had even seemed possible. He prepared to build her when they first started construction on the underground city, but didn't actually begin until after the fall, when he played off his access to the materials as coincidence. He made her out of the same materials that had been used to build the shelter, her skin from the suits they wore to withstand the blast of the flash bombs. What did they need them for anymore? There was no one left to attack them. He took these liberties with the law because knew his design was perfect and he knew they would need her.

She was programmed only to be useful. How simple was that? As a result, she was kind and gentle and could follow instructions as if they had been inventions of her own mind. However, as the most advanced thing in existence, Epilogue became the most obsolete. Dr. Knight was a man of progress, or at least he used to be before progress stopped. Now, progression meant going backward and he could be that man again. But that meant giving her up.

Dawn had trapped him into it, and a part of him would always have a dark spot in his mind for her because of it. Her logic was sound and her reasons were completely true. But he was Doctor Victor Knight, the saviour of humanity (although the other eight billion that were lost in the fall would probably disagree with this title). No one left alive would begrudge him the few hours' work he had to put into her every week. Or the one measly generator he would have to keep operational for her to charge herself. No one but his wife.

Still, Dawn's arguments were sound. She brought them all out in such a subtle way, that his fighting her would only admit that the jealousy she tried to hide was apt. Then she would tell him that she had seen the photograph. Even though—just by Dawn's behaviour—he knew it was true, having it out in the open would destroy them. As much as he hated Dawn for making him do this, he loved her and loved his family. They had survived the end of the world and he wasn't going to let an old girlfriend break them apart.

"Victor," Dawn called out.

He jumped out of his reverie with a gasp and looked to see her coming out of the tent. "Yes?" He walked to meet her halfway. Epilogue and three of the men were gathered near him and he didn't want them to overhear.

"What are you still doing sitting there?"

Dr. Knight sighed and gestured toward where Epilogue sat. Her eyes were wide and focused on Ronald Bishop as he droned on, smiling as if she were hearing the best story in the world. "She's just so—"

"'It' Victor, not 'she'—*it*."

He apologized. For a moment he had forgotten himself. He, his two daughters and most others of the community, referred to Epilogue as 'she,' but never when Dawn was around. "*It* is enjoying the evening. After all the work it's done...just give me—"

"This is happening tonight. I just told the girls."

"You what?" He gasped and shook his head. "We agreed to tell them afterward."

"Well, I just did, and I am certainly not doing that again. Poor dears are heartbroken."

His girls, Abigail and Emma, adored Epilogue. She'd been around their entire young lives. He tried to keep his ear on the chatter around him so that he wouldn't hear them crying. "You told them we shut her down?" Their agreement had been that they were going to tell them that Epilogue broke down and that, in the new world, they couldn't fix her anymore.

"Of course not," Dawn said, offended. "I just told them that *it* was broken. I stuck with the plan." She gave a hard nod back in the direction he'd come from. "I expect you to do the same."

The nod he gave her back was both heavy and weak. Her expression only grew harder before she turned away. He walked lethargically back to where the small group was gathered. "Epilogue, would you walk with me?"

"Of course I would." She smiled. "Would you like me to?"

He gave a little chuckle as he felt tears sting his eyes. "Yes, yes I would."

They walked away from the gathering and into the naked tree line. He kept her on the moon side so that the faint light lit her face. He was going to miss that face. He had worked on it so diligently to get it right. He should have destroyed the photograph once he had it perfected. But he couldn't part with it. That photo was of the real Anne and Epilogue was only a look-alike. In personality, she was nothing like the woman he loved so many years ago. He had taken great care with her programming to make sure that she wasn't. He wasn't trying to replace Anne. He just found it comforting to see that face.

The Last War had waged for seven years. Anne had been taken from him in the first wave, long before the other side had perfected the flash bombs that left such clean corpses. Anne had been badly burned, yet impossibly still alive, in the last moment he spent with her. Until he rebuilt that face he could not close his eyes without seeing the charred mess that had become of his beautiful sweetheart. He wasn't substituting Epilogue for Anne and if he thought they would survive the conversation he would have liked to explain that to his wife. Epilogue needed a face, any face would do, and he needed to build a very specific one to quiet his own mind. That was all.

They came to a clearing he knew well. Before his wife's earlier adventure—when she had stomped off in frustration and anger and ruined the Ascent for herself by going above ground— he had been the only post-fall human to walk these lands. Once he was certain that it was safe, he began venturing above ground to prove that certainty to everyone else. He had discovered that this was the only spot within their boundaries where he could see the army base he had been working in at the end. It was already a hateful spot to him, the place where they had perfected their weapons just in time for them to be completely useless. Just

~ Flashpoint ~

looking at it gave him a sinking heart. He didn't want to ruin another spot for himself, so he would do it here.

"Epilogue..." he began, but was distracted when the wind picked up her blonde hair. It moved around so much like Anne's had. That grief that already weighed inside him grew heavier with a sickening force. "You talked to Dawn earlier?"

"I did," she said, her smile growing so bright that it looked nervous. He wondered if she was, or if she was scared or sad. This was all ridiculous, of course. He hadn't programmed her to feel any of those things. But after everything they'd been through together, it felt so underhanded to just flip the switch without ever telling her and thanking her. He had to admit to himself that, in spite of everything, he was grateful to Dawn for shouldering that burden.

"And you understood what she told you?" he asked, delaying as tears blurred above the lower arcs of his eyes.

"Of course I did." She nodded. "It made perfect sense."

"Then you know what has to be done?"

She brought her hands together and nodded down at them in one quick motion. It almost looked like a bow. Her smile was larger when it fixed back on him. "I have to be useful."

He stopped. Did she understand? Dawn said that she made it perfectly clear. "Well, yes—"

"I've always been useful. Even things that you didn't need me to find, I found them. I kept them nearby in case you did need them. For future usefulness."

Poor girl, he thought. *Damn you, Dawn. Epilogue has no idea.* Could he still do it? Just shut her down? Or did he have to tell her? She was a machine. How would she know if she wasn't here anymore? It seemed cruel to tell her. It occurred to him that he was a coward and he stuffed that thought down again, as he always did when it popped up. He was just going to do it; tell her she needed a quick repair, open the casing beside her spine and flick the switch for the last time. He was about to say it when she spoke again.

"I was so useful after the fall."

He smiled. "You were and—"

"I will be again."

"Well...um, could you turn—" He stopped. The pieces of her ramblings clicked together and each connection formed like

~ Flashpoint ~

ice webs over his heart and brain. "Epilogue...what are the things you put away for..." He paused to recall her phrasing, "future usefulness?"

She gave him a playful swat as if he should already know. "The same things that made me useful in the first place. They were all at the base. It's time. Watch."

She pointed north, away from the ocean, beyond the celebration where his wife, children and the rest of humanity were in the open air celebrating the end of the end of the world, toward the old base.

The noise came first. A horrible sound he had had hoped to never hear again his his lifetime. Then the screams. The light came next. That awful, terrible green light of the flash bombs. Too bright to be anything at all, not hot enough to be fire or cold enough to be ice and yet you know it's going to kill you. Next came nothing.

Part Three: Epilogue

Epilogue's daily tests had been done and the results were just awful. She 'tsked' at the fuming air as she waited for the elevator. Dr. Knight was going to be very unhappy and he had been so unhappy lately that she had hoped for something good. She didn't think she knew much about how humans felt, but she read cues. Silence and refusal to move seemed to her to mean unhappiness. They were all unhappy.

Her first destination was the lab. On the walk through the underground village Epilogue worried that she might have to start testing the air inside. Dr. Knight had given her basic sense receptors, which was how she knew the air was starting to smell. It smelled like bad food mixed with the smell of that cow that just wouldn't eat.

Since she came to the kitchen before the lab she decided that she had better check in on Dawn, Abigail and Emma. The three of them were so unhappy lately that she was at a loss. She took them to all of their favourite rooms and she even still read to the girls everyday. Dawn was at the stove. It was off, but she didn't seem in any mood too cook lately anyway. Poor Dawn was as unhappy as everyone else and wouldn't stand up anymore. Epilogue had to use a ladder to prop her in front of it and used a rubber band to keep her grey and cold hand around one of her cooking spoons. The girls still sat at the table, still with the same book on the same page that she had set in-between them.

"Lazy, lazies," she said to them sweetly as she lifted them out of the chairs—one over each shoulder—and took them to their room. They smelled as bad as the air. She was tempted to bathe them again, but the last time she did that, part of Emma's face came off when she washed it. Epilogue glued it back on, but it still didn't look right. However, Emma didn't say anything when she asked her if it was all right so she left it alone. Once the girls were settled she started to the lab.

Dr. Knight sat in his chair, his head back like he was napping. But he wasn't napping. Since she took him back underground, he was just too sad too work. They all were. Every last person there was so disappointed to go back to the underground village that they wouldn't even walk there themselves. She had to carry every one of them.

"The results are awful," she told him.

He didn't respond.

Epilogue sighed and took a seat on the floor near his feet. "I really hope you get happier soon. Or someone does. Someone who can tell me how to make you happier." She looked at his face for any response. Nothing. If anything his expression and skin were even darker than they had been in the four days since they came back underground. She rested her head on his knee. "Sure is quiet here when everyone's so unhappy."

Her words echoed in the silent room. For a moment, she found that pleasant and continued to make small sounds bounce back at her, imagining that it could have been a conversation. She only did this for a minute before she realized she was wasting time. Epilogue stood and looked down at Dr. Knight. "Are you sure there's nothing I can do for you?"

Again, he didn't respond.

Epilogue nodded. "That's all right. I'll make myself useful. I always do."

~ Flashpoint ~

Jenn Tubrett is a writer local to Sydney, Nova Scotia. Her background is mostly focused in Theater, some of her stage works include: *Notte Del Partito* (2011), *The Apple* (As a part of *Tales From the Bottom of the Well II*, 2011) and *Ruby* (As a part of *This Hour Has 666 Minutes*, 2013). She has previously been published in *Unearthed*, (2012) with *Our Last Vacation* and is excited to be a part of *Flashpoint* with her new work *Epilogue*.

Battle Scars

"But you could do it, Baraster, couldn't you?"

The young lad looked up at him with eyes wide and watery. Clearly, he had been crying, and for a significantly long period. Baraster sat upon the cold stone, trying to force down the anger he felt, a rage in the pit of his stomach that longed to explode.

"Young one," he began, "it is never so simple. People like me need to be extra careful," his voice dropped to a sullen whisper. "The pain I could cause, should I lose control, far exceeds the good I could do." He pulled his grey cloak close about his neck and noticed for the first time the blood on his hands.

"Take me to the next wounded." Sliding off the stone where he sat, Baraster motioned for the lad to lead him away. Many of the wounded had already been attended to, and thankfully, most of the injuries here were minor.

Baraster walked carefully, stepping between those lying on the cold, damp ground. That would not help them recover, but there was little choice. They were several days from the nearest village, a warm fire, and a firm bed. Many were covered with boughs of fir and spruce, guarding them against the cool night chill. The few blankets the camp possessed were reserved for the very young, the very old, and the very sick. And there seemed to be no end to the need. It tore Baraster apart inside to see so many people in pain.

The boy led Baraster through a thicket of refugees, their lonely faces dark, dirty, and bloody. Beyond the mass of listless, tired bodies stood a group of middle-aged men. Dawson was the tallest, standing nearly nine hands high; he could look many horses in the eye. An imposing farmer, he was unusually gentle and soft-spoken. Beside him, holding a large map on a tattered papyrus scroll was Gunther, the local blacksmith. Short and stout, with powerful, thick arms, he was the most educated of the village elders, having apprenticed under the master blacksmiths in the Empire's Seat. Many looked to him for guidance and wisdom, just as Gunther looked to Baraster. Gunther looked up, and a smile equal parts relief and joy crept across his face.

"I'm so glad you're here, Baraster" he said, "we have much to decide."

Baraster shook his head immediately, "I'm attending to the wounded. Nothing more. I'll be on my way soon."

He held his breath, waiting for the pleas to come. But Gunther barely gave him a second look, instead refocusing on the map in his hands. "The rest of the wounded are beyond that rock bluff," he stated, gesturing to the small outcropping of stone some thirty yards away.

Baraster said nothing, and began moving quickly to the triage area. It was pleasing that Gunther didn't press him, but also very surprising. He didn't like being surprised. It usually meant he had missed something. And when he missed something, it usually meant danger was but a breath away.

Baraster climbed the low rock out-cropping. Perhaps a dozen bodies came into view as he crested the top, laid out across the hard surface, just below. The ground glistened in the moonlight, wet with their blood, and a confused array of persons ran forth and back tending to as many people as possible. Baraster spotted the young boy who had led him through the refugees.

"Jacob, come here, lad."

The boy ran quickly from the middle of the patch, careful to avoid stepping on any of the wounded. "Yes, Master Baraster, what do you need?"

"Take me to the most severe injury." He did not want to criticize the efforts of the villagers, but inwardly, Baraster thought the organization was horrific. With this mass confusion, most of the remaining injured would die. He knew that not all could be saved. Could he make the hard decision to let a man die, and move on to the next patient? Clearly, the villagers couldn't, as they scurried from one wounded person to another,

~ Flashpoint~

in a vain attempt to keep them all alive. Even Noria, the village
herbalist who ought to have known better, jumped vainly from
patient to patient. She had served in the Kingdom's armies. She
knew the reality of the post-battle world. All he could do was
shake his head. Jacob touched his robes gently, and gestured
toward the far side of the plateau.

They approached the figure of a young man, his clothes
dirty, torn, and blood-soaked. Baraster reached out with his
slender, bony fingers and lifted up the young man's shirt,
revealing a deep gash from his shoulder down to his hip. A sword
wound. Probably an old, dirty, rusty sword. The victim's eyes
were wide and glassy, his breath shallow and weak. Baraster
placed his hand upon his forehead, whispered 'sleep', and the boy
closed his eyes for the last time. Baraster took a deep breath
before looking up, and saw Noria bearing down upon them, with
balms and bandages in her hands.

"Noria. No." He shook his head. "This boy is beyond help.
Take those to someone who will benefit."

Her smudged, plump face reddened and her eyes narrowed
as she scolded, "How can you give up on him? I've known this
boy for fifteen years. He's like a son to me. I won't give up."

"Noria," Baraster insisted, "we would be wasting time. I've
put him into a deep sleep. He'll feel no more pain."

"But he'll never awaken!" Noria couldn't contain the anger
in her voice.

"No, he won't, and if we waste more time here, then many
more won't see the morning, either!" A glimmer of anger tinged
Baraster's voice now, and he raised his right hand to silence the
impending argument from Noria. "I'll see to the worst cases—and
put to sleep those that are beyond help. You already know who
you can really help. Go and do it."

Noria swallowed her retort. Baraster could see her
frustration, and in some small fashion, could understand her. As
an outsider, Baraster didn't have many close connections to
those in the village. Certainly, he had grown to appreciate and
like the villagers over the last three winters, but he was a solitary
man by nature. He only knew a handful of these people. His goal
had been to disappear from the Kingdom, and he had thought
Mastadon as good a place as any other he had ever visited. It
rested on the eastern edge of the kingdom, with the Horatia

~ Flashpoint ~

Mountains to the east and the Dulath Sea to the south. Protection on two sides, with the nearest village more than two days north, and the closest city nearly four days to the west, Baraster had been certain he could live out his days here in relative peace.

He was enjoying a cold ale alone in the tavern when Gunther burst in with news of the approaching troops, flying their Muraden King's banner. Gunther immediately called for help to prepare rations and billets for the incoming soldiers, but Baraster knew exactly what was afoot the moment he saw the familiar formation. This army was marching *to* conquest, not *from* one. Baraster directed Gunther to evacuate the village folk to the mountain caves, while the village guard initiated a defense.

The caves formed a complex web of tunnels, some delving deep into the mountain, others turning and routing higher to flat plateaus. Some of the tunnels were natural, while others had been deliberately cut years before humans settled at the location. Rumour had it that dwarfs had once mined these mountains for gold and jewels, but the veins had run dry a millennium ago.

The villagers had scouted and mapped the tunnels over the many decades that they had dwelled in the shadow of the mountain, believing it to be a safe, secure haven. They had even found many of the hidden passageways and rooms contained in the cold stone. In a stroke of brilliant foresight, Noria had stocked several of the rooms with rations and supplies. It was to those rooms that the defenders initially retreated, before being carried by Dawson and the other farmers to their current plateau. If not for those secret rooms, none of the young men would have survived.

As it was, Baraster felt he was still putting too many young men into their last slumber. It was only four, and it gave Noria the time to attend to six other youths, but that was little consolation. He prepared to put the fourth youth to sleep—the scrawny young man's chest had a deep, gaping, wound, his flesh ripped away. Somehow he still drew breath, but he was fading fast. Baraster laid his hand on the boy's forehead, and whispered the gentle spell one last time.

"Sleep well, son. Too few winters you have seen." Steadying himself against the makeshift table, he moved cautiously to join Noria with another patient. "How many more to attend to?"

~ Flashpoint~

"I think you've *helped* enough, wizard."

"Noria, don't judge me so harshly. They are asleep. They have no pain now. If we have time, we will go back and try to save some, but if we are too late, then they will die peacefully, in a deep slumber. Please. Let me try and help some more."

She nodded, and pulled back the covering on the chest of Aeral, a strong young man of barely fourteen. He had lost a lot of blood from a shoulder wound, but it was not fatal if treated.

"Get me some needle and thread," Noria commanded. "We have to sew this up."

"Wait," Baraster interrupted, "bring some light over here." One of the village women came over with a torch. Her blood and mud soaked dress stank of sweat, her face was streaked with tears. Baraster found her indiscernible from the rest of the village's women.

"See here," he said, pointing to the wound, "you see that dark spot. That needs to be cleaned out and sterilized. If we were to sew him up now, it would probably kill him."

"How should we clean that?"

Baraster thought for a moment before asking, "Do we have any rum in the store rooms? That may do the trick." Noria motioned for the women to retrieve the rum. "I'm not sure that's a good idea. I've seen men get much worse after using rum on a wound. I think we should just sew it up."

Before Baraster could argue with her, young Jacob burst toward him, a frantic expression on his face.

"They're coming. They found the tunnel!"

"Gather the elders. Quick!"

Jacob was off like a young deer, his spry legs bounding across the rock outcropping, gliding gracefully between men carrying lumber, supplies, and weapons. Baraster pondered the implications.

Surveying the plateau upon which their camp rested, Baraster suddenly felt boxed in. The plateau was wide enough to drop the entire village within its sheer walls, though it would be too short to include the harbour docks. The cliff walls rose straight up, cutting off his ability to see any movements—enemy or otherwise—beyond the rock wall. Reaching the top of those cliffs would be nearly impossible for the attackers, so they were unlikely to be attacked from above, but they were also cornered.

~ Flashpoint ~

He knew only of the entrance door they used to access the plateau from the storeroom, but given the size of the plateau, he could hope there were other escape routes. That's what he needed to discuss with Gunther and Dawson—how to get the villagers off the plateau and to safety. But that would be difficult, with enemy soldiers in the tunnels.

Jacob returned quickly with Gunther and Dawson. The large men strode across the rocky field with a grace befitting battlefield commanders. Gunther's eyes drank in every detail as he swept past. Baraster could feel those eyes bore into him—the dull jade barely hiding the fire behind them.

"Wizard," he spat, with no attempt to hide the aggravation in his voice, "I thought you were tending the wounded, and then would be off, away from us."

"My intentions seem to be in direct conflict with the circumstances of our existence. Gunther, if you will have my counsel, I will provide it."

Gunther looked him up and down. His posture was stiff, his large arms folded in front of him, his powerful legs spread shoulder width apart. The ends of his shirt were torn, frayed, and burned. He was as he had been in his forge. "I would have your assistance, wizard, more than your counsel. Are you not a Battle Mage of Aginor?"

Baraster bowed his head, taking a deep breath, trying with all his being to remain calm. "Gunther," he began, a slight catch in his voice breaking up his usual confident tone, "I am retired. I no longer fight—but I can offer guidance."

Dawson looked on from behind Gunther, though he towered over the man. Baraster could see him mouth the word *coward*, but he wouldn't say it aloud. Briefly, he considered challenging Dawson, but immediately thought better of it. Arguing with the man now wouldn't help anyone. They needed to build a plan if they were to save the villagers. For their sake, Baraster swallowed his pride.

Gunther, to his credit, didn't push further. "Jacob told us on our way over that the soldiers have entered the tunnels. It is only a matter of time before they find the secret rooms and the passageways to our temporary '*home*'."

"Why are you certain they'll find the hidden routes?" Baraster questioned, "Dwarfs are well-known craftsmen."

~ Flashpoint ~

"True, but I don't believe they ever really intended these passageways to be secret or hidden. We are but simple farmers and artisans, and we found them. Our best hope now is that the army follows the main path out the other side of the mountain, to the Dirage valley. And that they don't seek out the side passages and tunnels."

"And if they do?" Dawson asked, speaking for the first time.

"That," Baraster whispered, "is our task. Gunther, where are we on your maps?"

Gunther rolled out a tattered papyrus scroll, revealing a detailed outline of the mountain tunnels. Baraster looked down, utterly amazed. There were thousands.

"How long did it take you to map this?"

"My predecessors began it many, many years ago. We've been adding to it for over fifty years. We think we've found them all." He reached out with his thick, calloused hand and pointed to the top left hand corner of the map. "We are here," Gunther said, drawing his finger across the map to the lower right hand corner, "and the village entrance is here. The most direct route takes you across the mountain to the valley. If they find this tunnel," he indicated the third door on the western side of the main thoroughfare, "they would have a hard climb, but they could be here within an hour. If they find this door," he said, again pointing to an exit marked on the western edge of the main passage, "then they may be lost in a bit of a maze, giving us more time. But we need to get off this plateau."

"Agreed," Baraster said, his long brown beard scraping across the map surface, pointing to the area east of their present position, "but we can't go through these tunnels. Our movement would alert the soldiers. What are the exits from the plateau, and where do they lead?"

Gunther and Dawson both leaned over the map, studying it carefully. Occasionally, one would look up, point to an area of the cliff face, then put his head back down, whispering back and forth in hushed tones. Baraster stood back a step, listening as best he could. Gunther and Dawson debated various options. The more they discussed, the further they seemed to get from a potential solution.

After several long minutes, Baraster stepped between the two of them and asked, "What is our priority—run, hide, or

~ Flashpoint ~

defend?"

They looked up at him blankly, grasping for the right words.

"It does no good to look at routes and maps and tunnels if we don't know what the objective is," the wizard said, punching his fist into his left hand forcibly. "Always know your objective!"

"The battle mage has returned." Dawson sounded pleased.

"No!" Baraster's voice boomed, more intensely than he intended. He drew a deep breath, releasing it in a slow sigh before continuing in a controlled tone, "I will help you plan, but I will not fight. Now, is this," waving his hands over the plateau, "a defensible position? If so, how many entrances would we have to defend?"

Dawson rubbed his chin, grey stubble bristling against his fingers, and answered, "There are seven: three on the eastern wall, two on the northern wall, and two more on the western wall."

"We can't defend them all," Gunther flatly stated.

Baraster nodded his agreement. Protecting against all possible points of entry would spread their tiny militia beyond capacity. They would be overrun. "What if we split up and hid in some of the store rooms?"

Dawson and Gunther both shook their heads. Then Dawson, with a respectful head bow to Gunther, took the lead. "We can't take the risk to sacrifice some, in the hope that the rest of us find safety. Besides, we don't know how extensively they'll search, and small groups would be easily overwhelmed by their superior numbers."

Baraster nodded again. Running, then, would be their only reasonable option. He signalled Gunther to pull out his other maps from the sack on the ground, and lay them over the stone table. "Which way to the nearest village?"

"North," Gunther stated, pulling his last map out of his bag, "but I think it would be best to head out of the western door here." He smudged a corner of the map with his soot-blackened finger, "Then we'll have to follow the tunnels to the higher levels, before circling back and down, exiting about six leagues north of our village. From there, it be about two and a half days to Sansde. Maybe three, with the burden of the wounded."

Dawson drew closer to the maps, looking intensely at the options, and then nodded his agreement.

~ Flashpoint ~

"Then we prepare to move the wounded." Baraster waved Noria over, and gave her the news. Dawson signalled for a few of his farmhands to join them, and having given them instructions to scout ahead in the desired tunnels, released them to their task.

As Noria took her leave, a wave of nausea came over Baraster. His head began to spin, and he had to steady himself on the makeshift rock table. "Jacob," he called, "help me." The young man came running over.

"Hold on to my arm. Lean on me. I'll find you a place to rest." Jacob, though years younger and hands shorter than Baraster, took his full weight upon his shoulder, and guided him to a flat stone near the western facing. There, he eased Baraster down. "What happened, sir?"

Baraster gasped for breath, the nausea continuing to take him, his eyes unable to focus. "It's the magic, boy," he gasped, his voicing sounding every bit as ancient as his body felt. "Using magic is not good for one's health."

The young man patted him on the shoulder and, ensuring that Baraster was comfortably seated on the rock, rushed off to get some water.

Foolish old wizard, Baraster thought. It had been years since he had touched the magic; he knew the effect it would have on his body. Yet he did it to spare those young men pain. Few knew of the toll magic use took; fewer still would care as long as he did their bidding.

Jacob returned with a water skin, and Baraster drained it quickly. The cold, refreshing water invigorated him. The boy had good instincts—in another life, he would have made an excellent apprentice. Baraster handed the empty water skin back to Jacob, and nodded his thanks. Leaning his head against the cold stone, he closed his eyes. He hoped the young man would leave him be now, but he could feel the lad's eyes boring into the side of his skull. "I thank you for the water. Now, let me rest, Jacob."

"I...I don't want to bother you, sir, but really, what happened?"

Baraster leaned forward, resting his elbows on his bony knees, cupping his chin in his left hand. "What do you know of magic, Jacob?"

"It's powerful. And it's rare to find a teacher."

~ Flashpoint ~

"Do you know why it is so rare to find a teacher?" Baraster gave him a moment to absorb the question before continuing, "It is rare, because using magic slowly kills the user. Every wizard knows this; it is only a matter of time."

He reached around Jacob's shoulder with his right hand, pulling him close, so close that his grizzled old whiskers pressed upon the lad's smooth face. Pointing straight ahead with his left hand, he spoke in a soft voice, "Look at the spaces *between* the air. Can you see the dark spots, floating between the pockets?"

Jacob shook his head, and Baraster continued, "I'm not surprised. It took me three years before I could see them." He reached out with his left hand, and grasped at the air. He pulled it close and opened his fist, revealing a tiny black speck on his fingertip. He brought it close to Jacob's face.

"Is that ash?" Jacob asked.

"No—it is death. Death surrounds us, looking, searching for someone, anyone, to latch onto. The essence of magic," he whispered, as he blew the speck of black from his finger, "is to control death. I've learned how to pull it into me, control it, manipulate it." He looked at Jacob's wide eyes, registering the disbelief. "It wasn't easy." Laughter rolled into his voice. "I was at the academy for three winters before I could even see the death in the air. I studied another three winters before I could master the simplest of uses."

"So, that's why it kills you—because you take in death?"

"Excellent." Baraster's voice carried more than a hint of pride. He was right—this young man did have potential. Over the last couple of harvests, Baraster had gotten to know the young lad, and liked him a great deal. Jacob had prodded and probed, and it was obvious he was, at the very least, intrigued by the allure of magic. Perhaps he would take Jacob to the academy and see if he could be trained. It was a long road, and dangerous travel at the best of times. The recent actions of the King's army gave him cause to be concerned. Would taking him to the academy be worth the trip? Battle Mages were tools of the military under the best of circumstances—now, attacking his own people—Baraster wasn't sure he would want to subject anyone to that kind of life, especially a young lad he had become fond of.

"So, is that why you've stopped using it? Because you want to live?"

~ *Flashpoint* ~

Baraster thought for a moment. As he considered his answer, he heard Dawson consulting with some of the young militia.

"You see Dawson?"

Jacob nodded.

"Did you know he was in the King's guard?"

Jacob shook his head.

"I don't know if he remembers me. I didn't spend much time with the common soldiers. But Dawson, he's a memorable one. He towered over the other soldiers, and...the strength he possessed! I saw him crush a man's skull with a broken axe handle. The man had a plate helmet on. Left such a dent in the helmet, that you could have made soup in it afterward. He had everything they looked for in a soldier—strength, confidence, intelligence. He could have been a general by now, yet all he could talk about was serving his time, and returning here, to his farm. It was all he ever wanted; it's what made him complete. He had to be a farmer."

Jacob looked at him inquisitively

Baraster continued, "At some point in your life, you have to decide what you want to be. I was a tool, molded to kill, for more years than I can count. I had only two choices—continue to kill because it was all I ever knew, or never kill again, because it wasn't who I wanted to be."

"But can't you use your magic for things other than killing?"

"I never learned. When I was at the academy, the kingdom was at war. They needed battle mages, and battle mages were all they graduated. I have no idea how to do anything else with my power."

"What about your healing?" Jacob inquired.

He paused for just a moment, a bemused smirk catching the corners of his mouth, "I don't heal anyone, Jacob, at least not with magic. The spell I apply is a sleeping curse, one, which if used to full capacity, could kill. I would use the same curse to put guards to sleep before assassinating enemy commanders. Exceedingly efficient." He paused, as he noticed a puzzled look on Jacob's face, "But I'm certain you will be able to do more, learn more. When we get out of here, I'll take you to the academy." Jacob's face lit up, as if he had just won the prize hog at the harvest dance.

~ Flashpoint ~

The elation was short-lived. Before Jacob could respond, Dawson yelled to them, frantically waving his arms. "Come, Jacob, there is a problem," said Baraster.

"Our tunnel out of here collapsed. The scouts can't tell if it's natural, or if the soldiers brought it down." Baraster could never remember hearing such panic in Dawson's voice.

"Dawson, I know what you're going to ask. Please don't." Baraster pleaded. "It might be time to consider surrender."

Dawson's jaw dropped, his eyes widening in anger.

"Listen. If they come through those doors, they will kill us all. Our best bet to survive now is to surrender. We don't even know why they're here." Pain and anguish clouded his voice. "We have too many wounded, too many inexperienced men. I know that you don't want to kill anymore."

Shock rushed across Dawson's features. With the low growl of an angry bear, he retorted, "Don't speak of that."

"My apologies—I wasn't aware that it was a secret. I did share it with Jacob." Genuine regret tempered his voice. He understood the desire to leave the past far behind.

Dawson just shook his head, letting out a massive sigh of resignation. His body seemed to relax, finally, and he took in several deep breaths, his chest rising slowly as he filled his lungs with the crisp night air. "Fine." He stepped back, and called over one of his farmhands, sending him off to find Gunther. "I'll talk to Gunther, and recommend that we stay here, hoping that they don't find us; that they give up looking. If they do find us, we surrender, and look for mercy."

He looked around at the many villagers who were gathering their few remaining supplies; the far too young, the frail elderly, and many more who never held a sword other than to appreciate the intricate work of the hilt or scabbard. "I hope you are correct, Mage. Remember, they didn't offer a surrender when they arrived. I don't see why they would give an opportunity now."

Baraster watched him walk away, and his heart was heavy for the man. Both knew that the army would normally take prisoners, but ones as strong as Dawson, and likely Gunther, would never have the opportunity to surrender. He had seen enough combat to know how battle would progress: seek out the strongest, most dangerous, and cut them down first. The remaining opponents would then be easily rounded up. Still,

Dawson's warning resonated with him. There had been no offer of parley or opportunity for surrender upon the army's arrival. There was little hope they would be offered one now.

Baraster found the most comfortable rock he could to sit on, and waited. With their best exit cut off, and the soldiers closing in, their options diminished. Leaning back against the cold stone wall, he saw the first signs of morning creeping above the rim of the valley. A shallow red glow began to overpower the stars, and with a little sadness, Baraster watched as the northern star faded into the sea of red overhead.

Maybe, Baraster thought to himself, maybe they would actually survive this. Perhaps this army that had descended upon their quiet village would relent in the search, give up and return to their garrison, content in whatever it was they had hoped to achieve. He wanted to close his eyes and rest, and he nearly did, but he couldn't relax enough. He knew his hope was a long shot at best—he knew from his days in the military that they would not relent. If they were into the tunnels, then there was an objective outstanding, and the King's Army did not relent until successful or defeated.

Baraster sat there, and tried to calm his mind, thinking hard on his options. The sky burned a faint red from the rising sun, passing wisps of clouds creating a light pink hue just above the rim of the cliff. Then he noticed it: black flecks floating overhead, toward the eastern wall. At first he thought it was ash from the small cook fires, but then he noticed they were moving in the opposite direction of the cloud cover. His eyes traced their path, as they disappeared through the eastern wall.

"Jacob," he called, "come here." Jacob was at his side in an instant, ready and willing to act. "The western passages are blocked, correct?" Jacob nodded confirmation. "And the army is coming up the eastern passage."

Jacob looked at him quizzically.

"I can see their mage pulling death through the eastern wall—it won't be long before they burst through." Again, Jacob nodded. "Take as many as you can, and escape through the northern tunnels. No matter where you end up, it will be better than under the heel of a soldier's boot." Jacob nodded, and immediately called for assistance in moving the women, children, and the wounded.

~ Flashpoint ~

Dawson crossed across the camp, a small amount of confusion on his brow. "Where are you sending Jacob?"

"To safety, I hope. Gather what men you can, the army will be here shortly."

"Will you fight with us, if necessary?" Dawson's voice carried a morbid certainty.

Baraster reached out, putting his hand on the giant man's shoulder, "I wish I could, friend. I know you know how hard it is to kill. I cannot go back to that, no matter what."

"I don't know what evils you were forced to conjure when you served the King, Mage," his voice rumbled with grave concern, "but fighting for a free village is different than fighting for an army. These people matter. It would be for their lives, not to profit the King's coffers."

"He's right, sir!" Jacob interjected.

"Jacob!" Baraster scolded, "you are not to be eavesdropping. Your duty is to get as many people away as possible. Now go, be useful!" Jacob scurried off again. Baraster watched him gather a few children, and point them toward the northern exits.

"He is a good lad, Baraster. With your help, he can grow to be a great man." Baraster glared at Dawson, but before he could respond, Dawson raised his hands in surrender, and muttered, "Think on it. It's all I ask."

Baraster shuffled over to his favoured stone, sat down, and rested his head against the western facing of the cliff. He concentrated on the specks of death that floated between the spaces in the air. More and more flowed toward the eastern facing. The assault would come soon. He broke his concentration briefly to watch the preparations.

Dawson and Gunther had armed themselves with some old swords. Several of the other farmers had picked out the best remnants of weapons that the dwarfs had left behind ages ago, though they were rusted, pitted and dull. Most of the remaining men carried nothing but pitchforks, butcher knives and the broken handles of shovels and picks. Casting his gaze to his left, Baraster noticed Jacob assisting Noria with a sledge, packed high with medical supplies and food. Content that he could only slow their progress now, he put his head back and again focused on the movement of the dark specks in the air.

Most floated about harmlessly, carried by the breeze and

~ Flashpoint ~

the inadvertent desires of those around them. It amused Baraster that so many people touched magic, using magic without really noticing that they had. In such minute amounts, they would never feel the effects, or recognize the impact they had on the world around them. The longer the specks floated without purpose, the safer they all would be. No sooner had the thought crossed his mind, than he noted a discernible change in the pattern. Where only a small stream had floated through the eastern wall, suddenly a torrent flowed through the stone. A river of black so obvious, he wondered briefly how even the untrained eye could miss it.

The assault exploded upon them.

"Take cover!" he yelled as he jumped up from his rock. There was virtually no time to react as the eastern wall exploded, sending stone debris across the plateau. One of the shards flew straight at Baraster, taking him in the chest and driving him hard against the western facing. He felt ribs break and fell to the ground as his head bounced against the wall; his ears rang and he became briefly disoriented. Crawling to his knees, eyes blurry with pain, he saw enemy soldiers burst through the gaping hole in the rock face, archers letting arrows fly with impunity.

Gunther and Dawson stood in the front line, hands held up above their heads. They shouted in surrender, but soldiers ignored their pleas, instead battering their torsos with a barrage of arrows. Most bounced off their makeshift armour, but the impacts caused both men to fall back, blood seeping through their tunics, as they drew swords from the sheaths at their belts. If there was to be no surrender, they would go down fighting for those they loved and lived with. More soldiers poured through the hole, their swords already drawn, ready to meet the meagre resistance. The wizard who had blown out the wall wasn't visible, nor was there any obvious commander.

"Stand down! We surrender!" Baraster yelled as he struggled to his feet, his knees wobbling, and his breath short and painful. "Don't attack. We surrender!" he repeated. Excruciating pain ran through his chest with each breath he took and each word he spoke.

Still they came. The soldiers descended on the poorly armed villagers with sword and pike, the archers falling back. Gunther fought on and on, despite several arrows protruding from his chest and shoulders. He defended a small knot of villagers, but was overwhelmed quickly by the superior numbers of the attacking army. Baraster struggled to stay on his feet; the nausea and dizziness consumed his body. He staggered towards Dawson's position, where he held his own against a formidable group of sword-wielding men. Several dead soldiers lay at his feet, but he was pressed against the wall, and with his blood loss, could barely stand. Before Baraster could act, he witnessed Dawson finally succumb to the onslaught, swarmed by the mob, penetrated by half a dozen swords. The soldiers rolled past the lifeless Dawson, and descended upon the remaining villagers behind him. A group of soldiers broke toward the northern wall, rushing after the retreating villagers with Jacob at their rear.

"Stop! They're civilians. Let them be!" Baraster screamed, but still they advanced. Jacob turned from the entryway to face the on-coming soldiers, holding the lid of an old barrel for a makeshift shield and the broken handle of an old axe as a weapon.

Baraster could do nothing to help as one soldier pushed past Jacob, knocking him aside, and a second slashed at his torso. Jacob deflected the first slash with his barrel lid shield, turning his body aside, but he didn't anticipate the offhand knife, and Baraster watched as the soldier plunged the knife into the boy's upper body.

"No!" Baraster yelled, despair and rage swelling in his breast.

Jacob fell to his knees, anguish and pain washing over his face. Witnessing so many innocents, people he now called his friends, falling to the enemy onslaught was more than Baraster could stand. Unable to resist touching that well of anger and hatred he had buried for years, he succumbed to the powerfully violent urges inherent in his training.

Extending his arms wide, Baraster focused intently on the tiny dark specks floating about him, drawing in as much of the floating death as he could hold, then drew in even more. Streams of tiny black specks sped toward him, enveloping his body, penetrating his skin, filling his lungs, flowing through his veins. He absorbed as much as possible, savouring the power at his control while simultaneously fighting against the sickening nausea that threatened to overwhelm him. Holding more magic

~ Flashpoint ~

than he had ever held, he turned his palms outward and from his outstretched fingers erupted a flame that incinerated the soldiers pursing the escaping villagers.

Baraster staggered from the nausea, steadied himself against the wall, and drank in yet more power before firing another stream of fire toward the soldiers who filed in the gap between the eastern and western walls. He glanced to his left, and saw Noria crouched beside Jacob, lying on the plateau floor, the life ebbing from him.

With nothing left to lose, Baraster pulled in yet more magic from the surrounding air. There was so much death in the area and he absorbed all of it, willing the black specks to pour into him like water filling a bucket. Slowly, he brought his hands together in front of his chest, focused his thoughts on nothing but destruction, and pulling his hands apart, he released the energy in a brilliant red and blue arc of fire, pushing it out toward the cliff walls, causing them to crumble and fall. Further and further he pushed the semi-circle of fire and percussive power, cutting through the upper reaches of the tunnels and collapsing tonnes of stone on top of the soldiers still below. Rocks cascaded down through the tunnels, clogging exits and crushing bodies beneath.

When Baraster finally released the spell, he had cut off the entire Eastern side of the mountain; the plateau now extended to the horizon, the yellow gold glow of the rising sun hovering over the plateau's edge.

"I'm sorry, Jacob. I should have acted sooner," he whispered to himself, as he fell to his knees, overwhelmed by the pain in his chest. He felt the sickness wash over him again. He had taken in far too much death. He nearly fell face first on the stone, barely bracing himself with his hands at the last moment. Darkness crept into his vision. Try as he might, he couldn't muster the energy to rise. The harder he tried, the closer he came to the ground. His vision was failing and he closed his eyes, just before he felt his body collapse to the plateau floor.

A hand lifted his face off the cold stone.

"Master,"Jacob's voice called to him, "you did it. You saved *our* people."

Baraster opened one eye, and through the blur saw that Jacob had crawled over to him, a short blade still protruding from

~ Flashpoint ~

his shoulder. Baraster tried to speak, but couldn't form more than a grunt. He could not even force a smile. Finally, unable to keep his eye open any longer, with his face pressed against the warm touch of his only true friend, Baraster felt the last remnants of his life flee his body.

"Sit still, will you!" Noria scolded, as she carefully packed more bandages on Jacob's wound.

Jacob continued to squirm and pull away, anxious to check on Baraster, holding onto the desperate hope that he might yet revive.

"He's dead, Jacob." Her eyes welled up again. "There is nothing to be done. It was a magical death—and there are too many wounded people here to take care of. Baraster wouldn't want me to kill twenty others while I tried to save him. You know that."

"How many?"

"I think we number thirty-five in all, now."

"And the army?" Jacob queried.

"There's no sign of them. Gunther's apprentice made it down to the village, and reported that it remains empty. It would appear all the soldiers were in the tunnels or on the plateau fighting us. The mage bought us time to regroup and escape. There," Noria stated, affixing the last bandage to Jacob's shoulder, "that should hold until we apply a proper poultice." She put her tools down and wiped her brow with the back of her meaty hand, "You still want to be a wizard like him, after seeing him die like that?"

Jacob considered for a moment before replying, "Yes." He reached up and touched the wound on his shoulder. "I may still lose the arm?" Jacob questioned, but didn't expect an answer. "There's no way I'll ever be able to be a farmer, or an artisan. But I could be a mage. I can learn. I can go to the academy, and learn."

"I fear," Noria said, "that you'll never be able to attend the academy in our kingdom. I do not understand how we are now enemies of the King." She paused, letting the reality of the situation sink in, "We'll have to cross the border, through the

~ Flashpoint ~

Dirage Valley and start a new life in Dower."

Jacob smiled, pleased with the thought that had crept into the back of his mind. His smile broadened, and his eyes lit up. "I'll find another academy. Maybe they'll be able to teach me a better way to use magic—a way that won't kill me. I can be a great wizard. I can make Baraster proud."

Noria shook her head in the motherly fashion he despised. "Let's get ourselves off this plateau first, and head to the border. We'll need some help bringing the wagons up from the village, to carry those who are still too weak to move on their own. Make yourself useful and go ensure the others are hitching the wagons properly. Guidance only—I don't have time to mend the arm again."

Jacob stood, smiled at Noria, and pulled a blanket around his shoulders to protect against the crisp morning air. He looked out over the plateau, lingering over the carnage that was still visible. Baraster's body lay twenty paces from where he now stood, covered with branches as there was no time or place for a proper burial. Jacob gave him a respectable bow as best he could, as he imagined one would for a departed king. Pride in the old wizard fended off much of his sense of loss, for now. Wiping a tear from his cheek, he moved toward the surviving tunnel, intent on getting the remnants of his village to the neighbouring kingdom to begin his new life.

While many were moving west, Patrick M. Charron came east to Cape Breton in 2007 for a Controller Position at an automotive plant in North Sydney. As fate would have it, the plant shuttered in 2009, but he and his family had become so enamoured of the people and places of Cape Breton they couldn't bear to leave. Patrick found employment with the provincial

~ Flashpoint ~

government and a local Marion Bridge store. Now his family continues to enjoy the amazing arts available on the island, performing in dramas & musicals at a variety of venues, including the Savoy, Wentworth Park Bandshell, and the Boardmore. While clearly the least talented member of the family, he will endeavour to continue to write fantasy in his free time.

Peter Andrew Smith

Invasive Species

Wolf sighted in Highlands National Park the headline screamed. James folded the newspaper under his arm and started back up the long driveway toward the house. Every time someone saw a large coyote they cried wolf. His face broke into a smile. Jillian would have laughed for days at a crack like that.

He stopped and let the memories wash over him. Then he wiped his face and took a few deep breaths of the clean, crisp air. He listened to the birds singing and watched a squirrel scamper in a nearby tree. He loved living on a winding country road where the trees hid the abandoned houses on either side. This was what he needed, quiet and solitude.

An explosion lifted off the porch roof and blew out the side window. James leapt into the ditch as shingles reached toward the sky and the telephone pole crashed to the ground. After the debris stopped falling, he lifted his head and surveyed the damage. Even at this distance he knew the front part of his house was gone and, given the flames licking out the side window, the rest was not far behind. He picked himself up and headed toward the nearest neighbour.

The door in the house across the street opened. A young woman, her short blond hair framing a cherub face, glared at him.

"I don't know you. You're not someone I've met."

"I need to use your phone to call the fire department," James said.

"Gran already called. They're on their way." The door slammed shut.

"Welcome to friendly Cape Breton," James muttered.

The door flew open.

~ Flashpoint ~

"Sarah's from Toronto." An old woman, same face but with wrinkles, stood in the doorway leaning over her walker. "You're that fellow from out West who bought the Cameron place."

"I am."

"You haven't been over to visit since you moved in last month."

"I haven't."

"High time we got to know each other." She looked him up and down. "I'm Agnes MacDonald. Everyone calls me Gran."

James gestured over at the flames across the street. "Not really a good time."

"You realize no power means no pump and no water don't you?"

James nodded.

"Fire Department will take ten minutes to get here. You can stare at the burning house like an idiot or come in and have some tea like a good neighbour." Agnes turned her walker around and started in. "Close the door behind you or this place will smell like smoke."

"So did you leave a cigarette burning?" Sarah asked from across the table. "That can cause a fire you know."

"He doesn't smoke," Agnes said. "I know because I watch him go for his jog each morning. You should too. He sometimes takes off his shirt. You'd like that."

Sarah turned the colour of James's burning house and tried to disappear under her chair.

"Oh, for God's sake sit up," Agnes said. "No one wants to marry a slouch."

"Gran! You're embarrassing. You shouldn't say things like that."

"Never be ashamed of the truth." Agnes pushed a plate of biscuits toward James. "You sure you don't want honey on these? Or we have meat pie if you would prefer."

"Just the tea is fine," James replied. "How long did you say the fire department would be?"

"I'll call and see." Agnes grabbed her walker and stumbled out of the room.

"Sorry about Gran," Sarah said twirling her hair around a finger. "I don't want to be here but my parents think she's too old to stay alone and might need to go into a home. Sometimes she

~ Flashpoint~

forgets things—like turning off the burner." She stopped playing with her hair. "Maybe that's what happened to your house. Do you suppose that caused the fire?"

"They're a couple of minutes out." Agnes cuffed Sarah on the back of the head before falling into her seat. "Did you not hear the explosion? Leaving a burner on causes a fire, not an explosion."

"Maybe something exploded because of the fire. That could have happened."

"Nonsense child, there is only one explanation. Only one possible reason for such a terrible thing to happen." Agnes leaned forward and pushed a wisp of her grey hair to one side. Her hazel eyes locked onto him and her voice dropped to a whisper. "Coyotes."

Sarah rolled her eyes and the sirens sounding in the distance rescued James.

James threw a blackened chair out the hole in the side of his house as he picked his way through the debris. He noticed Sarah coming up the driveway, dressed in a red windbreaker and carrying a basket which he expected contained a selection of food from her grandmother.

"You know what caused the fire? Or are they still waiting to find out why your house exploded?"

James hauled the remains of his table to the growing mound of debris. "Propane tank."

"A propane tank? You mean like from a barbeque?"

"Yes."

"I didn't know you had a barbeque. I like hamburgers cooked that way."

"I don't."

Sarah looked into her basket. "Then I should probably go back home. Gran said I should bring over the stew, but I told her you might be a vegetarian."

James sighed. "I don't own a barbeque."

Sarah's brow furrowed. "So if it was a propane tank, and that's what exploded but you have never owned a barbeque, then how come one exploded in your house?"

"Someone put it there."

~ Flashpoint ~

"Who would do that?" Sarah asked. "I mean, what reason would anyone have to do that?"

James shrugged. "What's in the basket, Sarah?"

"Oh, Gran was watching you work and figured you would be hungry. So she sent over some stew and biscuits with honey."

"Tell Agnes thank you, but no."

"How can you not be hungry? I mean, your whole kitchen exploded." Sarah took the top off the stew and the delicious aroma of deer meat assaulted James. Damn, he wished Agnes would mind her own business.

"I can fend for myself."

"Why would you do that? I mean why would you turn down perfectly good food from your neighbour?"

"Sarah." James locked her in his gaze. "What type of kin are you?"

Her eyes flashed. "That is just plain rude. You don't ask that."

"And what do you think your grandmother is doing?"

"Gran is being a good—" Her mouth closed as her brain caught up to the conversation. She looked at him carefully from the bottom of his soot covered work boots to the top of his sun kissed hair. "How can you tell we're kin?"

"Like the half-form, it is something older kin can do." James held up his hand and Sarah swallowed her next question. "Your grandmother wants me to choose food so she can figure out what I am. What's in your basket besides stew?"

"Biscuits with honey, rabbit pie, and iced tea. Plus all the stuff you need to eat and drink because, well, you know." She gestured at the devastation.

James saw movement in the window across the street.

"Okay. Let's eat.

Sarah's eyes widened. "What would you like?"

"A smile spread across his face. "Everything."

James savoured the return of silence as Sarah disappeared across the road with the dirty dishes. He looked at the remains of his house and headed for the backyard. He needed to burn off some anger and frustration but he couldn't really let go with nosy neighbours watching. Instead, he strolled through the small field into the woods behind the house, listening to the wind and breathing in the scents of the trees. He stood and felt calm wash over him. This was why he'd moved to rural Cape Breton.

A high pitched scream cut through his thoughts and the snarls and barks that followed sent him racing for the house. He burst from the trees to the sight of a coyote pawing at a small hole near an old stump at the edge of the clearing.

James picked up a stone and threw it at the coyote's hindquarters. It yelped and turned toward him in surprise. A second coyote appeared from the underbrush. A third emerged from the other side of the clearing and snapped at the hole as a small red snout peeked out.

"Are you stupid?" James yelled.

All three froze in place and tilted their heads to one side.

"Always run from humans."

White teeth answered from the largest coyote.

James shook his head. "Wrong. Coyote attacks bring trappers and hunters."

Two of the coyotes started to back away toward the trees. The largest stayed in place.

James clenched and unclenched his fists, trying to control his rising fury. "You really don't get it, do you?"

The remaining coyote began to crouch.

"Everyone loses if you attack a human. You see one, you turn and run."

The coyote leapt.

James let his anger flow and his body shift. He felt his muscles come alive as his true nature rose to the surface. His nose became a snout, but he forced the shift to stop in half-form so he had the best of both human and beast shapes. He flexed his claws and bared his fangs.

The coyote twisted in mid-air to escape, but James easily snatched it by the scruff of its neck. He held on tight and pulled the wide eyed animal close to his sharp teeth.

"My territory," he growled.

The coyote snapped at him. He forced its mouth shut with his other claw.

"You do not hunt in my territory." He shook the coyote violently from side to side. "Do I make myself clear?"

The coyote went limp. James threw it to the ground and

~ Flashpoint ~

allowed it to crawl into the safety of the forest.

He exhaled the rage pumping through his veins in a series of deep breaths as he sat on the ground. He felt his snout push back into his head as his body returned to human form.

The birds began to sing again. He opened his eyes to see the fox emerging from her hole.

"Yeah, they're gone," James said. "You and the kits are safe."

She sniffed the air.

"Does it matter what type of kin I am? I haven't bothered you all month."

The fox cautiously crept to where he sat in the grass. He reached out a hand and she dashed forward, licked it, and then retreated beyond his reach. She looked over at the house and then back to him.

James bit his lip. "They're going to be back, aren't they?"

She let out a short yip and growl.

"Are there enough local kin to stand up to them?"

Black eyes stared at him without blinking.

"Damn."

He had to go talk to the neighbours again.

James held out his cup for a refill. "Any idea when we might get around to talking about the coyotes?"

Sarah shrugged.

James sighed and sipped his drink. He sat through gossip about neighbours and talk about the weather while waiting for kin to arrive. When the last one came through the door, Agnes declared a necessity for tea before they could talk.

Chairs ringed the living room, with Agnes in the large comfortable recliner. Edith, a middle-aged woman whose eyes never stopped moving, sat on one side of her and Sarah on the other.

Sally and Bertha, two sisters who spilled over the sides of their chairs, took turns laughing at what Agnes was saying and nibbling on biscuits dabbed with honey. Doug, a hulking man who seemed normal size seated between the siblings, was soaking his biscuit in a small jar of honey.

James swallowed the last of his tea and cleared his throat

loudly.

"Sorry to interrupt, dear." Agnes touched Sally's hand to stop a rambling discourse about army worms and gardening. "Someone is impatient to start."

Sally glared at James for a moment before nodding at Agnes.

"We speak for all the kin on the Island and—"

"—what about her?" James asked.

A petite, pale woman with flaming red hair stood just outside the screen door.

"Karla," Agnes hissed. "You have some nerve..."

"The coyotes attacked my den," Karla said.

Sally and Bertha's faces clouded over and they murmured about the need to keep cubs safe.

Agnes waved a hand and Sarah brought a chair in from the kitchen and put it next to James.

"Your kits are okay?" Sally and Bertha asked as Karla sat.

She touched James' hand. "Yes."

"The coyotes are an invasive species who need to be run off the island," Agnes said.

"They left us alone before," Karla said.

"The little fox is right," Doug said. "Even we bears notice they have become different in the last months."

"Everyone is talking about the coyote as big as a wolf," Sarah said. "It was even in the paper."

"That's just nonsense," Agnes protested. "Never believe anything you read in that rag."

"There is no giant coyote," Edith said and then flushed as everyone looked at her.

"Exactly," Agnes announced. "It doesn't matter why they're acting this way now. We need to drive them out of Cape Breton and send them back to wherever they came from. Get the foreigners out!"

"By that logic I should leave," James said.

"Nonsense. I heard your mate was from here, so you're just coming home."

"Jillian's family came from Cape Breton, but that was generations ago."

"Good enough. Now that your branch of kin are back we can stand up to these interlopers. When you roar at them, they'll turn tail and run!" Agnes shook her fist. "The time for talk is over. Now is the time for action!"

Sally and Bertha clapped enthusiastically. Agnes grabbed her walker and launched herself vertically.

"Sarah, go get more tea. Alice, go into the cellar and break out the big bottle of honey for our allies and some deer meat stew for our champion. It's time to celebrate our victory!"

Doug and the sisters rushed forward and pumped James' hand and thumped his back. When the food arrived they retreated to their side of the room.

James turned to Karla. "What just happened?"

She rolled her eyes. "Lynxes are crazy."

James snagged Sarah's arm. "Am I missing something?"

"Gran says you're the answer to the coyote problem. She has everyone convinced you can make things right."

"Why?"

"You tried to hide, but Gran figured it out. She's smart like that," Sarah said. "You stay alone and aren't very sociable. You like deer meat and your kin used to live here."

"So?"

"Gran guessed your secret." Sarah gave him a shy smile. "She knows you're a cougar."

James pushed Sarah away and shouted for everyone to be quiet. He opened his mouth to explain their mistake when the world exploded with the sounds of coyotes howling.

Agnes threw herself at the door as she started to shift. "Those ill-begotten canines will rue the day."

"Gran!" Sarah shrieked. "You can't shift to beast form with your angina!"

Agnes snarled at her but stopped her shift in half-form and threw open the door to the twilight.

"Get off my lawn!" she shouted. A dozen of the boldest coyotes backed up as she stumbled down the steps, leaving her walker behind.

"Sarah, you and Alice stop her and bring her back before they attack," James barked.

Soon two lynxes stood between the raging Agnes and the coyotes trying to encircle her. The two cats started inching their way back toward the house despite Agnes' protests that she was ready to whip the insolent curs. A trio of coyotes slipped behind

~ Flashpoint ~

her, avoiding her claws as she tried to keep upright.

James narrowed his eyes. Things were moving too fast.

"I need Agnes out of the way and safe." James turned to the bears. "Can you convince those coyotes that trying to get behind her is a very bad idea?"

Bear paws started swatting and soon the bold coyotes were back into the large grouping. Slowly Sarah, Alice and the still angry Agnes had their backs to the step and coyotes on only three sides. The bears took up defensive positions with the lynxes as the coyotes paced back and forth in front of the steps.

James turned to Karla, cowering behind him. "I'm going to try to convince the coyotes to leave, but I need you to shift."

Her eyes went wide. "They'll tear me to pieces."

"I need your eyes and nose."

"What difference can that make?"

"If I can't convince them as a group, maybe I can sway their alpha." He put his hands on her shoulders. "Hopefully he is as clueless as Agnes."

For a moment, a slight smile touched her face. "But what if they won't listen?"

"Then you need to run when the fighting starts."

Karla shifted and a small fox trotted out to the front of the standoff.

"You're sending the little one? Come out here and teach these mutts a lesson!" Agnes stumbled, as an adventurous coyote snapped at her. James grabbed her walker and thrust it into Agnes' claws as he pushed to the frontline.

"What are you doing?" Agnes said. "Change form and drive out these invaders. Reclaim our land from them."

"You are not helping," James snapped. "This is wrong and needs to stop."

Fifty or so coyotes shifted their attention to him. There were too many of them to fight. This was not going to end well if he couldn't defuse the situation. A limping figure at the back caught his eye.

"You. Yes, you. The addled-looking male at the back trying not to be noticed. I thought I made myself clear when I threw you back into the woods that being aggressive like this is a stupid move."

The coyote in the spotlight made a half-hearted attempt to

growl as it started to slink off. A couple of others began falling back. James felt a flash of relief. They were listening. Perhaps it was going to be easy and he could be alone in the quiet again.

"Damn you, stop talking and fight them!" Agnes roared.

"Agnes," James yelled. "Shut up."

"The old cat is ours. The rest of you can go." A deep voice boomed from the darkness. "That offer will expire soon, so take it unless *you* want to expire."

The coyotes stopped retreating and paced nervously back and forth in front of them. *So much for the easy way of doing things.* Karla pressed up against his leg. She stared into a clump of coyotes near the underbrush. Great. The alpha was hiding.

"Why does your strongest and bravest cower like a human politician?" James asked.

The coyotes shifted their attention to the dimly lit area that Karla had pointed out.

"You try my patience." A tall man with a tangled beard stepped out from the darkness. "We are taking our rightful place. No more will we be despised and shunned by the kin. This land will be ours!"

James ignored the speaker and watched the gathered coyotes. Many of the males were snarling but a few were not. Most of the females were silent. Karla growled softly, the vibration rippling against his leg. James moved his feet slightly and black eyes turned to him. She bared her teeth and James sighed. She was right. There was no other choice left. The solitude had been nice while it lasted.

"Have your pups been safer these last few months?" James raised his voice. "Will war with the other kin give you more prey to hunt?"

"They will not listen to you. They are my pack, my coyotes." The man laughed. "You cannot challenge us and hope to win."

"I have no intention of challenging them," James said. "You, though, are weak and a coward. I challenge you for the leadership of the coyotes."

"What the hell? You're not supposed to—" Agnes' words were cut short as bear paws covered her mouth. The lynxes looked the other way.

The man spit on the ground. "None of our kin will ever

~ Flashpoint ~

follow you."

James knelt down and Karla licked his hand and growled at the man. The coyotes went deathly still. James flicked his hand and the fox raced back to where Agnes and the others waited. He stepped forward and let the coyotes quietly form a circle around him and the alpha.

"So you can impress a fox. That means nothing. I am the greatest coyote to enter Cape Breton. I have the heart of a wolf." The man shifted form to an oversized coyote and bared his teeth.

James locked eyes with the beast. "Just the heart?"

He released the rage he felt at having his home destroyed, his privacy violated, and his solitude broken. His body shifted form and grey fur broke forth to cover him from tail to snout. He threw back his head and let his howl tear through the stunned silence of the onlookers. The oversized one snarled and James flashed his sharp white fangs. The coyote turned and tried to run but James leapt and forced his opponent to the ground. He released through his teeth and claws all the anger and grief he carried in his heart over losing Jillian to the car accident six months ago.

The second time James threw back his head to howl, the coyotes joined him.

"I'm not supposed to let you in because Gran is mad at you," Sarah said, opening the door. "At least I think she is because she isn't speaking to me."

"Karla can't hunt because one of her kits is sick. Go get her some fresh rabbit from my woods." James walked past Sarah into the kitchen.

"I have nothing to say to you," Agnes snapped from her seat at the table. "You made me look like a fool."

"The coyotes are not a problem any more," James said. "Isn't that what you wanted?"

"I never would have let you in if I had known you were a wolf." Agnes pushed a cup toward him. "But since things are safe for Sarah and the other lynxes I'll keep my mouth shut. Tea?"

James nodded. "Just one minor detail."

"What's that?"

"You're going to fix my house."

~ Flashpoint ~

"Why in heaven's name would I do that?"

"Because you blew it up." James put a bit of milk in his tea.

"The coyotes blew up your house."

"First question I asked them after I put down that mongrel with dictatorial aspirations," James said. "They didn't do it."

"They're lying."

James smiled. "No one lies to you when you have the blood of the previous alpha on your teeth."

"I'm an old woman with a walker."

"One who can get along without it in half-form." James sipped his tea. "You owe me a house."

"You weren't doing anything about the coyotes, " Agnes protested. I needed you to be angry with them."

"You could have killed me or injured me."

"I didn't though, did I?" Agnes' eyes narrowed. "Besides I thought you were a cougar."

"That would have made it all right?" James shook his head. "Karla was right. You cats are crazy."

"I was desperate."

"Now you are not, and the price just went up," James said. "A house and an apology."

Agnes hissed and spat for a few moments as James sipped at his tea.

"All right. I'll call in some favours and pay for the work," she said.

"And?"

"I'm sorry I blew up your house."

"Yes, I suspect you are." James drained his cup. "I called your daughter last night, and you're moving into the nursing home next week."

Agnes was loudly cursing and swearing as James let the door slam behind him. He emerged into the beautiful morning sunshine and smiled at the sight of yapping fox kits playing with a blond lynx beside the remains of his house. This really was a good place to be.

He heard a car in the distance and started to yell for the kin to take cover but stopped. Instead he shifted to wolf form and raced across the road toward the delighted youngsters. The newspaper would probably report this tomorrow but he didn't

~ Flashpoint ~

care. After months of grief and anger, James was at peace. He was finished hiding.

Peter Andrew Smith lives and writes in Antigonish, Nova Scotia. He and his wife Meredith share a house with their dog Sophie who bears no resemblance to either a coyote or a wolf and will not eat anything but dry dog food and carrots. A list of Peter's serious and not so serious publications can be found at www.peterandrewsmith.ca.

B.R.A.N.E., Inc.

The first odd thing I noticed was the pale blue sticky note pasted on the bottom of his shoe. He knelt in front of the dark, silent copier and had already removed an access panel without saying more than "Good morning" to me with a brief nod and a not-quite-smile when he arrived at the office. The embroidered badge on his limp cotton shirt read *Leonard* and he was cute in a grim, planes-and-angles sort of way. Hadn't even asked me yet exactly what the trouble was with the copier. I debated whether to explain the problem or tell him about the paper stuck to his shoe as I surreptitiously checked my hair with my phone camera.

When he shifted his weight to reach inside the guts of the machine, I saw the bottom of his other shoe—and the blue square of paper there, too. I squinted. They looked like sticky notes, but they were held in place with packing tape. So I figured that a) he must know about them and b) I might as well just explain about the copier, even though he hadn't asked.

"It was fine yesterday afternoon, but then this morning when I went to print out the dailies, I just got gibberish," I told his back, repeating what I'd said to a bored-sounding dispatcher over the phone.

He didn't turn around, just nodded, his hand still deep inside the copier.

"I turned it off and then on again a few times, and I unhooked it from the network, and then I tried again, but I got the same thing," I added, because for some reason I wanted him to know that I wasn't the type of girl who just throws up her hands when a machine or piece of tech screws up.

He sat back on his heels and glanced at me over his shoulder. A smudge of something dark marred the back of his shirt, as if he'd brushed up against something dusty. "You still have what it printed?"

"Sure." I retrieved some sheets out of the recycling bin and showed them to him. Each page bore just a couple of illegible lines. "But like I said, you can't read it. I don't even know what font this is." The characters were printed in a weird symbol font I didn't recognize.

He glanced at the pages and his back stiffened. Suddenly the office felt very still.

"What was it you were trying to print?"

I shrugged. "Just the dailies—blank timesheets, schedules, appointment lists. I do it every morning, before everyone else comes in. I send them direct from my computer." *Just the first of the day's usually mind-numbing tasks,* I added silently.

"How long have you had this copier? About two months?"

I thought for a second, nodded. "Yeah, it's about that."

He nodded. "I think you might have gotten the wrong model, by mistake. Anything strange ever happen with it before?" Now he was looking at me—really noticing me for the first time, I thought. He hadn't even looked at my tattoos before, which most guys do, whether they like them or not—they still notice. Sure enough, now his eyes did linger over the new ink on my forearms —some cool symbols I'd found on the Internet. He had pushed his ball cap way back on his head and damp dark curls peeked out from under its brim. Why was he sweating? The office AC hummed along just fine. I noticed that his eyes were mismatched —one dark hazel green, one deep amber. It was oddly attractive.

You're the weirdest thing so far, I thought, but I only shook my head. "Folks will start arriving in about half an hour. Do you think you can fix it by then?"

"Do my best," he said, getting slowly to his feet. He stared at the copier for a minute, like he was thinking over his next move. Finally he said, "I have to get some equipment from the truck. Don't let anyone else in here until I come back, okay? And you should probably stay away from the copier now that it's open. Maybe over at your desk."

This got stranger and stranger, but I wasn't getting a bad vibe from the guy, just a weird one. "Sure."

I went and sat at my desk when he went out, but I couldn't settle in to any work. The exposed inside of the copier looked dark and deep, and even though he'd unplugged it, an

~ Flashpoint~

intermittent yellowish light flickered within it. I turned to my computer and started checking email, deftly deleting the overnight spam, but my eyes kept straying back to that oddly-lit blackness.

Leonard came back, lugging a rivet-covered silver toolbox. He bumped the door shut behind him with his hip and set the box down about five feet from the copier.

"What's your name?" he asked me. Not in an *I'd-like-to-ask-for-your-number* kind of way, but more like an *I-need-to-call-you-something* kind of way.

"Nicole."

"Okay, Nicole, I'm going to need your help." His mismatched eyes caught and held mine, looking very serious. "I called the office from my truck, but I don't have time to wait for backup and we want to have everything straightened away before anyone else gets here, right?"

Backup? Copier repairmen had backup? "Uh, sure," I said, although I didn't understand. No-one would miss the dailies for once, and it wasn't like having a repairman in the office was going to freak anyone out.

He put his hands on his hips and considered me. I felt his gaze flicker again over my ink and piercings, but it lingered longest on my eyes. "I'm going to be straight with you, because I think you can take it. There's something living in your copier. Now, that's not bad news in itself—"

I resisted a sudden urge to pull my feet up off the floor. "What? What lives inside copiers?" Images of spiders, cockroaches, and various other many-legged horrors skittered through my brain.

Leonard took a deep breath and blew it out through pursed lips. "Brownies."

I squinted at him, trying to decide what game he was playing. It didn't seem like a joke, though. "Brownies?"

He nodded, his eyes serious. "You know I don't mean the kind you eat, right?"

"Well, duh. I might think you're crazy, but I don't think you're suggesting the existence of sentient baked goods. You mean, like, fairies."

"Best not to call them that," he cautioned with a grimace and a shushing motion. "They really don't like it."

~ Flashpoint ~

"Right." I stood up from my desk. "So, supposing for a minute that I grant you the existence of brownies, why would they be in my copier?"

"Well, they live in a lot of copiers. That's not the problem," Leonard said. "The problem is, you've also got a flashpoint indicator, which is why I'm probably going to need your help."

He didn't say what a flashpoint indicator was, but it didn't sound good. He knelt down and flipped up the catches on the metal box, opened the lid and took out what looked like a pair of 3-D glasses. The old-school, one-red-lens-and-one-blue-lens kind, but the lens colours matched his eyes, green and amber. He slipped them on and scanned my printouts from this morning. "*Skitkarl*," he breathed, and although the word was foreign to me, it sure sounded like cussing.

The phone rang, and I jumped. "Schneider and Ali, how may I help you?"

"You called this morning about trouble with your copier?"

"Yes." I thought I recognized the bored-sounding dispatcher. She still sounded bored, and now her voice was tired, too, as if it had taken all her current energy reserves just to call me back.

"I'm sorry, but we won't be able to get anyone out there until at least noon." She didn't sound all that sorry.

I frowned at Leonard. "You can't send anyone to fix the copier until noon?" I repeated back to her slowly, for his benefit.

His eyes widened behind the absurd green and amber lenses and he shook his head. He stabbed at the paper with his forefinger.

"Okay," I said into the receiver. "We'll wait." When I hung up I put my hands on my hips and glared at him.

"We monitor calls when the readings in a certain area get unusually high," he explained. He pulled another pair of glasses out of the metal box and handed them to me. I put them on and looked over the printout. Sure enough, the strange symbols resolved into words.

FLASHPOINT ALERT. Portal breach imminent at coordinates 3514.259.4158.SWCNA

I looked up at him and pulled the glasses down on my nose. "You know what, Leonard? My mood has been pretty much going down the toilet since I came in this morning, but I have a little bit of patience left. About five minutes' worth. That's how long you have to explain all of this to me."

He swallowed. Maybe he was used to people just accepting it when he came barging into their offices to announce that their equipment was full of imaginary creatures, but I didn't get to be office manager at twenty-five by being a sucker. And I wasn't about to lose that job, boring as it might be, at the hands of some whacked-out repairman with a few pairs of funky glasses.

Even if he was cute.

I tapped my foot a couple of times to let him know his five minutes were ticking down.

Leonard glanced at the copier and sighed. "Okay, long story short. I think this copier shouldn't be here at all. We had some shipping mistakes a few months ago—"

"Who's 'we'?" I interrupted.

"Oh, we're brain," he said.

"Brain?"

"B.R.A.N.E., Inc.," he spelled out. "It stands for Bureau of Realms and Netherworlds Enforcement. Anyway, as I was saying, some of the units meant for our field offices went to mundane operations, like yours. Unfortunately we've had a hard time tracking all of them down."

"And these 'special' copiers have 'brownies' living in them?"

He nodded, apparently oblivious to the sarcasm. "They're not all copiers, but yeah. See, brownies like to live in houses and offices. They do little chores in return for a roof over their heads. They seem to like big copiers especially—I don't know why. Maybe the warmth. You notice the office is a lot tidier since you got this copier? Cleaners seem to be doing a better job? Maybe people are picking up after themselves more?"

I frowned and thought back over the past two months. He could be right, although I'd thought it was just a result of my nagging people not to be such slobs. I shrugged, not ready to buy into his story just yet. "Maybe. So what's with the gibberish printouts and this 'portal breach' stuff?"

He knelt to the metal box again and rummaged inside. "Brownies are especially sensitive to the links between worlds," he said, "particularly between Earth and the faerie realm, the demon planes, and the ethereal realm. Earth is like a way-station or hub connecting them all. Which unfortunately also means it's full of potential flashpoints. Brownies can sense these. Think of them as an early warning system. They tried to send a message about it, but since the copier is in the wrong office, you got it instead of one of the team."

I blinked. "So you want me to buy into the idea of brownies, other faeries, demons, *and* other worlds? Just because my copier is futzed?"

Leonard found what he was looking for and held out two items that looked almost like a motorcycle helmet and a gun. Almost. "In a couple more minutes, if we don't move to contain the breach, you're going to have a lot more to worry about than a busted copier."

When I didn't move to take the objects, he juggled them into one hand and pulled out his own sort-of motorcycle helmet with the other. Both of them bore an odd logo I didn't recognize: colourful strands woven together in a sort of circle. He slid one over his head, then stood up again and stared at me intently. The effect was somewhat diluted by the green and yellow lenses of the glasses he still wore. "Are you going to help me, or is it all too much for you?"

I snatched the things out of his hands. He might not have convinced me of all this ridiculous stuff, but I wasn't going to have him think I was some vapid keyboard bunny about to cower, snivelling, under my desk. "If whatever goes down here costs me my job, you're going to hear about it," I muttered, slamming the helmet on. So much for the hot rollers I'd spent twenty minutes on this morning. It was comfortable and light for its bulk, though, and I quickly forgot that I was even wearing it. I pulled off my shoes and kicked them under my desk, too. I didn't think heels were going to be appropriate footwear in the next little while.

"So where's this breach going to happen?" I asked him. "Right here in the office? 'Cause I've never been aware of any kind of portals in here, except the normal kind of, you know, *doors*."

Leonard shook his head and glanced down at another gadget he'd pulled out of the box. It looked a little like a tricorder from *Star Trek*. "Not here in the office, but nearby," he said. "Up on the roof, I think. It's actually pretty lucky that the copier ended up in this building by accident. This must be a new portal, just opening up."

Yeah, I feel really lucky. I held up the gun-like thing. "All right, show me how this works."

"You hold it like a gun, point and shoot at the target," he said. "But we call it an equalizer."

"That's original."

He shook his head. "No, not like that, because it's not a gun—no bullets are going to come out of it."

"So, like, a force-field or something?" I asked, pointing it around experimentally. "I think I'll just call it a gun, okay?"

"Sure." He studied the readout on his gadget without looking up. I pointed the gun at him for just a second to see if he'd notice. He didn't seem to. That struck me as pretty trusting, considering we'd only met about twenty minutes ago. I pointed it at the copier.

"Don't do that," he said. "Makes the brownies nervous."

I swung the gun away, but really—I hadn't even seen these hypothetical brownies yet.

"It's definitely the roof," Leonard said, holstering the gadget in his belt and pulling another gun-thing out of the box. His was bigger than mine. *Men.* "Do you have access to the roof directly from this office?"

I shook my head. "Nope. There's just one staircase at each end of the building, as far as I know. If you turn right from here, the closest one is at the end of the hallway."

"We'll have to deal, then." He knelt in front of the copier and held a low-voiced conversation with the putative brownies. It occurred to me that if he was just some nut, I was going to feel mighty silly when everyone else arrived for the morning and found me wearing a not-quite-motorcycle helmet while some guy talked to the copier. However, since it looked like we were going up to the roof, I took the opportunity to dig my sneakers out from under the desk and slip them on. I have to walk a block to the bus, and I don't do that in heels.

Leonard turned from the copier and dug inside the metal box again. He tossed me a small baggie and said, "Stick these on the soles of your shoes."

They looked just like the squares of blue paper I'd noticed on the bottoms of his own shoes, but when I took these out of the bag they each bore a thin film that peeled off to reveal an adhesive. I applied them and they stuck extremely tightly at the slightest touch. I hoped they didn't have to be straight, but he

~ Flashpoint ~

hadn't mentioned that. And his own were only attached with packing tape.

When I looked up from having stuck on the blue things and tied my laces, I was glad I'd sat down. A group of small beings, the tallest maybe six inches high, was in the process of jumping one at a time out of the open access panel of the copier. They reminded me of garden gnomes, although less rotund. Most of them did have pointed hats. Hair colour varied, but their skin was uniformly a deep-tan brown. Pointed ears stretched as high as the tops of their heads, and ended in fluffy tufts of hair. Their faces were, for the most part, fine-featured and a bit pouty. They wore a varied assortment of pants, jackets, and tiny boots in earth tones, except for one rebel who sported a miniature motorcycle jacket in black leather and a blue do-rag knotted at the back of his head. Most of them ignored me, but the biker-type regarded me with an extremely cranky frown. I wondered if I'd been somehow mistreating the copier. Or maybe he didn't approve of some of the jokes I'd copied last week.

Leonard looked over at me and I snapped my jaw shut. "They can help us, but we have to get them up on the roof, and we can't let anyone else see them. They're already annoyed that they have to expose themselves to you."

"Let's hope *that* won't be necessary," I muttered. Louder, I said, "There's hardly anyone around this time of the morning—I get here early because the next bus makes me too late. They can probably just walk."

The brownies started shaking their heads before I finished talking. Leonard did the same. "They won't take a chance," he said. "It's a big deal for them to be out of the copier at all when anyone's around."

I glanced around the office. "Well, there's this," I said, grabbing my oversized purse off the back of my chair. I'd brought my pink and white "Hello Bunny" bag, because I'd been feeling sort of whimsical when I left the house this morning. The cranky brownie looked aghast and I felt a pleasurable surge of vindictiveness. "They'd fit," I pointed out.

Leonard seemed to be trying hard to smother a grin. "They would," he said seriously. "And it would make good camouflage. That thing is huge. I think you could even get the equalizer in there."

~ *Flashpoint* ~

The brownies exchanged glances and one started to protest, but the tallest one—not the rebel brownie, but one with a flowing white beard and tiny glasses perched on a bulbous nose—held up a hand. Apparently the decision had been made. I put the gun inside, then set the purse on the floor on its side and held it open. With as much dignity as they could manage, the brownies marched in. I scooped the purse up gently and swung it over my shoulder with care. "Okay, Leonard," I said. "Let's do this thing, whatever it is."

He nodded and closed up the metal box. After a quick press of a button on one end, the whole thing contracted until it was about half as big as before, and he tucked it up under one arm. With the other hand he picked up his toolbag. "Lead the way."

The hallway outside the office was deserted, so Leonard gave me a low-voiced briefing as we walked.

"When the flashpoint portal starts to open, we'll have about a minute and a half to shut it down before it stabilizes enough for anything to pass through," he said. "That should be plenty of time, because with both of us and the brownies working together, we'll be able to hit it with a concentrated amount of anti-thaumatter."

I almost chuckled. If Leonard was making this all up or delusional, he'd thought it through.

"Anti-thaumatter. Right," I said. "Where do we get that?"

"It's what comes out of your equalizer," he said. "That's why we call them that. A portal can only open when the thaumic force on one side of the brane becomes greater than on the other side, and stabilizes that way. The equalizer exerts thaumic force to compensate for the other side's attempts to thin it on their side."

"So it's not like antimatter, then," I said, trying to make it sound like I understood. Most of my notions about antimatter came from old *Star Trek* episodes. "We don't have to worry about particles colliding and cancelling each other out and destroying the world or anything."

"Um, no," he said. "That would only happen if two thaumically identical but opposite things from different sides of the portal came in contact with each other. I don't think even that would destroy the world. It could destroy the two things, I suppose." He kept his voice low but walked faster. "Anyway, all the equalizer will do is re-stabilize the portal so it can't open. And those blue squares you put on your shoes? They're anti-thaumatter grounds, to keep you from being sucked through the portal when it's unstable."

I was glad they'd stuck so tightly. But I frowned. "Seems like portals could be opening all the time if you weren't there to catch them."

Leonard shook his head. "They can only initiate at a place where the brane between the planes is weak to begin with—we call them flashpoints," he explained. "Luckily, there are relatively few places like that. That's why we monitor them. Although," he added, his voice sounding tired, "there seem to be more weak places developing all the time. We're spread really thin trying to cover them all. But once we deal with this attempt, we'll get a team in here to try and patch up the thin portion of the brane as soon as possible, so it won't happen again," he added.

We'd reached the end of the hallway and I pushed open the door that led to the stairs. "Why are they happening more frequently? What's causing the change?" I asked him.

"No-one's sure," he said. "But we're working on it." He didn't sound all that hopeful.

"Humans," a voice said from behind me, and I jumped and whirled. The hallway lay empty.

A chuckle came from inside my Hello Bunny bag, followed quickly by a *shhhhhhh!* I felt a hot wave wash over my face. *Damn brownies.* I'd forgotten about them for a moment.

"We don't know that," Leonard argued, and I had the distinct impression that this was a conversation he'd had before.

"Humans are weakening every other aspect of the Earth," said the same voice, and I realized the voice was female. "Why look any further for an explanation for this weakening as well?"

Leonard threw me an exasperated look and rolled his eyes.

"But still you're helping us," I threw over my shoulder at the bag.

Someone snorted a tiny snort. "It's our world, too," said the brownie. "We know you humans think you have some kind of superior claim to it just because you've spread your nasty—"

Whatever else the brownie was going to say was cut off by an even louder *shhhhh!* and lost in a burbling noise that sounded

~ Flashpoint ~

like someone had clapped a tiny hand over someone else's tiny mouth.

That little exchange got us up to the top of the stairwell, and I slid back the bolt that secured the door leading to the roof. Before I pushed it open, though, Leonard laid a hand on my arm. His skin was cool, and just a little clammy. It was reassuring that he felt a bit nervous. I was doing my best to ignore the butterflies careening around in my stomach and the tightness in my chest, and I felt glad that I wasn't the only one.

"All you have to do up here is follow my lead," he said, looking intently into my eyes with his mismatched ones. I couldn't help thinking again that the difference was intriguing. "Point where I point, shoot when I shoot or tell you to shoot. Stop when I say it's okay."

I nodded. "Got it."

"You think you can hold your aim steady? The area of the portal should be at least a couple of feet in diameter, so you don't have to hit a really small target."

"I've played laser tag and paintball with my brothers," I said. "Neither one had the fate of the world hanging on it, but we're pretty competitive."

He flashed me a rare grin. "You'll do great."

"When should I let the...er...brownies out of the bag?"

Leonard consulted his gadget. "I think we'll have at least a minute or two once we're on the roof," he said. "The levels haven't reached critical yet. After we close the door we'll look for a spot with some cover, I'll transmit the actual coordinates of the flashpoint, and you can set them down then. No sense making them run further than they have to, since their legs are short."

"We heard that," said the voice from the bag.

"No offense," Leonard said. "But you can't say it isn't true."

When the brownie didn't seem to have a retort for that, Leonard pushed the crash bar down and swung the door open. The sun hadn't been up all that long, but it burst into the gloomy stairwell with a searing brilliance. My eyes watered and I blinked as I followed Leonard through.

The rooftop was typical office-building style, with physical plant intakes and outflows, tin-plated sheds and stacks and other things whose purpose I couldn't identify. Any one of them would have afforded us some cover, but we didn't have time to take two

~ Flashpoint ~

steps toward them because obviously Leonard's gadget was wrong. A three-foot wide, shimmering grey globe with a mercury-like sheen hung in the air about twenty feet from us, spitting tiny forks of black lightning.

Leonard swore and dropped to one knee, scrabbling with the metal box.

"What's wrong? Let us out!" yelled a brownie, and something sharp stabbed into my back, just below my shoulder blade.

I yelped. The Hello Bunny bag slid off my shoulder and slipped out of my sweaty grasp. The bag plopped to the pebbly rooftop with a *thunk*. Brownies grunted and groaned and spilled out of the bag, muttering what I assumed were brownie curse-words.

I knelt and pulled the equalizer out of the bag once the little creatures were out of my way. "Should I shoot it?" I breathed at Leonard.

"Yes!" he snapped. "It's already worse—"

A clear calm washed over me as I raised the equalizer and took aim. This was going to be easy. As a target, the globe was huge compared to the skinny frames of my brothers. I squeezed the trigger.

Nothing happened. I released it and looked at Leonard.

"Keep shooting!" he yelped.

I aimed and shot again, but I still couldn't see or feel any effect. Keeping my aim steady at the globe and my finger pressed on the trigger, I said, "Is anything happening?"

"Yes, you just can't see it," he said, fumbling with the box. He opened the lid and did something inside. "Come on, boot up," he muttered.

"You could have *told* me that."

Meanwhile, the brownies seemed to have taken up a formation utilizing my legs as their cover. They peeked around my ankles and over the tops of my shoes, gripping tiny versions of my equalizer that they had produced from somewhere. They all pointed and presumably shot at the crackling globe, but it was disconcerting that there was no visible indication that anything at all was happening.

If this were a movie, I thought, *there'd be some kind of cool beam or light or something.* Like the spitting, crackling energy

~ *Flashpoint* ~

beams in *Ghostbusters*. I mean, you *knew* something was happening when you engaged a proton pack. With the absolute lack of feedback from the equalizers, I couldn't even tell if I was hitting the target or not. Nothing on the globe gave any sign that our actions were affecting it at all.

Leonard continued clicking buttons inside the box.

"Is this working?" I demanded.

"No," he said curtly. "Don't stop, though," he yelped, as I let my hand start to drop. "You're slowing it down—maybe even holding it steady—but it's not enough to close it."

"Would you consider helping, then?" I tried to bite down on the sarcasm in my voice, but it came through loud and clear. The weirdest part was how quiet all this was. The globe was virtually silent, except for the sharp pops of the lightning crackles, and the weapons made no sound at all. I wondered if the globe could be some kind of hologram and this could still turn out to be an elaborate prank.

I glanced down at the brownies clustered around my feet and dismissed that thought. They were damn real. One had his forearms braced firmly on my instep.

"I'm trying," Leonard said. "I don't think my equalizer is going to make the difference we need, so I'm trying to tap into the global net, see if I can pull in energy from anywhere else. Trouble is..." he broke off and I heard the stutter of keyboard typing, "...the presence of the portal is disrupting my signal."

"What about other—agents, or whatever you are?" I asked him. "You said there wasn't time to call for backup, but maybe there's someone else in the area already. Can you check on that?"

My arms felt heavy. The equalizer wasn't much of a weight, but the strain of holding my arms out and steady would soon start affecting my aim.

His lips pressed together in a pessimistic line. "I can try—"

Whooomph! Without warning the globe expanded, growing from three feet wide to six in a single burst. It was like someone had forced high-pressure air into a balloon. I actually felt the air displacement hit me, and staggered back a step. Leonard swore.

The air slapped my face, fiery hot and smelling like a compost heap, the heat and stink making me blink watering eyes. My aim faltered for a second, and wavered away from the target despite its increased size. Without the invisible field of anti-

~ Flashpoint ~

thaumatter pouring into it—or onto it, or however it worked—the globe shifted from silvery grey to translucent, and I glimpsed what lay on the other side of the portal. I had three impressions: glowing yellow eyes, a jagged-clawed hand, and tattered black wings. And—definitely more than one. A scorched, burnt-meat scent tickled my nostrils.

I twitched the equalizer back on target and the globe shuddered and greyed out again. It didn't shrink at all. My trigger finger was starting to go numb from squeezing so hard. I had an unwelcome thought.

"Is this thing going to run out of—anything? Energy, or whatever?"

"Eventually, yes," Leonard said. "Look, we'd better switch. I'll take both equalizers and you try to get us some help."

"But I don't know—"

"I'll tell you what to do." He stood from the box, levelled his equalizer one-handed at the globe, and depressed the trigger. The globe shuddered again, and shrank back a bit, losing maybe a foot or so of its diameter.

Leonard held out his other hand and waggled his fingers for my gun, and I carefully eased it into his grasp, keeping the trigger depressed until his own finger closed over it. I let go with relief, quickly flexing my hands to try and get some feeling back into them. The brownies skittered away from my feet as I moved over and knelt at the box. Inside was an industrial-looking laptop computer, with a standard keyboard and an overlaid skin of weird symbols. A program resembling an Internet browser displayed on the screen, with a bunch of tabs open across the top. Relief washed over me. A computer, I could deal with.

"Press the F7 key," a voice instructed from my left, and I realized that the cranky rebel brownie had clambered up the side of the box. She was also the owner of the female voice I'd heard earlier. She'd passed her weapon off to one of her comrades and had come over to help guide me through whatever I was going to do here. The tone of her voice hadn't softened any, but I was glad of the assistance. I did as she said.

More of the weird symbol font from the printouts scrolled up the screen. I felt in my pocket for the 3D glasses and slipped them on, and the characters resolved into something I could read.

Unfortunately, not something I could understand. It was

~ Flashpoint ~

just a bunch of numbers, and I had no idea what they referenced.

The cranky brownie frowned and shook her head. "That's just data on the portal strength," she said, "and the available energy flux in the area. If we're looking for backup, we want F12."

I duly pressed F12 and another window popped open, displaying a map that I recognized after a moment as the city core. I used the arrow keys to hone in on our block.

"Chaltos-A for nearby agents," the brownie directed.

"Well, if I knew which one of these symbols was *chaltos,* that might be helpful," I said.

"For Mab's sake, you've got one on your arm!" The brownie snorted and pointed to a key with a two-pronged curlicue.

I froze, startled. She was right—part of the new tattoo was a sigil that looked identical to the one inscribed on the key. The globe crackled as a finger of electricity raced across its surface, and I shook myself. Whatever the coincidence meant or didn't mean, I didn't have time to worry about it just now. I pressed the curlicue and the A key together. Two purple dots appeared on the screen, one that I figured must be Leonard himself since it was exactly where I thought our building would be, and another one very close. I moved the cursor and clicked the nearby dot, and a dialogue box opened up.

"That's for sending a message," the brownie said. "Do it quick!"

"What do I say?" I asked, but I started typing the first thing that came to me. *Portal opening. Request immediate assistance.*

"Keep it short. Something like, 'Portal opening. Request immediate assistance'," Leonard said.

I clicked *send.* "Now what?"

"Better come and take back your equalizer. My arms are burning."

As I stood, he slid one foot toward me so I could reach my equalizer better. In the still-eerie silence, broken only by the globe's intermittent crackling, I heard a faint ripping-peeling noise. Leonard seemed to hear it, too, and we both realized in the same instant what it was.

The sound of one of his jury-rigged anti-thaumatter grounds peeling off the sole of his shoe on the uneven rooftop.

He had just time to meet my eyes in a horrified glance

~ Flashpoint ~

before the force of the destabilized portal pulled him a few stumbling steps toward it. I grabbed for my equalizer, but his finger slipped off the trigger before I could get mine on, and the globe surged again. Worse, with Leonard trying to resist the pull of the globe, his aim wavered, and there was a moment once again when the globe gained power, turned translucent, and gave me another look at the world beyond.

I gulped.

This time, since the globe was bigger, I saw more of the other side. The creature I had only glimpsed before was much taller than I had realized. Taller—and even more terrifying. The ultimate stereotypical devil-type demon—with the addition of an extra set of horns, more teeth, more muscles, and a few assorted tentacles. Some additional clawed fingers and a set of blade-tipped wings. *That's* who was knocking at the door.

I grabbed desperately and caught Leonard's hand with one of mine, while I brought the equalizer to bear on the globe and squeezed the trigger. An opaque skin slid over the surface of the globe, but it didn't shrink. The black lightning bolts streaking across its surface seemed to have grown, too, and one sizzled out and hit the pebbled surface below it. Dirt particles flared and smoked.

The force drawing Leonard toward the globe was incredible. He leaned back, trying to counterbalance it, and I tightened my grip on his hand. It was as if he hung suspended over a gorge, as gravity dragged at him. My arm ached already with the strain of trying to hold him back. There was no way we could do this alone.

"Any reply?" I yelled to the cranky brownie.

"Nothing."

"We have to get Leonard's weapon back on target," I told her. Leonard was still trying to aim and shoot, but he couldn't get a steady bead while he fought to keep from being dragged closer to the globe. It seemed to have grown again, although it remained opaque. I was thankful for small mercies. The eyes of that creature on the other side promised things I didn't want to think about.

"What the heck is going on here?"

The voice came from behind me, and I threw a quick glance back over my shoulder. A girl stood beside the box holding the computer, hands on her hips and a disapproving glare taking in me, Leonard, the globe, and the brownies all at once.

No, not a girl, I realized. Well, female, but not human. I saw upswept, pointed eartips poking through long, straight hair—blonde hair, but oddly tinted with green overtones. Her eyes, large and cornflower blue, tilted up at the outer edges, lending her a puckish look belied by the glare. Her legs and arms were a little too thin, her torso a little too long. All tiny things, but they added up to decidedly not human.

I tilted my head down so I could look over the tops of the 3D glasses I still wore—an instinctive action since I wasn't used to wearing glasses and it just seemed that I should be able to see her better without them. I may not have seen her *better*, but I certainly saw her differently.

Without the benefit of the special lenses, she looked like a perfectly human, perfectly cute, perfectly stylish young woman.

"Amber!" Leonard shouted. He hadn't looked around at her, his attention being quite fully taken up with trying to aim his equalizer and battle the attractive force of the globe at the same time, so he must have recognized her voice.

I felt a weird twinge of...something. Jealousy?

"I hope you're here to help," I said. "As you can see, we're in some trouble."

"Who's your *friend*, Len?" she asked, ignoring me. "Here, let me do that," she said to the cranky brownie, brushing her away from the keyboard rudely. Granted, the brownie's small size hindered her efforts to call for more help, since every key on the keyboard was as big as one of her hands.

Leonard slid a foot closer to the globe, his feet skittering across the rough pebbles underfoot. I had a momentary fear that his other anti-thaumatter grounding pad would be scraped off.

I was about to yell at "Amber" to come and lend a hand, but she beat me to it. "I'm sending out a global emergency call, and trying to suck down some extra-thaumic energy," she said. "I don't really have any upper body strength on this plane, so I can't help keep Leonard back from the portal. I'll bet one of his grounding pads came off, didn't it? Did you tell the human girl, Len, how I kept telling you to get them fixed or get new ones, and you kept telling me how they were 'just fine for now'?"

To do her credit, her thin fingers were flying over the

~ *Flashpoint* ~

keyboard as she spoke; she wasn't just scolding Leonard, she really did seem to be trying to help.

"I don't think this is the time—" he started, but his words cut off abruptly as the globe enlarged like a balloon being blown up, and both his feet slipped out from under him. I lost my grip on him and his equalizer flew out of his hand and bounced across the gravel. He went down hard on his back.

He flipped himself over and clawed for purchase on the ground, but slid inexorably toward the globe.

I didn't think. I dropped my own equalizer, grabbed his hands, and braced myself, careful to keep my own feet flat on the ground.

It worked. To an extent.

Leonard stopped sliding toward the globe. Some of the brownies swarmed toward his feet, and I saw that they carried his lost grounding pad. If they could stick it back on, maybe we could salvage this yet. I pulled against the force even harder, to give them time to work.

However, with both equalizers off the target, the globe burst suddenly to a full seven feet in diameter, turned completely transparent, and sent a flurry of black-tentacled lightning strikes toward the ground. They caught and held like living mooring ropes, sizzling and hissing.

And the demon stepped through.

I heard Amber swear in that weird language. I knew without a doubt that it had to be a curse. No one in their right mind would say anything else at that moment.

The brownies scurried back towards us as the pull against Leonard abruptly ceased. I fell backwards, half-pulling him over on top of me, and pain shot up my back and down my arms as I landed hard. I felt, rather than heard, his breath whoosh out in a rush, and behind it a wave of fetid heat from the portal. The brownies had fixed Leonard's anti-thaumatter ground. Once he'd fallen down, they could get to the soles of his feet.

Well, that was ironic, because the demon—or whatever it was—was through now, anyway.

It looked around, and its massively muscled chest rose and fell as it took a deep breath. I wondered crazily if it felt fresh and cool after the heat of the plane it had come from, or unpleasantly cold. It didn't seem to mind, anyway, because the first thing it did was reach down, pick up Leonard's dropped equalizer, and casually crush it in one fist.

That can't be good.

I struggled to my feet, because if I had to face some creature from another plane, I wasn't going to do it sitting down. Leonard tried to help me, but it was more the other way around. He'd fallen hard, too, and held one arm as if it really, really hurt to move it.

"Amber," Leonard half-hissed, although the demon was standing right there and could no doubt hear perfectly well, "Amber, do we have anyone—anyone at all?"

To her credit, Amber had apparently just kept on working as the portal opened and the denizen from the other side stepped through. "Help is on the way," she hissed back, although for all I knew it could have been a bluff for the demon's sake. Leonard seemed to stand a little taller, anyway, so I guess what she said gave him some hope. He was probably thinking we just had to contain things for a couple more minutes on our own.

Me, I wasn't thinking that way. Maybe I'm just not one to put my faith in other people, or last-minute rescues or *deus ex machina*. I was sizing up that crimson sucker and wondering where his weaknesses might be.

He stood a good seven feet tall, now that I could see him clearly and we stood on the same level. Crimson skin, covered in rune-like markings that could have been tattoos of some kind, or possibly were naturally-occurring marks, like demon birthmarks or something. Some of them looked familiar. In fact, I recognized a two-pronged curlicue that matched the one on the keyboard—and my arm. A chill like a slow trickle of icy water skittered down my back. What could that mean?

"What do the runes mean?" I hissed at Leonard, because if we were going to pretend the demon couldn't hear us, I could go along with that. Maybe it could hear us, but not understand English. It still hadn't made a move beyond crushing the gun, surveying us with slitted, lizard-like eyes, as if wondering whose head it was going to rip off first. Yeah, that kind of look.

"What runes?" he whispered back, even though he was staring at the demon just like I was.

"The ones covering his hide," I said impatiently. "I don't know, maybe you guys call them something else. Symbols?

~ Flashpoint ~

Sigils?"

Leonard shook his head. "I don't see them."

That freaked me out for a second, because I started wondering if it even looked like a demon to anyone else (the way Amber looked different with or without the glasses). I realized I was still wearing my glasses, but Leonard had lost his when he fell. I lowered my head and peered over the top of the lenses, like a gimlet-eyed librarian when your book's three weeks overdue. Huh. He looked exactly the same, except for—no runes.

"Greetings," he said finally, breaking the awkward silence. His voice sounded like stones slithering over each other in the bottom of a streambed. "If you care to try and bargain with me, I'll hear your pleas now."

That definitely didn't sound good. At. All.

Leonard chose that moment to stand up to the guy, maybe still thinking that help was only seconds away. He took a deep breath and stepped slightly in front of Amber and the brownies and me, and squared his shoulders. "You are neither welcome nor permitted on this plane. You are in violation of the Inter-Planal Reciprocal Exclusivity charter, and as a recognized agent of B.R.A.N.E., I demand you return to your own plane at once."

I had to admit he sounded pretty official and serious and threatening. If it were me, I would have scatted back to my own plane pretty quick.

However, the demon was not me. He regarded Leonard though narrowed eyes for a moment and then burst into laughter. The streambed rocks were now granite boulders, tumbling down a scree-littered slope and crashing into each other. It was actually painful. I barely stopped myself from covering my ears with my hands, but I somehow thought the creature would like that and I didn't want to give it the satisfaction.

He glanced over at me, still chuckling. I felt his hot gaze flick over me, assessing and dismissing. Instinctively, I took a step closer to Leonard and moved my arm just a little behind his, so the creature wouldn't see my tattoos. Then he seemed to really notice Amber.

His eyes narrowed to even-more-unfriendly slits and he hissed, "Shifter."

I tore my gaze from the demon to see her reaction, just in

time to catch her—unbelievably—glance up at the extraplanar horror and flip her middle finger at him.

"Natural enemies," Leonard whispered to me.

"I got that," I whispered back.

I wasn't sure how she did it, but Amber returned her gaze to the keyboard in such a way that it was a deliberate insult to the demon. She also kept typing, and spoke to him without looking up again.

"You heard my colleague," she said. "This isn't going to work; you might as well go back."

He crossed to her in a few quick strides and swung his clawed fist in a wide arc. I gasped, certain he was going to decapitate her in one strike, but instead he batted the laptop. It sailed away from Amber in a shallow arc and hit the pebbled roof fifteen feet away. Miraculously it didn't smash into a million pieces, but I seriously doubted it would still be in working order if one of us managed to retrieve it.

Amber leapt to her feet and hissed something in that odd language. Then she was gone. The demon whirled to watch as a long-haired blonde cat—with an oddly greenish tint to its fur—darted between his legs and toward the crackling black fingers of electricity anchoring the globe.

I took advantage of the distraction to grab Leonard's glasses off the ground and jam them onto his face. I wanted to be sure he could see everything I was seeing.

"Runes," I told him, sticking my arm in front of his face. "*Runes.* What do they mean?"

I'd noticed that it wasn't just the two-pronged curlicue on the demon that matched both the symbol Leonard had called "chaltos" and part of my new tattoo. The rest of my tattoo—an oval with a wavy line through it and a squiggle that looked like some Greek letter whose name I could never remember—were also replicated on the demon's crimson hide. The three ran together in a line across his midriff in exactly the same configuration as on my forearm.

Leonard's eyes widened as he glanced from the demon to my arm and back again. "*Theros, chaltos, lunata,*" he said. "They —match. I don't understand." He shook his head as if trying to clear it, pain making his eyes dull and unfocused.

The demon roared, making both of us jump, and Leonard

~ Flashpoint ~

hissed in pain at the jolt to his arm. The demon swiped at the cat, missing her tawny hide by mere inches as she bolted through the spitting electricity below the globe. I gasped, expecting her to be injured, electrocuted, or sizzled on the spot, but instead the bolt she touched retracted into the globe for a moment. As soon as she was clear, though, another spiked down to take its place.

"Where are the brownies?" Leonard asked distractedly.

Good question. I hadn't noticed them since they'd helped get Leonard back on his feet. I hoped they hadn't been inside the case when the demon had sent the laptop flying.

Dull red light flashed and the globe shuddered, going opaque for a moment before clearing again. I looked down to see that the brownies had gathered around our feet again, and had all their equalizers trained on the globe. It was a nice gesture, but I knew it was futile. Theirs and ours together hadn't been enough to stop it, so I didn't see how theirs alone had much of a chance.

A clatter and clang from behind the physical plant marked Amber's progress as the demon chased her.

"Psst!" It was the rebel brownie, standing on my right instep and gesturing frantically for me to pick her up. I knelt quickly and scooped her into my palm. As I straightened, she scampered up my arm and onto my shoulder with an agility I never would have guessed at. In the next instant she was pulling painfully on my earlobe.

"Ow! What?" I couldn't turn my head to look at her for fear of knocking her off my shoulder.

"You have to do something!"

Amber flashed into view again. Now she bore the shape of an agile, lizard-like thing with pale, green-tinted scales. The demon was still on her heels but she skidded to a stop, whirled, and breathed a jet of blue flame toward him.

"Look," I said, "I'm with you. But what can I do?"

She tugged on my earlobe again. "You have to stop him!"

"Ow! Stop doing that!" Leonard seemed to be going into shock, sagging against me with more and more of his weight. I didn't know how much longer I could keep him upright, or how much longer the demon would be distracted by Amber's antics. Where was that backup she'd supposedly called for?

I tried to give Leonard a little shake, although it was difficult to shake him and support him at the same time.

~ *Flashpoint* ~

"Leonard, come on!" I urged him. "What should I do? How do we fix this?"

He turned to look at me, pupils dilated behind lids he struggled to keep open. "Can't...think," he managed. "But the runes—"

And then he slumped toward the pebbled rooftop, my arms finally giving out.

"Watch out!" I yelled at the brownies, and they scattered out from under his descending form. The one on my shoulder caught hold of my collar with one hand and my earlobe with the other, and held fast.

"What did he mean, 'runes'?" she asked.

"Well, that thing is covered with them," I snapped, fighting the urge to swat her away like a bug.

"I can see that," she answered me, no less snappishly. "But what can we *do* about it?"

"Aren't you the experts?" I hissed at her. The instinct for self-preservation was the only thing that stopped me from yelling, because I knew that attracting the attention of the demon would be worse than anything I had to put up with from a snippy little brownie in combat boots.

"We don't get into the field very often," she admitted in a whisper. "We're usually on the other side of the operation."

And that's when Leonard's earlier words came back to me with the force of a blow to the solar plexus. *If two thaumically opposite things from different sides of the portal came in contact with each other...it could destroy the two things.*

The demon's runes. My tattoos. They were the same, but different...from two different sides of the portal. Were they thaumically opposite? Did that follow? Would bringing them together eradicate the demon...and me with it?

I had no idea. But it was suddenly, blindingly, obvious to me that I had to try. That thing couldn't be allowed to stay on this side of the brane.

I take an inordinate amount of pleasure in the fact that the demon never saw it coming. I'd seen him dismiss me as inconsequential. He didn't even really look at me when I approached him. Amber had shifted this time into a creature I didn't recognize, which, on reflection, is fine by me. I really wouldn't want to live in a world where something that big, with

~ Flashpoint ~

leathery wings and so many claws and that evil-looking hooked beak is easily recognizable. The only thing that kept me from fainting at the mere sight of it was the fact that its hide was a pale blonde colour, with greenish accents, so I knew it had to be Amber.

And, I suppose it was slightly less terrifying than the demon itself.

Anyway, Amber was dive-bombing the demon and it was batting at her in return with its long, wicked-looking claws. She'd managed to open a pair of deep, parallel gashes in the demon's right shoulder; in exchange she sported a fresh, ragged tear in the leathery skin of one wing. It didn't seem to be stopping her, though. I wondered briefly if shapeshifters could regenerate and heal injuries when they shifted. Too bad I probably wouldn't be around long enough to find out.

So the demon wasn't looking at me as I stole up beside him, threw my arm out to the side with my tattoos facing his runes, lined them up as well as I could, and smacked my forearm into his midriff.

His flesh was hot—not hot enough to burn, but like a really high fever. It wasn't enough to make me scream, but the pain that lanced through my arm, beginning where the runes had touched and radiating all the way up to my shoulder and down through my fingers—yeah, *that* made me scream, and wrench my arm instinctively away from the excruciating contact.

Except it wouldn't come away. My arm was stuck fast where the sigils had connected.

To my shock, the demon screamed, too. Truthfully, his was more of a roar, but it tended toward a scream. Pain more than rage. Not that the rage wasn't there. But it was—overshadowed.

So, this was a big mistake, I had time to think. At that point, a fiery conflagration that immolated both of us might have been a bit of a relief. Instead, the demon picked me up, turned around, and ran for the globe.

Oh no. Not the world I'd glimpsed on the other side of that portal. Fiery conflagration looked better every second. The pain in my arm increased, and so did the heat emanating from the conjoined symbols. I felt certain that we would burst into flames at any second.

~ Flashpoint ~

But when I twisted my head reflexively to see where we were going, the globe was blessedly grey again. I spotted Leonard on the ground where I'd left him. He'd come around, somehow, and found my equalizer. The brownies were arrayed alongside him. All of them had their equalizers pointed at the globe. Leonard's face was grey with fatigue and pain, but his aim was unwavering.

The demon skidded to a stop in front of the globe and swiped it with a claw. His hand passed right through.

"NO!" The demon snarled and tried again to push my arm away from his midriff. His hands were hotter now, clamped over my shoulder and wrist, and I wondered which would happen first —my shoulder would dislocate, followed quickly by my arm being torn completely off my body, or all the flesh would simply peel off it as he ripped me away. I couldn't quite feel bones being crushed yet, but it felt imminent. My arm would not budge, although the skin stretched alarmingly. The matched runes and tattoos would not let go of each other.

The heat coming off his body was intense now, as if I were standing much too close to an open fire. Waves rolled over me, stinging my skin and blistering my cheeks. *How can there be this much heat without any smoke?* I wondered hysterically.

The demon changed tactics, turning back to the globe and trying to thrust me inside it. Where his hand had passed through it, it remained solid against me, like a medicine ball at my back. I could feel the curve of the sphere as the demon shoved me against it and my spine bent painfully to match. At least the globe was a cool counterpoint to the heat blasting from the demon, which seemed to intensify with every passing second. I couldn't believe my hair wasn't smoking by now.

Still, I preferred going up in flames to passing through to the world I'd glimpsed on the other side of that portal. Bracing against the unyielding, steady globe at my back, I pushed my rune-inked arm harder against the maddened demon's midriff. And without even thinking about it, I repeated the names Leonard had given the runes.

"*Theros, chaltos, lunata,*" I said through gritted teeth. "How do you like that, you big ugly bas—"

I wouldn't have thought it possible, but the demon's face turned an even brighter shade of crimson. The yellowish sclera of

~ *Flashpoint* ~

his eyeballs bulged, tiny red veins arcing through them in a weird echo of the black lighting below the globe. And the world exploded in blazing white and crimson, and then blessed, blessed, darkness.

Being dead was nothing like I'd ever expected. I mean, I didn't anticipate any kind of conscious thought at all—just a deep, never-ending sleep in which awareness didn't enter into the picture. But there was definitely an unaccustomed weight on my chest, something uncomfortable digging into my back, something strangely cool and comforting on my face, and something else that seemed to be trying to pull my head off. So maybe there was a chance that I wasn't dead after all.

With a supreme effort, I opened one eye. Leonard's mismatched green and amber ones hovered over me, beneath a brow furrowed in concern.

"She's back!" he yelled, and the faces of Amber and the rebel brownie joined his, all wearing similar expressions of relief. He finished slipping the not-quite-motorcycle helmet off my head.

"Give the crazy girl some air, would you?" I muttered, trying to wave them back. My right arm wouldn't move at all, but I managed to lift my left one and bat ineffectively at Leonard's shoulder.

The faces pulled back slightly, and Leonard pulled a cool cloth from my cheeks.

"Put that back," I ordered, and he did. I noticed that his injured arm seemed fine now.

"Are you okay?" he asked.

"There's a stone digging into my spine, and my chest feels heavy," I said. I felt too weak to actually raise my head and take an inventory of myself.

"Oops," the rebel brownie said sheepishly, and scampered off my chest and onto Leonard's shoulder.

Leonard slipped a hand under my back and found the offending pebble, flicking it out of the way.

"Much better," I said. "What about you?"

He flexed his arm. "Amber healed it. A little stiff, but it'll be fine."

I wondered if and when the prickly shapeshifter might get

~ Flashpoint ~

around to healing me. Then I had to know. "What about the—"

"Gone," Amber answered with a smirk. "You killed that sucker good, human girl."

A residual tension I hadn't even recognized fled, and my body felt limp enough to sink into the gravelled rooftop, where I'd realized I still lay.

"I'm curious, though," she continued.

"Shhh," Leonard told her, but she ignored him.

"How'd you know to use the runes, and say the spell?"

I closed my eyes. "Good question," I admitted. "Sadly, I don't have a good answer. I took a guess. Dumb luck?"

"Or fate?" Leonard suggested. "Not anyone could have done that, you know. It wouldn't have worked if you didn't have...something...unusual, in your blood."

Leonard set the helmet down next to me and I could see that it was blackened and smoking. Runes that hadn't been visible before now glowed eerily on its surface.

Leonard saw me looking at it and nodded. "Probably saved your life," he said. "Once you and the demon were—connected, it was the only thing stopping you from crossing the portal."

I shivered. If the demon had realized that, he could have just wrenched it off my head and—

Rebel brownie piped up and said, "Well, we owe you one. You were the only thing that stopped this from being a major incursion." She patted my arm with a tiny hand.

Amber looked like she was about to argue the point, but closed her mouth without saying anything.

"Yeah, there's usually a reward for saving the world, isn't there?" I joked. I managed to move my right arm where I could see it, bracing myself for the sight of burnt and ruined flesh. It was, however, intact. My tattoos were still there, and there was no evidence that the appendage had come close to combustion just a few moments before.

No, scratch that. The tattoos now held a sheen, a faint glimmer, that they hadn't had before. Almost like an internal glow, as if they'd taken some of that unbearable heat and absorbed it. They were completely healed.

Leonard looked sheepish. "I don't have much to offer," he said, "except maybe...a job? Ever considered flashpoint patrol as a career?"

~ Flashpoint~

"I didn't even know there was such a job an hour ago," I said, struggling to prop myself up on my elbows. The rest of the brownies huddled beside Amber, watching me and quietly whispering among themselves. The tall brownie still held his equalizer loosely in one hand, glasses pulled low on his nose, watching me over the tops of them. Expectantly. Everyone was waiting to see what I was going to say.

I smiled at Leonard. His mismatched eyes were warm and hopeful. "Hell, that's the most interesting morning I've had at work in a long time," I said. "I'm in."

"Excellent." He grinned, and the others cheered. He reached out to help me up, but I stopped him with a palm.

"As long as someone fixes the photocopier before I leave," I added. "If things don't work out, a girl's got to have good references."

S herry D. Ramsey is a speculative fiction writer, editor, publisher, creativity addict and self-confessed internet geek. When she's not writing, she makes jewelry, gardens, hones her creative procrastination skills on social media, and consumes far more chocolate and coffee than is likely good for her.

Her debut novel, *One's Aspect to the Sun*, was published by Tyche Books in late 2013 and was awarded the Book Publishers of Alberta "Book of the Year" Award for Speculative Fiction. The sequel, *Dark Beneath the Moon*, is due out from Tyche in 2015. Her other books include *To Unimagined Shores—Collected Stories*, and *The Murder Prophet*, an urban fantasy/mystery.

Visit Sherry's blog and website at sherrydramsey.com, or keep up with her much more pithy musings on Twitter @sdramsey.

~ Flashpoint ~

Donald Tyson

The Fire-Eater

In the darkness, the boy squeezed between the middle and upper strands of the barbed wire fence, cringing away from the sharp points when they pricked his skin. He stood in the meadow and listened. The weight of invisible thunderheads massing overhead pressed a clammy mist from the summer night. It would rain before morning, but until then the air would remain hot and sticky. He could not see where the sky met the crests of the hills or even the outline of the lightning-blasted oak he knew to be on his right. Only the yellow lanterns of the carnival were visible, flickering beacons that had lured him in his striped pajamas from the cool, white cotton sheets of his bed.

His name was Thomas Hammond, and he was exactly nine years old. At suppertime there had been a blue and white birthday cake with candles, fresh-churned ice cream with strawberry preserves, and presents. Best of all had been the silver dollar, shimmering and glowing with mint newness.

"This is for luck, Tommy, not to spend," his father had said with a smile, pressing it into his hand and closing his fingers around it.

He held it now, clutched tightly in his right fist, afraid that he might lose it in the thick weeds. The serrated edge of the coin bit and left its pattern in the heel of his palm.

With uncertain steps he felt his way down the slope of the hollow, straining his ears for sounds from the wagons. He heard nothing but the rustle of his own bare feet on the grass. A mixture of fear and excitement caused his heart to thud against his ribs when he began to make out corners and edges of their wooden shapes in the dull light from kerosene lanterns that hung from several of them. He could not see them all but knew they were thirteen, having counted them the previous afternoon from his upstairs bedroom window. The window was high enough that he could see into the hollow, even though the wagons were hidden from view when he stood on the front step of his house.

A man from the carnival had come to the house that morning and asked to pay Tommy's father for permission to camp on his land and drink his water. The boy had watched from down the hall, peeking shyly around the edge of the kitchen doorway.

"Well I don't know," his father said, scratching his head. "I don't usually allow itinerants to stop here. Some like to steal things."

The carnie was so thin, his dark suit hung from his arms and shoulders as though empty, and his black top hat made him look seven feet tall as he stood framed in the light of the open doorway. When he talked and grinned, the funny little moustache on his upper lip moved up and down, but his eyes were covered by dark green glasses with round lenses.

"It's cash in your hand, Mr. Hammond, just like it fell from heaven. I never knew a farmer yet who could afford to pass that up in these hard times."

His father hesitated, but money was not so plentiful during the Depression that he could cast it away. Finally he shook the man's bony fingers, then lingered uneasily in the door until the carnie's rattling Ford truck passed out of sight.

Throughout the day, the boy watched with wide blue eyes from his bedroom window as the trucks pulled their wagons into place in the hollow, and the men unfurled gaily-coloured tent canvas for mending. His father would not let him get closer.

"I don't want you talking to them, Tommy," his father told him gravely. "They're not like us. They don't work, they just travel around and trick folks out of their money."

All afternoon his father kept an eye out to make sure no damage was done to his trees or fences. By suppertime he was satisfied enough to smile when Tommy blew out his nine candles —all but one. He even let the boy drive the tractor as a special treat.

~ *Flashpoint* ~

Nearer and nearer Tommy crept until he was close enough to spit on the peeling paint of the billboards on the sides of the wagons. Not a soul stirred. The wagons sat like a field of garish tombs. Each panel proclaimed the art of its sleeping resident. He moved down the line, squinting to decipher the faded letters, forming the words with his lips. The Strong Man. Gypsy Fortune Teller. Thin Man and Fat Lady. Sword Swallower.

One wagon, drawn apart from the rest, sat like an outcast on the edge of the weak lantern gleam. Its great iron-rimmed wheels and ornately carved woodwork gave it an ancient look. The painted letters on its side were too faint to be read from a distance, yet the boy feared to get closer. Unlike all the other wagons, which were closed tight, this one's door stood open in mute invitation. A little set of wooden steps led up to the yawning shadow.

Tommy started toward them, but a creak of wood against wood sent him running back like a startled fawn. He stood trembling on the beaten grass, angry at himself. He was no sissy! The black mouth mocked him and dared him to come nearer. He shifted his weight to his right foot, then back to his left. Finally he stopped still and listened as hard as he could for the faintest brush of movement from inside the old wagon. When none came, he forced his heels forward in short, reluctant steps until the wagon towered over him, its wooden axles level with his shoulders.

Once, twice, three times he traced in the air with his finger the painted legend on its side—each time losing its thread in its confusion of lines and curves—before he knew its meaning.

"The Fire-Eater," he breathed, his voice reverent with the demonic power of the words.

The red paint, dulled by decades of sun and rain, had not lost its magic. It raced flickering in loops and swirls up and down the billboard front, flaring over the edges in elemental exuberance, scorning the patches of bare, weathered wood as though certain of its ultimate victory. To the boy, its coursing energy was the embodiment of the words it spoke.

"Come on in, kiddo," said a voice with a strange accent from the dark interior. It sounded like two rusty knives rubbed edge on edge. A wooden match flamed brightly.

Blinded by the sudden flash of light, Tommy darted back,

~ Flashpoint ~

stopped, ran a few more yards, stopped again. His heart beat like a hammer on a rail. He waited in the shadows, ready to bolt.

The light died to a dim candle flame. After a minute the boy screwed up his courage, gripped his silver dollar tight, and inched his way into the yellow rectangle cast through the door on the grass. Inside the wagon, an immense disproportionate shadow rippled across the wall and ceiling.

"H-how did you know I was a kid?" Tommy's voice quavered despite his effort to make it belligerent. He hoped the other had not heard him run away.

"You was watchin' us from the top window of the house today, hidin' behind the curtain," purred the shadow.

"I wasn't hiding."

"You shoulda come down to see us. We'da given you a private show and taught you some tricks."

Tommy's heart ached. He wished now that he had disobeyed his father.

"Why didn't you come? We was expectin' you."

"I don't care about old carnivals."

The shadow remained silent. Uneasily, Tommy shuffled his feet, not wanting to stay but unable to leave. The siren-song of the magic entranced him. His mind filled with visions of one who could hold live coals in his hand, could bathe in flame as though it were water and drink it like buttermilk. It was an awesome fascination, one he had dreamed night after night for years, though the face in his visions always remained shadowed.

"Are you the fire-eater?" he asked the empty doorframe.

The laughter of the shadow clashed like metal plates.

"What it says on the wagon. Why don't you come in and see for yourself?" The voice was like the widening of a cat's eye just before it springs.

Tommy began to back away. "I got to get home now," he said, watching the doorway.

"Don't you want to see some magic?" said the voice, pursuing him. "I can swallow daggers white hot and fan a blowtorch over my chest without gettin' burned."

Tommy hesitated.

"I can teach you to light the stove with your fingertips and hold flaming matches on your tongue."

He stopped dead, marveling.

~ Flashpoint ~

"You ain't afraid to talk to me, are you, kid? Is that it? You scared?"

The mockery in the fire-eater's tone cut to the boy's heart. His lips tightened in defiance. "I ain't afraid!" he said. "I ain't afraid of nothing."

Stiffly, he mounted the awkward little flight of wooden steps leading up to the doorway. He had to use his hands to climb onto the first step, which was higher than his knee. The wood of the well-worn treads was smooth beneath the soles of his bare feet. Inside the wagon, he peered past the candle flame at the flickering shadows. The wagon looked empty. Then he saw the fire-eater.

The big man sat in a cane chair behind a square wooden card table, one of his long legs extended casually, the other bent, his hand resting loosely on his knee. He wore a pair of black leather tights, high black boots, and a broad belt with a silver buckle. His muscular, naked torso, mahogany in colour, glistened with sweat, and his long black hair lay brushed flat against his skull. Beside the candle on the table stood an open bottle half-filled with amber liquid.

Tommy saw nothing but the fire-eater's eyes. They glittered like volcanic glass, dark mirrors that reflected the candle flame as two dancing red sparks. When the boy met them with his own, they filled his sight and became immense midnight pools, vaster than the sky. He sank through them, drowning in their depths, suffocating on their emptiness. Somewhere, deep inside them, he felt a burning.

"Sit down, kid," the man rasped. He tilted the bottle off the table and raised it to his lips.

Tommy perched meekly on the edge of a wooden chair. A slurred thickness to the fire-eater's tongue frightened him.

The fire-eater studied him with a half-smile on his withered lips.

"Do you know what a fire-eater is?"

Tommy knew. He had dreamed about it all his life. It was the rolling curl of the fat orange flames and the dangerous invisible hiss of the blue. It was the gasp of farmers' wives and the voiceless gawk of children, the smell of gasoline and popcorn and charred wood. It was the prickly red glow on your cheek and the sparky-curl of singed hair. It was the knowledge that nothing

~ Flashpoint ~

on earth would ever frighten you again.

"You put lit torches in your mouth?" It sounded hollow in the boy's own ears.

The fire-eater nodded, once.

"And fire—do you know what fire is?"

Tommy hesitated.

"Fire is life," the man rasped. "It keeps us warm. It cooks our food. It scares away the wolves from our doors. Fire is life, but it's death, too."

He took another long draw on the bottle, and the liquid seemed to sizzle down his throat. He spoke softly, as though to himself.

"Give fire half a chance, and it crawls across your skin, peels the flesh off your bones and melts your skull like wax. It gets inside your guts and burns your soul to ash."

The dark man stopped talking and eyed the boy, who trembled visibly on his chair, his freckled cheeks pale in the candlelight. The man unclenched the hand he had tightened into a fist on his knee, and once again smiled with just the corners of his scarred lips.

"Fire always needs a master. Watch. I'll show you."

Reaching behind his chair, he took up a long rod with a fluffy bulb on one end. Tommy thought it looked like the bulrushes that grew down by the creek. Onto its head the fire-eater poured some of the rusty liquor he had been drinking, unconcerned when a portion of it slopped over his thigh. He held the bulb of the rod against the candle. It burst into a bluish-green flame that glowed red at the base.

"Now you watch this." The sparks in his black eyes flickered. "See who cracks the whip in this outfit."

He passed his bare hands slowly through the flaming wand one after the other. Tommy saw the fire lick hungrily around his fingers. The man gave no sign of pain. He fed the torch along his arms and rubbed it over his chest like a bar of soap, washing himself clean. His face became sensual with pleasure. Tilting his head back and opening his mouth, he inverted the torch and pressed it between his lips. The blue flame fluttered over his charred and blackened teeth and he brushed it playfully with his tongue. Then he closed his mouth to seal the burning brand deep in his throat. When he drew forth the torch,

~ Flashpoint ~

it was cold.

Tommy sat spellbound. He had never seen anything to match this display of skill and daring. It was beyond fairy tales and comic books. It was like the miracles the preacher's wife read aloud in Sunday-school class.

The fire-eater laid aside the extinguished brand, watching the boy's reaction from the corner of his eye.

"Most folks wonder where the fire gets to after I swallow it," he said in his metallic whisper. "You want me to show you?"

Tommy nodded, not trusting his voice.

Tilting back his head, the fire-eater opened his mouth and stroked the sides of his throat with his fingertips. An enormous gout of orange flame roared past his lips and leapt to the ceiling of the wagon. The room filled with blinding hellish light. Tommy put his hands up to shield his eyes.

The man laughed his harsh, clashing-steel laugh. Then it was a laugh no longer, but a retching cough that went on and on until Tommy thought it would never stop. It left the dark man doubled over and clutching his belly, agony written across the angular planes of his gaunt, lined face.

When at last he could sit up, he glared at Tommy with a look of such hatred, it made the boy cringe. The fire-eater seized the bottle and drank with slow, deep swallows. For the first time, Tommy noticed the ragged thinness of his neck and the webbed lines around his eyes.

"Are you sick, mister?"

"What makes you think I'm sick, kiddo?"

Tommy hesitated. "Your cough is real bad, and you sweat so much—like you got fever."

The fire-eater bared his scorched teeth in pain. He regained his composure and resumed his relaxed pose.

"Fever?" he murmured in a soft rasp. "I guess you might call it that."

Tommy cast a furtive glance toward the blackness of the open doorway. He wanted to leave the wagon, but was afraid to move.

"Fire makes me sweat," the man said slowly, his eyes staring into the empty dark outside the wagon. "When I was a green buck, I thought I was fire's master. I figured I could make it jump through hoops and sit up and beg like a dog. But I didn't

~ Flashpoint ~

know nothin' about nothin'. One night in some hick town just like the one you got down the road, I swallowed the fire, and guess what happened?"

He turned his black gaze on the boy and leaned forward.

"It didn't go out. I could still feel it, burning up my vitals and running through my veins like molten lead."

He chuckled to himself at the memory.

"Devil alone knows how long I screamed. The rubes got their dime's worth that night." He hit his glistening chest with his fist so that it thudded like a drum. "The fire's still in there, kiddo. It keeps flamin' away, trying to reach my heart, and there's only one way I can put it out."

He took a slow pull from the bottle and set it on the table with a heavy hand.

All the magic of the man was gone. Another bout of coughing wracked his frame, shorter this time and less violent. Through his slack jaw, Tommy imagined he glimpsed a flickering red glow on the roof of his mouth.

"I got to go now," he said, in a small voice. "My daddy's going to be looking for me."

He stood up, quivering with tension, ready to bolt at the slightest move from the dark man.

"Not yet, Thomas," the fire-eater whispered. "I still ain't showed you the best trick of all."

"I don't want to see. How do you know my name? Did you talk to my Daddy?"

"Just one last trick, kiddo. Better than the others, I promise you. Somethin' to keep with you for the rest of your life."

He cocked his gaunt head and smiled with the corners of his lips. Tommy hesitated. Outside the wagon, the wind sighed through the pines and heat lightning flickered silently along the horizon. The boy let out his breath and inched back closer to the table. He sat on the edge of the chair.

"That's a brave little trooper. I knowed you was brave first time I seen you watchin' from the window of your house. Now I'll show you what fire can do. No more cheap tricks for hayseeds. I'll show you somethin' special."

He extended his hand across the table. On the palm was a black circle with strange, angular markings inside it. Tommy looked at this tattoo in fascination.

~ *Flashpoint* ~

"No carnie ever gives it away for free, kiddo. I need a coin. Any coin'll do, even a penny. Course, it works better with a nickel, and better still with a quarter...but it's best of all with a silver dollar."

He looked at Tommy, and suddenly in some way he could not have explained, the boy knew that the man knew everything about him. About his ninth birthday party, and how his dog, Rusty, had eaten one of the candles from his cake. About his mother and father, and how they had met at the winter fair. About his baseball bat with the chip out of the handle, and about the dead sparrow he'd buried last spring in the north field under a flat stone. Even about the very first tree that had fallen beneath his grandfather's ax when the farm was still forest, long years before his father had even been born.

The silver dollar felt too big in his sweating hand. He pressed his fingers tightly around it, but he sensed it shining through the spaces between his knuckles and sticking out past the heel of his fist.

"Do you have a coin, Thomas?" the fire-eater whispered.

Unwillingly, Tommy laid the silver dollar on the man's lined palm. It fitted right over the tattoo. He wanted to snatch it back and run, but knew it was too late. He tried to stand up but could not move his legs.

"Watch the coin," rasped the fire-eater.

Tommy stared at the silver dollar—token of a father's love, symbol of his very existence—glimmer softly in the candlelight on the motionless brown palm. When he glanced up, he saw that the fire-eater was looking, not at the coin, but at him. Anticipation rattled in the dark man's laboured breaths.

Without warning, the surface of the silver dollar turned sooty-black. Tommy felt a wash of heat rise up from it, and drew back his face. The heat continued to grow until he thought the skin would peel from his cheeks in curling sheets. Still he could not turn his gaze away. He watched the silver disk glow red, then yellow, then at last blue-white with blazing intensity that made his eyes water.

"Stretch out your hand, kiddo," the fire-eater commanded.

Cringing, but unable to resist, Tommy extended his trembling palm. With a deft movement the fire-eater turned his own hand and dropped the glowing coin onto the hand of the boy.

~ Flashpoint ~

Tommy heard his skin sizzle and saw it smoke. Strangely, no pain came. The blazing disk settled into his flesh. He felt heat run up his arm and flicker along his nerves, play over the surface of his heart like fluttering fingertips, and race down the marrow of his bones. The coin did not cool on his palm. Instead, it got hotter. His eyelashes and the hair on his forehead begin to curl.

"I waited a long time," the fire-eater rasped. "Almost too long. It nearly got me. But it's all yours now, kiddo."

With a hiss, the glowing disk of silver vanished in a bubbling froth of liquid metal. A spray of fine molten droplets peppered the boy's face and made him yell with surprise.

He blinked away blue spots and tears. His empty hand swam before his eyes. In his palm, the impression of the hot silver had left a circular black brand with a strange geometric design in its center. He reached to touch it without thinking. His fingers felt the heat of it, like the top of his mother's cook-stove, but his fingers were not burned.

The boy found his legs and hurled himself blindly through the open doorway into the blackness. He hit the ground on his feet, almost fell to one knee, then regained his balance and ran wildly between the silent wagons back the way he had come. The world swam before him in a red sea of pain. From behind, rasping laughter pursued him. His bare feet found the path in the darkness, and with ankles twisting and knees buckling he flew up the slope.

He had forgotten about the fence. The barbed wire caught him full in the chest. Bruised, cut, and bleeding, he struggled to get between the steel strands.

"Everybody's gotta retire sometime, kiddo." The slurred voice of the fire-eater reached him faintly through the darkness. "Come see me again tomorrow night. I'll teach you all the tricks."

Tommy knew the mark on his hand would never wash off. It was a brand for life, like the brand on his father's cattle. He felt the fire alive inside his body. It raced along his nerves, restless and angry, seeking a way out. It did not burn him—he would never be burned again—yet somehow he knew that it would burn everything in his world, and keep on burning, until there was nothing left but ashes.

~ Flashpoint ~

Donald Tyson was born in Halifax, Nova Scotia. He began to write professionally after finishing university and has pursued this career for the past forty years. He writes a broad range of fiction and nonfiction based in the Western esoteric tradition. His short stories have appeared in such recent anthologies as *Black Wings II*, *Black Wings III*, *Searchers After Horror*, *The Weird Fiction Review*, and *A Mountain Walked*. A collection of his John Dee and Edward Kelley occult-mystery stories, titled *The Ravener and Others*, is available from Avalonia. Presently he lives in Cape Breton with his wife, Jenny, their American bulldog, Ares, and their Siamese cat, Hermes.

~ Flashpoint ~

And Again

You step out of the bookstore into the evening's frigid air. Snowflakes slip from the sky sparingly, as if the darkness is too cold to give up anything more than a sprinkle. You step onto the nearly vacant sidewalk, onto the slush that has frozen in the evening chill. Your shopping bag bumps against your knee, and now you think, with that very modern sense of commercial regret, that you will never read *The Universe in a Nutshell*. It caught you in a moment of weakness, perhaps in that moment when you were too determined to improve yourself, learn something new, or perhaps in that other moment when you felt abysmally dull and hollow and needed something to change all of that.

The sad neon lights of the Dairy Queen buzz slightly with the snapping of electricity. How fittingly archaic for a place in the middle of December where the only good product is ice cream.

You notice the muted throb of a few cars crunching as you reach the intersection. Across the street sits a tiny park. Its three benches, surveyed by a bronzed Robbie Burns, are vacant. Really, the night could use a rousing reading of something.

Opposite the park you see the Public Gardens, its wrought iron fence hemming in trees that nonetheless spill over into the night. You wonder how hard it would be to get in after closing; to find that little bit of peace in the middle of the city; to wander along the faintly lit paths, admiring the covered beds, the empty ponds, and the looming arms of shorn trees. Well, the top of every iron column has a sharp point. That would definitely be a problem. Still, there might be an open gate or—

The man ahead of you in the heavy brown parka is already half way across the street. You step closer to the road and are hit with the wind's brass knuckles, a squeal of breaks, the yelp of a horn. The man does a frantic dance that's interrupted when the Jeep plows into him. All the little details you will wish were never there collect in your mind: his neck's lurch toward the vehicle as the rest of his body hurtles away, the soundless sliding of his body along the surface of the road, the small pool of scarlet expanding underneath his head. Then he lies still, caught in the headlights of the vehicle that is bleeding passengers. And now, frozen in the middle of the sidewalk you realize that all the cold has gone out of the night as your fingers move for the phone in your pocket, busying themselves with being useful. The streetlight across the road flickers.

You step out of the bookstore into the evening's cool air. It snowed heavily earlier, so the darkness is backlit by the white sidewalks and the night-stained streets. You step onto the nearly vacant sidewalk, onto the soft carpet that constantly threatens to slip you up. Your shopping bag, one of those reusable canvas ones, flops against your leg reminding you that it's still empty. It's like you have to warm up to Christmas shopping. Every year you start off determined to get some decent presents early, to actually plan a few things out, but then this happens. It's not really a warming up; it's a way to avoid wearing out. Sure there were a hundred books in there; everyone you know should read one. But it was a present, you told yourself, not a homework assignment. Twice you almost picked one out: *Picasso*—who couldn't be interested in something about his life and work? Or *Fast Food Nation*—entertaining and alarming. But then you hesitated; you weren't sure. And having decided something better would come up, you are on the sidewalk with nothing at all in the shopping bag and a slightly more hopeless feeling in your chest.

The over-sized neon lights of the Dairy Queen flicker with the snapping of electricity. It's surprising how many people are lined up inside considering the temperature and the fact that the only thing they sell that's worth eating is ice cream. The crunching noise of a few cars on the snow-paved road is louder at the intersection. Robbie Burns has a touch of white hair and looks a bit silly, but there's no one on the benches to appreciate his new coiffure. Looking diagonally across the street, you see the Public Gardens—wrought iron black against white bushes. The larger trees hold up the snow and create drier spots on the sidewalk. You wonder if any homeless people find their way in. It would be a little island of peace in the middle of the city. But so cold and sad to wander along the faintly lit paths, the covered beds, the empty ponds, and the heavy arms of weighted trees. Still, there must be a place in there better than the sidewalk. The top of every iron column has a sharp point; that would definitely be a problem. But, there might be an open gate or—

The man ahead of you in the dark coat is already half-way across the street. You step into the street and a gust of wind turns the world into a recently-shaken snow globe. And then the squeal of breaks, the cry of the horn, and the man in front does a dance to avoid a car that slides between you and him and comes to a stop on the wrong side of the street. You panic without moving, and your heart, belatedly, starts to bash against your ribs. You can't believe how fast it happened, as if a strobe light had cut half the frames out of time. Finally, with the red feeling of too much blood in your head, you rush across the street to the man, lying on his back. His face is ashen and as you bend down to ask if he's all right, you find that your hand has already dug your cellphone from your pocket. Above you, the streetlight suddenly comes back to life, as if trying to help.

You step out of the bookstore onto your very sore ankle. Brilliantly lit fluffy flakes snake from the heavens, but their beauty is quickly overwhelmed by the deep throbbing pain shooting up your leg. *Damn. Idiot.* The new layer of snow was like butter on the sidewalk ten minutes ago when you hit that spot by the bank. For a moment you had been proud of your reflexes, how your body's unthinking reaction kept you off the ground, kept you from being the fool sitting on the sidewalk. Now the price to be paid is clear.

One more strike against the holiday shopping season. Could there be a better engineered way for a society to revel in its excess? Was there nothing the marketplace could not render into a disgusting industry? And the sickening part of it is the guilt. There is no way out. You don't begrudge spending the money on your friends and family; no, it is just the set-up, the background noise, the artificial atmosphere that sets in a month too early, the

~ Flashpoint ~

expectations, the compulsion to buy something satisfactory. As if you could solidify love and friendship by covering it in wrapping paper. But really, how much of this is your ankle talking? Doesn't everyone go through these little fits in the midst of shopping?

You try to appreciate the gentleness of the flakes as you hobble up the street towards Dairy Queen. But it's crazy to walk home like this. Beneath the over-sized neon lights that flicker softly in conversation with each other, you shift your shopping bag back to the other hand and get out your cell phone. What's that cab number? 8800?

You get it right on the second try (8880), and they say they'll just be a few minutes. The Dairy Queen is pretty busy, so you don't step inside. Instead, you look diagonally across the street at the Public Gardens limned by snow-lined wrought iron. The snowflakes caught in the light are endlessly replaced. Just like humanity. We fall from the heavens, cover the ground and melt away in the spring-time. Well, that's where that analogy dies. Your fingers, holding the shopping bag, are cold and you think of the book inside. Really, you don't know if she'll like the book anyway; it's more that bookstores are the most tolerable of the shops. Your eyes drift back to the park and you are just beginning to think about what's inside when the yellow cab pulls up.

You hobble over and jump in the back. "Just over to Kent," you say, and the driver, a small man in a rumpled grey coat nods. He is going to be one of those cab drivers who says nothing but the price. He catches the end of the turning light and whips through the intersection, cutting off a man with a heavy brown parka. Behind you a streetlight suddenly dies. But what stays in your mind is his shocked expression, inches from the car, as the driver says, "Idiot."

You step out of the Dairy Queen into the December evening's cool air. It looks like the snow might pick up now that the night is becoming slightly milder. Why did you buy that sundae? It'll be Christmas in a week, won't there be enough junk-eating then? But the hot fudge, and the nuts...well, it's not like there will be homemade pies or anything anyway.

~ Flashpoint ~

It seems like there might be some accumulation after all; the small flakes are really beginning to come down. You should be shopping, but this year you've decided to chill out—maybe that's why you're eating the sundae. Christmas always works itself out, doesn't it? You'll just pick a few things up as you see them.

The sidewalk's pretty empty, and considering the time of night, it's not surprising. You notice that the Dairy Queen's neon lights aren't working anymore, which, all in all, is not such a bad thing. Another bite of the hot fudge and you turn toward the intersection. A sharp breeze cuts into your bare knuckles and you decide you'll have to handle the big red spoon with gloves on after all.

At the intersection you glance at Robbie Burns, and realize that you can't name one thing he wrote. Maybe it's time you looked into that—you see his statue every bloody day. Looking across at the Public Gardens, you recall again your wish that they were open in the winter. It's probably lovely on a sunny winter day. Just wander through and appreciate the contours of the path, the little frozen ponds, and the stark naked trees.

Your tongue's desire for more hot fudge pulls you from your reverie and you see the man in a brown coat in front of you move into the crosswalk. You step forward while lifting the rapidly cooling fudge up to your mouth and notice that the light is still red. And then you hear the horn and see a taxi almost on top of you. And now your hands are reaching out, and the sundae is in the air as you grab the hood of the brown coat and pull back. The cry of surprise, the man crashing down on top of you, and the muffled shriek of the taxi's brakes all register at once in your startled brain. Now the man rolls off you, his astonished face as white as the snow in the park. The cab driver rushes toward you armed with a cellphone and a look of panic mixed with rage. The cab's flashers blink, blink, blink as you close your eyes.

You step out of the bookstore into the glistening winter air. The cold air shrivels something small and important inside of your lungs, but you enjoy the feeling. Taking a deep breath, you turn toward the intersection and make your way up the crowded

~ Flashpoint ~

street hoping—

You step out of the drug store laden with gifts to find that the evening's frigid air has been quietly filling itself with the immaculate splinters of winter. Practically all of your shopping done in one stop, you make your way back up the sidewalk to—

You are sick and can barely open your eyes. Is this what it feels like to be poisoned? Has someone been poking holes in all of your cells? Has—

You look out the window of the coffee shop at all the Christmas shoppers, and enjoy your mocha more and more. It's time to—

Sitting in the Public Gardens, surrounded by winter's frozen stillness, you—

You wait at the bus stop freezing and—

You zip up your brown coat and—

You step out of a book—

~ *Flashpoint* ~

Bruce V. Miller says, "I am writing this bio in my kitchen in Margaree, against the background noise of my two-month old's swing—though to be honest, his snoring is louder. Outside, the sunflowers are just starting to bloom. Inside, my two young daughters are immersed in some sort of pony game, which sounds like it might be life or death. My wife, Krista, who would surely disapprove of a present-tense, first-person bio, is currently doing housework and, like me, regretting that the end of summer is approaching rapidly. This means I will return to teaching and she will have to sort out how to get the baby to sleep and mediate pony games single-handedly, among other things. In the past I have had several short-stories published and written some poetry and songs; in the future, who knows? Currently, I am writing a brief bio."

Fever

Lily followed Quinn into the farm house.

"Happy one hundred and twentieth birthday, old man!" Quinn's best friend Dimitri said, hugging him. Dimitri, the head of all the vampires in the area, had insisted on hosting a little party.

Lily scanned the room. Quinn's friends, the werewolf siblings, were already here. Eric sat in a bean bag chair, holding a beer and scarfing down a burger. His sister, Faye, stood close by. She held a wine glass, and was talking to a woman dressed in flowing black clothes, whose dark hair hung in messy curls. The woman had olive skin, and looked both exotic and familiar.

"Hey Quinn, who is that?" Lily asked, pointing to the woman. She still wasn't familiar with everyone in the vampire's social circles.

"Gabrielle, but everyone calls her Gabby. She's a witch."

Lily nodded. She remembered now. She'd seen Gabby in a picture with Faye at the werewolf's shop. Faye said that she was an old friend and would be inviting her to the party. She hadn't mentioned what made her "super" at the time so Lily had assumed she was a werewolf too.

A tall man sat in the corner. Lily had a hard time taking her eyes off him. He was thick and muscular. He wore no shirt, a blue and black kilt, and black leather boots. Dark brown curls spilled onto his shoulders. Lily watched as the man stood and walked towards them. He was at least seven feet tall.

"Well, Quinn, 'tis been awhile," he said, with a thick Scottish accent.

"Indeed it has. How have you been, Gareth?"

"Well, as usual. This must be the infamous Lily." He took her hand, and kissed the top of it. "'Tis a pleasure to meet you."

"Nice to meet you as well."

"I have lived a long time, lass, and 'tis been a long time since I have seen beauty such as yours."

Lily felt her face redden.

"Are you a vampire as well?" she asked.

"Nae, just your run-of-the-mill immortal highlander," he replied, winking at her.

"Move over, big boy," a woman said. It was Gabby.

"Go chat with the men and leave us ladies, bloodsucker," she said.

Quinn laughed, then bent and kissed her on the cheek. "A pleasure as always, Gabby. I'll be over there," he said, pointing toward Eric.

As Quinn and Gareth walked away, the witch turned towards Lily.

"Finally! I've been waiting a long time to meet you," she said pleasantly, and embraced Lily in a hug.

"It's nice to meet you as well. I've only met a handful of Quinn's friends so far."

"Yes, well, I'm glad they had this little shindig. It's a small crowd, but it's better this way. Often, so many kinds of supernatural beings don't get along so well, but we are the few that intermingle. They are all good people and allies. So, tell me, how did you save not one, but two big bad vampires?"

Both Quinn and Dimitri overheard and gave Gabby sidelong glances. They hated being reminded that a human had saved them. And on more than one occasion, to boot.

"It's a long story," Lily said.

"So, you and Quinn are an item now, huh?"

"Yeah. He's really sweet. A great guy."

"That he is," Gabby said. "A vampire, yes, but someone's eating habits shouldn't interfere with a relationship."

"How could I resist him? He's dazzling, pale and mysterious," Lily said with a smile.

Quinn, who had what looked like a glass of blood in his hand, yelled, "Don't you dare say I sparkle!" This sent the two women into hysterics.

Lily chatted with everyone and ate until she thought she was going to burst. There was enough food to feed an army. She danced with Quinn and knew he was happy. She could feel it, thanks to their blood bond.

"You know what we should do?" Gabby said, as she turned down the music. "Let's have a little game of truth or dare."

Eric groaned. "I hate that game."

"I didn't mean the human version. We can take it easy on Lily, though"

"What do you mean?" Lily asked.

Dimitri piped up. "It's not just a regular game of truth or dare. This is a supernatural version. It tends to get interesting."

"This is Quinn's birthday, not yours," Faye said. "Maybe he doesn't want to play."

"Sounds fun to me," Quinn said.

"I don't know if the lass could handle it," Gareth said.

Lily scoffed. "Excuse me, but I survived being vampire bait, helped catch a couple of bad guys, dealt with a vamp virus, and you wonder if I could handle a game of truth or dare? I say bring it on."

Gareth laughed. "She is full of spirit."

"Perfect," Gabby said. "Everyone get comfy."

They formed a circle on the floor. Dimitri took the bean bag chair, while others grabbed big pillows from the sofa. The lights dimmed and candles were lit. The fireplace glowed a faint purple from a spell Gabby used.

"Reach into the bag and pull out a stone," she said to Lily.

Lily's fingers brushed the soft leather bag as she did so. She looked at the stone. "It says five."

"Then you will go fifth. Pass the bag," Gabby instructed.

Lily handed it to Quinn, who sat on her right. "Three."

Faye took the bag and reached in. "Four."

Dimitri was next. "One."

Then, Gabby. "Seven."

Gareth took the pouch. "Six"

"I wonder what number I got," Eric said sarcastically, as he reached in. "Two."

"Whenever you're ready," Gabby said to Dimitri.

"Quinn, truth or dare?" Dimitri asked.

"Dare."

Dimitri smirked. A shiver ran down Lily's spine. She hated that look on his face. She and Dimitri had made an uneasy peace, but you never knew what was going on in that mind of his.

~ Flashpoint ~

"Quinn, I dare you to feed some of your blood to Lily. She's done it before, she can do it again."

"Doesn't seem like much of a dare," Gabby said.

"Oh, on the contrary. You see, each time Lily drinks from Quinn, their blood bond gets deeper. The deeper their bond gets, the stronger the connection. A stronger bond means they will eventually be able to read each other's thoughts."

Lily looked up at Quinn. "You don't have to," he told her.

"I know." Lily thought for a minute. She had already developed a bond with Quinn on many levels. She loved him deeply. "I'll do it," she said, "but what if you don't like the changes?"

"I wouldn't have a problem with it." He held her hand.

"So, are you going to do it or not?" Dimitri asked.

Quinn's fangs slid out, and he held his wrist to his mouth. "You sure?"

"Yes," she said.

He sunk his fangs into his flesh. Lily watched blood ooze out from the wounds as he held his wrist out to her. She gently took his arm, put her lips to his skin, and swallowed a mouthful of blood.

"That lass has a strong stomach," Gareth said, grimacing.

"Oh, like you don't," Eric said.

"It is one thing to cause or witness bloodshed. It is a whole new thing to actually drink the stuff. Good going, lass."

Lily grabbed a napkin to dab at her lips. The grin she formed for Gareth faltered as a wave of heat washed over her. She glanced down at the bloody napkin in her hand. It wavered slightly as perspiration broke out on her forehead and on the nape of her neck.

"Lily?" Quinn said, his voice edged with concern.

Lily glanced up at him, but he wasn't even looking at her. He was deep in conversation with Eric. Confused, she shook her head, folded the napkin and used it to pat the sweat on her forehead, which had begun to drip from her hairline.

"Lily," Quinn whispered as he gently sponged her brow. Her eyelids remained closed, her eyes twitching beneath them. "She's not getting any better," Quinn said, looking over at Dimitri.

~ Flashpoint ~

"You fed her your blood, didn't you?" he asked.

"Yes, hours ago. It should have worked right away...I don't understand."

Quinn was frustrated. And scared. It wasn't often he felt this vulnerable. This...human. He looked down at Lily, whose fever continued to spike. Her face was flushed.

When he'd visited the night before, Lily had said she wasn't feeling well. She had tried to work up the energy to talk about his upcoming birthday and he'd played along, because it seemed really important to her that they do something special. But she just couldn't focus. She had a slight fever, so she took some Advil and lay down to get some rest. She fell asleep in his arms before too long. He stayed with her as long as he could, but when dawn approached he left quietly, not wanting to disturb her. He figured by the time he got back she would be feeling better.

But she wasn't. She was worse. When Quinn returned, he found her still in bed, and after a quick look around he could tell she hadn't gotten up since the night before. Everything in her apartment was exactly the same, nothing touched.

Duke, the tabby cat, meowed loudly. Quinn fed him and went back to Lily's side. Her skin burned under his fingertips. That was when he called Dimitri.

Dimitri sat in the corner chair, legs crossed. "Our blood heals. If all she had was the flu, she should have been better by now. Hell, she should be bright eyed and ready to go, not still..." Dimitri trailed off. He had a look of concern on his face. That made Quinn cringe. Dimitri rarely showed any worry.

"I know. I dread dawn. I can't just leave her alone all day. What if..."

"Call Faye," Dimitri said. "She'd do anything for you."

Quinn had been an honorary pack member since he'd rescued Faye when she was a teenager. Her brother Eric was one of his closest friends. He knew Faye had nursed a crush on him ever since. They had been through a lot together over the years, and he loved her as if she were his sister.

He dialed her number. After several rings he heard a groggy "Hello?"

"Hey, Faye."

"Quinn," Faye said, suddenly sounding brighter. "How are

you doing?"

"I'm...okay. Listen, I need your help."

"What's wrong?" Faye asked. Her tone deepened with concern.

Quinn filled her in on Lily's condition.

"So you need me to look after her while you're down for the day."

"I'm sorry. I know it sounds like playing nurse, but I really am worried. My blood isn't helping her, so I don't think a hospital would, either."

"It's okay. I'll bring some of my books on healing. I'll be there before daybreak."

They said good-bye and hung up.

"Told you she'd do it," Dimitri said.

In the hours that passed, Quinn kept cold wash cloths on Lily's face and neck, stroked her hair, tried to get her to eat. He got her to take a little more of his blood, but it still had no effect on the illness.

"Remember the other effects your blood will have," Dimitri warned.

"What do you mean?"

"You know damn well what I mean. The more of your blood she drinks, the stronger your bond will grow. It won't be long now before she will be able to start reading your thoughts."

Quinn didn't know how she was going to react. Frankly, he didn't care. Whatever was wrong with her was scaring the hell out of him, and he would do whatever it took to help her. Even if it meant she was going to be pissed afterwards.

"Looks like it's my turn." Eric scanned the group, and his eyes landed on Lily. "Truth or Dare?"

"Truth."

"The night you first met Quinn is when you rescued him from the alley. If you had known he was a vampire before you removed the silver chains from him, would you have still saved him?"

"Like she's going to say she wouldn't have," Faye said.

"Actually, she can't lie. None of you can. The stones had a truth spell put onto them. It will only last the duration of the game," Gabby said, a grin on her face.

Lily looked up into Quinn's eyes. "I would have saved him regardless," she said. "Satisfied, Eric?"

He smiled. "Yup. Quinn, your turn."

"Dimitri. Which will it be?" Quinn asked.

"Dare."

"Are you sure?"

"Why wouldn't I be? I can handle whatever dare you throw at me."

"Okay then. I dare you to drink some of Eric's blood."

"Sure, serve me up on a silver platter, you bastard," Eric said, and grunted.

Quinn laughed. "We take a shot glass, put a bit of your blood into it, and Dimitri downs it. No sweat, eh Dimitri?"

Dimitri scowled, while the rest laughed.

"What's so funny?" Lily asked.

"Dimitri says werewolves smell like dogs and taste revolting," Quinn told her.

"To which I take offence," Eric said, but betrayed his lie by snickering.

"I will do it. But don't drop any fleas in it," Dimitri said.

Eric flipped Dimitri the bird.

Gabby snapped her fingers and a shot glass appeared. Eric grinned as he took it. "Bet he doesn't drink it," Eric said.

They watched as Eric nicked his forearm with his pocket knife, and let the blood drip into the small glass. Lily covered her nose, but the tangy aroma of the blood hit her nostrils anyway. Each time she had tasted Quinn's blood, all her senses heightened for the next few days.

Eric passed the shot glass to Dimitri. The vampire took the glass, held it up, and looked at it with disgust. "Smells foul."

"No, it doesn't," Quinn said.

Dimitri lifted the glass to his lips, and tipped back the mouthful of blood. He swallowed it and grimaced.

Quinn burst out laughing. "You've become a bit of a food snob in your old age."

"Oh, and you haven't?"

"I don't murder. That's not being a snob."

Another look of disgust came over Dimitri's face. "Damn it Eric, what the hell do you eat?" Dimitri covered his mouth and gagged.

Quinn laughed even harder.

"What the hell? I don't taste that bad," Eric said, clearly offended that a vampire had just gagged on his blood. "Least I know you won't come looking for me when you get hungry."

"I can't even begin to put into words what you taste like," Dimitri said, and tossed the shot glass into the purple flames. The glass hit the back of the fireplace, shattered, and tinkled into the fire. The heating glass cracked and popped. "And if you ever make me do something like that again, you will rue the day that we ever met."

A cat meowed, startling Lily. It was odd for Dimitri to have a cat around. He referred to her cat as an 'overgrown rat.' Must be a stray hanging around outside.

"Now that we have that little mess over with," Dimitri said, glaring in Quinn's direction, "who is next on the list?"

"My turn," Faye said. "Eric, pick your poison."

"Truth," Eric said.

"What's the worst thing you have eaten while in wolf form?"

Eric turned a shade of green. "Well, one winter back when I was a teenager, I travelled farther than I should have. A snow storm came up. Even with my enhanced vision, I couldn't see anything but snow. As the night passed I got so hungry that had a human come up, they would have been dinner. Finally, I found a cave and smelled...something...inside it. I found..." Eric trailed off.

"What?" Gabby asked.

"A dead bear, rotten and full of maggots. I ate it like it was a Thanksgiving feast."

Everyone was silent. Lily's stomach churned.

"I had to eat. It was that or starve," Eric said defensively.

"And you kiss women with that mouth," Gareth said, making everyone laugh. "Looks like I'm next. Faye, truth or dare."

"Dare," she said.

"Why don't you show everyone your new trick?" Eric said.

Faye glared at her brother. "You know I wanted to keep that secret, just for a little while. Until I, you know, get it down pat."

"Oh come on, Faye. Show us," Gabby urged.

~ Flashpoint ~

Faye sighed. "Well, the thing is, a lot of people don't realize that when werewolves change, it's into their full form. But there are some of us who can develop a rare skill."

Faye rolled her sleeves up and lifted her hands for everyone to see. She closed her eyes, brows furrowed in concentration.

The air around Faye shimmered and her hands began to grow, her fingers elongating. Her nails lengthened to seven inches long, sharp as a knives.

Lily watched in amazement. Faye was still her human self, but she had managed to shift her hands into a large set of deadly claws.

"That is epic!" Quinn said.

He was right. Lily knew that was impressive. She began to feel boring. What could she offer Quinn? She couldn't protect him with claws, or wow him with something supernatural. One time she had to drink his blood to give her strength so she could protect herself. She felt mildly pathetic, as if she did not fit in with them.

I don't belong. That's why.

Quinn turned his head towards her, eyes narrowed.

You belong with me.

Lily gasped. Quinn had heard her thoughts.

She turned back to Faye. Her hands were back to normal, dainty human ones.

Eric patted her on the back. "I'm jealous," he said.

"You should be," Dimitri said. "She's got the looks and the talent in the family."

"Oh, ha ha," Eric quipped back.

That would be so cool, to be able to have an ability like that. Lily couldn't help but feel a green-eyed monster eat at the back of her mind. *I hate feeling jealous.*

Quinn looked at her and she heard: *Well, that's only fair, since Faye is jealous of you.*

The doorbell rang. Quinn ran out to get it. "Thank God you're here," he said, enveloping Faye in a hug.

"How is she? Any change?"

"No, still the same."

~ *Flashpoint* ~

They walked through the town house to the bedroom. Lily murmured in her sleep.

"Nice to see you, Faye," Dimitri said.

"Wow. No dog insults?"

"No, not tonight. I think Quinn would rip my head off if I made one misstep tonight."

Faye walked over and put a hand on Lily's forehead. "She's burning up."

"I know."

"I'll do all I can, Quinn. But there has to be more to this than a regular flu. If your blood has done nothing for her..."

"What do you think it is?"

"I don't know, but I'll help you figure this out. I brought some things from my store. I called Gabby, too, for ideas. Hope you don't mind."

Quinn shook his head. Lily needed any help she could get.

Faye had a vast knowledge of the occult. She had been obsessed with it ever since she was a child and learned about what she was. After high school she opened her store, selling everything from books to crystals, candles, and potions. Now she began to pull tea leaves, oils, and crystals from a large green bag.

"I owe you big," Quinn told her, as he was about to leave. He felt a faint wash of nausea, but shook it off. The sun was close to rising, and he had to get back home.

"I haven't done anything yet. Just try to rest. I'll take good care of her."

Quinn reached out to brush white cat hairs from Faye's sleeve. "You're a good friend," he said. Then, to cover the awkward moment, "What did you do, rumble a cat on the way over here?"

Faye brushed at the hairs herself, as well as some that clung to her skirt. "Very funny. Gabby brought me some things, and you know you never see her without a cat or two."

Quinn smiled, then leaned down and whispered into Lily's ear. "I love you. Keep fighting." As he kissed her fevered cheek, he heard Lily mutter, "I can't believe Faye did that." Then a moment later, "Faye can't be jealous of me."

"I'm next," Lily said. She thought for a moment. What would a human ask or dare any of these unique people? She was at a loss. Then, her eyes landed on the highlander.

"Gareth, truth or dare?"

"Dare!" he said, and took a swig of his beer.

"I...I dare you to prove to me you're immortal."

Gareth laughed. "Anything for a beautiful lady," he said. "Besides, I like to show off."

He reached into his boot, pulled out a dagger and put it over his heart.

Lily held her breath as she watched him sink the blade into his chest.

Gareth gasped, his eyes rolled back, and he fell forward onto the floor.

Lily felt paralysed.

Eric got up, flipped the man over, and took the dagger out of his chest.

"That's going to stain," Dimitri said, as he watched blood pool onto the rug. "What a waste of perfect blood." He sighed.

Lily watched the gash from the blade slowly heal.

Gareth twitched, coughed, and sat up. "Coming back to life always feels funny."

Lily stared at the big man. Aside from the blood smeared on his chest, he looked fine, as if nothing had happened. She let out a sigh.

He smiled. "Takes more than that to actually kill me. God knows, I've tried."

"I don't understand," Lily said.

"When I was a man of twenty, I pissed off someone. Someone powerful," he said, his voice becoming deeper, his eyes in a faraway place. "The long and the short of it is this: he cursed me with being immortal. One would think that being able to live forever would be a good thing. But, to watch the people you love grow old, sick, and die, is torture. Every time you come to care about someone, you know that in time, they will be taken from you. One good thing about being friends with vampires is that they stick around longer." He sighed, a wry grin on his face. "But even then, things happen. Hard to kill, but not as hard as I am."

Lily felt Quinn's arms wrap around her.

"Aye lad, you know all too well of what I speak."

~ *Flashpoint* ~

Quinn walked quickly down the busy street toward Lily's apartment, wishing he lived closer. He made his home in an old warehouse, which offered him the shelter he needed.

His cowboy boots thudded loudly on the pavement as he walked. Some vampires could be graceful and quiet. Sleek, as if they were the shadows. Dimitri was like that. You never knew when he would make an appearance. Even Quinn sometimes didn't sense his approach. But Quinn was big, loud, and rough around the edges. Sleek didn't suit him. He never managed to perfect that trait.

This evening, agitated, he didn't even try. Lily's words, from the night before, still haunted him.

I can't believe Faye did that. Faye can't be jealous of me.

Quinn thought about that last part. It was no secret that Faye had a crush on him since she was a teenager. Is that why Faye was jealous? Or was it something deeper? He had tried to tell himself that it was just the fever talking. But Lily's words nagged at him until he slept. Even in his dreams he could hear her mumbled words.

What did Faye do?

Quinn looked up to see Dimitri sitting on the stairs of Lily's building. He was surprised his old friend wasn't wearing his usual suit and coloured tie.

"Slumming it, are we?" Quinn said, and nodded to Dimitri's attire. He wore a tight red t-shirt, black running pants, and sneakers.

"I didn't know what to expect. If she projectile vomits, I don't want a good suit to get hit."

Quinn grunted.

"Come on. Let's get inside. Maybe Faye has her awake," Dimitri said, and stood.

Inside, the scene wasn't the one that Quinn wanted. Lily lay in bed, her hair plastered with sweat.

Faye fussed with the bed sheets around her. "She's been tossing and turning for the last hour or more. Her fever breaks, but then comes back."

Quinn put his hand on Lily, and knelt to kiss her. Her skin was hot under his lips. He couldn't read her thoughts when she was unconscious, but he could sense her pain. Now he

~ Flashpoint ~

sensed something new.

Fear.

"How has she been since we left?" Dimitri asked.

"The same, if not worse. She hasn't woken up at all. I tried getting tea into her throughout the day. I've tried different ones, to see if anything would help. Most of it got spilled, but I managed to get some into her. At least she won't be dehydrated."

Faye sorted through the items she'd taken from the green bag earlier, and picked up a stone. "I didn't try this one yet. It's an energized crystal," she told Quinn. "They have healing properties."

Faye pulled back the bed sheet. Lily's clothes were damp from sweat, and tangled from restlessness. Faye ran the crystal over Lily's body.

Quinn's eyes blurred, nausea roiling his stomach. "I don't feel so—"

A scream erupted from Lily as her body convulsed.

Pain lanced through Quinn and he landed on the ground, his body pulsing as if electric shocks had shot through him. After what felt an eternity, the pain stopped. Quinn lay on the floor, panting.

Dimitri fell to his side.

"Lily?" Quinn gasped.

"Whatever that was, it's passed. Are you okay?"

"I think so." He sat up, and slowly got to his feet.

Faye still held onto Lily. She'd turned her on her side during the seizure.

"What the hell was that?" she asked.

Lily's words echoed in his ears. *I can't believe Faye did that. Faye can't be jealous of me.*

Faye seemed tired and wary. But she was here because he asked her to come. Or was she? "Are you sure you don't know, Faye?"

"What's that supposed to mean? Why would you say that?"

"Because my bond to Lily is gone. You tell me what the hell that crystal was."

"I'm the last one and I have something for you all," Gabby began. "I dare you to let me cast a simple vision spell. It will be the finale of the night." All agreed.

"Close your eyes, and stare into the blackness that is in front of you. Breath in deeply and relax." Gabby's voice became hypnotic, and Lily felt her whole body ease, starting with her neck and shoulders, working its way down to her toes. She sat comfortably, her mind fogging. She heard the rustle of Gabby's skirt as she walked around them, and felt the witch touch her shoulder as she passed.

"When I tell you to, slowly open your eyes, and look at what lies before you. Do not be scared."

Her voice was soft, soothing.

This isn't too bad. It's okay.

Gabby's voice sounded far away. Lily heard a whisper. "Open your eyes." Lily did so. At first she thought the lights were out. It was pitch dark. She turned her head to the right and saw Quinn staring at the ground.

She followed his gaze. There, Lily saw her gravestone, grass perfectly tended around it. It bore her birth date, but she was unable to tell the date of death. A single tear slid down Quinn's cheek.

She looked around.

Eric stared up at a glowing full moon.

Faye screamed as she ran from men carrying rifles. Hunters.

Dimitri watched, horrified, as flames licked up around his body.

Gareth was surrounded by dozens of clocks spinning in front of him, calendars passing year after year.

These are our worst fears. Quinn fears losing me. He may try to forget, but he knows I will grow old and die.

Lily looked before her. Quinn knelt on the ground, staring up and away from her. The light began to glow above her, and she realized that the sun was rising. "Quinn! Run!" she shouted, but he didn't move. The golden rays touched his pale skin, and he began to wail, as his flesh disintegrated and flaked away.

Lily stared in horror. When it was over, a pile of dust and ashes lay at her feet. Tears stained her cheeks. She lifted her head to the black abyss. He was gone. She couldn't feel him.

Gabby stood off to the side, watching them all as they faced their fears.

~ *Flashpoint* ~

How can she do this? Why would she? Why am I the only one who's looking around?

Was it because she was human and the spell affected her differently? Or was it because she had the strength to pull her eyes away? Her eyes locked with Gabby's.

"Why?" she screamed, but no sound came out. She pushed with all her might for the word to be spoken, to be heard. "Why?"

Gabby just smiled.

"You can't possibly think I did this to her," Faye said, eyes wide from shock.

"I don't want to believe it," he said, "but I've been putting some pieces of this puzzle together."

"Whoa, Quinn, do you really think Faye would do this to Lily?" Dimitri asked.

"Why not?" he asked, anger coursing through him. It was all starting to make sense. The facts were adding up, and it wasn't pretty.

"That's crazy!" Faye spat.

"Okay, both of you calm down," Dimitri said. "Quinn, you're not thinking straight."

"I won't calm down! After all these years, Quinn, you actually suspect—" Faye turned from him, put her face in her hands and sobbed.

"What makes you think this is Faye's fault?" Dimitri asked.

"She's been jealous of Lily, for starters," Quinn replied.

Faye spun around and stalked towards him, her face wet with tears. "Me? Jealous of her? A human?"

"Don't even try to deny it. I saved your life once. You drank my blood. I don't have the connection with you that I have with Lily, but I sense enough to know that you're jealous and hate her."

Faye glowered at him. "I might not have liked her much at first. But we're friends now. You know that."

"Unless you have alternate motives for being so close to Lily," he countered.

"You know, I think Dimitri's right. Because on a good day

you would never think I would do something so horrible," she told him. She wiped her eyes with her sleeve.

"Quinn," Dimitri said, putting a hand on his shoulder. "Think about this, buddy. Faye's been like your sister for a long time."

Quinn shook him off. "You know as well as I that people can turn on you, no matter how long they have been in your life."

"*You* asked *me* to come," Faye said. "And I did. I've been giving her teas all day, rubbing salves on her, making pastes. I've tried every remedy I could think of."

Quinn pointed to the green crystal, on the floor beside Lily's bed. Faye had dropped it during Lily's convulsions. "That didn't feel like a remedy."

Faye bent to retrieve the crystal. She shook it at him. "Gabby gave me this!"

A blood-curdling scream erupted in the room. All three of them turned to Lily, flailing in bed.

Quinn clasped Lily's hand. "Whatever you're doing to her, stop it!"

"Quinn, there has to be another explanation," Dimitri said.

Quinn looked toward Faye, but she had tuned out both of them. She lifted the crystal up and peered at it, frowning.

"What?" Quinn demanded.

She pursed her lips, but didn't look up at him. "A seam," she muttered. "A healing crystal shouldn't have a crack running through it." She turned the gem around in her fingers, then suddenly raised her hand over her head and smashed the crystal down onto the floor.

The vampires jumped as shards flew everywhere.

"What the hell?"

She fished a small object out of the debris and examined it.

"What is it?" Dimitri asked.

Faye held out the object. "A feather, I think. Dipped in something...maybe blood."

Dimitri took it from her, examining it. "This is dark magic." He turned to Quinn. "It could be blocking your bond with Lily."

Quinn glared at Faye.

She stared back and said in a low voice, "I do not ever practice black magic. You know that, Quinn. I know things but

I'm not a witch like Gabby!"

Lily screamed again.

"If that's what broke the connection, we need to destroy it," Dimitri said.

Quinn whispered in Lily's ear, quieting her.

"No," Faye argued. "We aren't sure what it can do and what risks are involved."

"What's the worst it could do?" Quinn asked.

"It could potentially kill her. Dark magic...It scares me."

"So what do we do?"

"I don't know, but I'm telling you, this wasn't me. The crystal came from Gabby."

Lily wailed again.

Gabby stared at her, a smug look of satisfaction on her face.

"I've had to wait a long time, Lily. But revenge is always sweeter when it comes at the most perfect moment. The final death is too good for Quinn. I wanted to make him suffer, like he has done to me. When I heard that Quinn was in love with a woman, a human one at that, I knew the time had come."

"Revenge for what?"

Gabby sighed, her face softened. "I have been waiting forty long years. I've waited patiently, knowing that at some point Quinn would become close to someone. I had seen it in one of my visions. I just didn't know when. The fact that he fell in love with you made my task much easier. Another supernatural could have a stronger immunity to this spell. A human is weak as a kitten against me."

"You look so young," Lily said, trying to make sense of it.

"I'm a powerful witch. I may not be immortal, but I will live a long time, thanks to my spells. You see, your precious Quinn was not always the upstanding vampire he's made himself out to be. Sure, he's a good guy now, but he hasn't always been like that. There was a time when he fed from whomever he pleased, killing his prey more often than not. Somewhere along the line Quinn grew a conscience.

"Forty years ago, Quinn had quite the party with some vampire friends. For weeks they killed every night. Blood is to vampires what liquor is to humans. The more they drink, the more powerful and invincible they feel. They get drunk on their feasting. During these weeks, he killed my partner, Suzi. He didn't care when the light from her eyes dimmed and vanished. I know because that is when I got there. I was too late. I watched as Quinn raised his head, fangs out and mouth bloody. He vanished before I could do anything. I held Suzi and promised she would get her justice."

Gabby walked to Lily. She raised her hand and lightly brushed her fingers to smooth away the hair from her face.

"Then why not kill me outright?" Lily asked.

"She suffered in her last moments. So shall you. He took my love from me. An eye for an eye."

Lily screamed, and lurched towards Gabby. Gabby vanished from her grasp, but her laughter echoed in all directions.

"What the hell was that about?" Quinn asked once Lily had quieted.

"Say that name again, Faye," Dimitri said.

Faye lifted her eyebrows and looked thoughtful.

"Why?" snapped Quinn.

"I have a theory. Humour me."

"Yes, he does, and you'll listen, Quinn. It's the least you can do after accusing me," Faye said. She took a deep breath and said, "Gabby could—"

Lily screamed again, her body flailing.

Quinn enveloped Lily into his arms, and whispered to her until she quieted again. "Why on earth would...that name cause this?"

"I don't know, but she's powerful. Ga—She could do this."

"But why?" he asked. "I haven't done anything to her."

"Is there any other powerful witch you or Lily might have pissed off?" Dimitri asked.

"Most witches stay away from vampires," Quinn said in a low voice. "*She* is the only witch I really know. Why on earth would she do this?"

Faye looked thoughtful. "You know, it could make sense. Gabby told me something once."

"What?" Quinn asked.

~ Flashpoint ~

"We were talking about past relationships. She said she lost the love of her life to a vampire. She vowed revenge, even if it took forever."

"I didn't know even Gabby until forty years ago," Quinn said, whispering the name, so as not to upset Lily. "We met at a party you held, Dimitri."

Dimitri rubbed his hands over his face. "There were all kinds of vampires there. I had invited a coven, but only Gabby showed up. She approached me beforehand, saying she thought we all needed to get along. I remember you didn't want to go. The party—Fuck."

"What?"

"It was a few months after that big binge we had. After that you swore you would change your feeding habits. You told me you didn't like how those weeks were a blur and you had little memory of it. You were afraid my party would set you back into a frenzy again."

Quinn remembered, all right. He remembered the weeks of feasting and killing.

"Maybe you killed her partner," Faye said, softly.

"But when I met her at your party she came up to me to introduce herself."

"What better way to plan someone's torture than by getting to know them?" Dimitri said.

"Gabby has a motto, Quinn. An eye for an eye."

Lily screamed.

She had to fight. But losing her bond with Quinn was terrifying and made her doubt what was real and what was illusion. Was he really dead? She couldn't just let this bitch win, and whether Quinn was gone or not, he'd want her to fight. But how?

Quinn's vision about her dying might come true.

Not if I get out of this.

Lily tried screaming, hitting herself, anything that could wake her up from this nightmare.

From the blackness, a deep laugh emerged. "You can't escape me, you pathetic human!" Gabby appeared in front of Lily, looking wild. Her hair bounced around her head as if electricity flowed through it. Her eyes were wide and red. "You will die!"

~ Flashpoint ~

Lily felt helpless. Gabby had years to plan this. She was smart and callous and hell-bent on revenge. She wouldn't have made any mistakes. Her only hope was the bond with Quinn that no one, not even Gabby, could break. She shut her eyes tightly to block out Gabby's face, so full of anger and hate, and tried to reach him, crying out with her thoughts.

Quinn! Quinn! QUINN!

Quinn felt like a block of ice had settled in his stomach. *Could I have been so wrong?* "Faye, I—"

"Save it," she said, voice curt.

Dimitri went to his side. "Gabby could pull this shit off, and she has a perfect motive."

Lily mumbled.

"I think she's trying to fight the spell," Faye told them.

"How the hell am I going to find Gabby? Lily's getting worse. She can't stand this much longer."

"She'd have to be close. Like, really close, Quinn."

Quinn thought for a minute. "The town house next door is vacant. I know because Lily asked if I might be able to move in there."

"That would be close enough," Faye said.

"You stay here with Lily," Quinn told Faye.

"No way. Lily is beyond our help here. After what you accused me of, I deserve to go. Gabby set me up."

Quinn huffed and turned to leave the house, Dimitri and Faye in tow. Now was not the time to argue.

Outside the autumn air was crisp. The street was quiet. The street lights hummed, and a dog barked off in the distance.

"That's the empty one," Quinn said, pointing to the house on the left.

"Um, what about that one?" Faye asked, indicating the one on the right. A half-dozen cats circled around the house, meowing and rubbing up against it.

"An elderly couple lives there. Why?" Quinn asked.

"I think she's there. Cats love her. Wherever she goes, there are always cats."

Quinn nodded, recalling the cat hairs on Faye's sleeves.

"Let's try there first," Faye urged.

~ Flashpoint ~

The cats hissed and ran off as they approached.

"What about the people who live here?" Quinn asked. They would be in deep shit if they barged in on innocent people.

"We'll worry about that later," Faye said.

Quinn turned the doorknob and was surprised to hear a small click. It was unlocked. As he slowly opened the door his nostrils flared, catching the scent of dead blood.

Blood covered the kitchen floor. The couple lay in the middle of it, their limbs in unnatural positions.

"Gabby needed to spill blood for a spell so powerful," Faye whispered. "She found them useful to her cause, it seems."

"I hear something down the hall," Dimitri said.

Quinn listened.

"Is that chanting?" Dimitri asked.

"She's probably in a trance, working her magick. As long as she's in it deeply, she shouldn't hear us approach," Faye told them.

Quinn made his way down the hall, his friends following close behind. Quinn peeked around the corner leading into the living room. Gabby sat cross-legged in front of the fireplace.

"We can take her," Dimitri whispered into Quinn's ear. "She's in a whole other world."

Gabby's body convulsed and spasmed as she continued working her spell.

"If we don't do something soon, she's going to kill Lily while we stand here," Faye said.

Before Quinn could react, Dimitri became a blur. He sped across the room toward Gabby. Just as Dimitri reached her, she stood, grabbed him, and tossed him across the room. He hit the wall and landed with a thud.

"Did you really think I didn't know you were here?" Gabby asked. Dirt streaked her face. Her clothes were torn and stained with dried blood.

"Am I the one who killed your partner?" Quinn asked. "Is that why you're hurting her?"

A low rumble sounded as the house began to quake. Next to the fireplace a large hole broke open in the floor, debris falling away as it cracked open and crumbled in on itself. A hellish orange-red glow lit the room.

"A portal," Faye whispered, her eyes growing bright. She

pulled the dark feather from her pocket, hurried to the edge and dropped it into the opening. It disappeared, seemingly sucked away. "There. It can't hurt her anymore."

Gabby sneered. "Hurt her? Hah. She's already dead. She paid for your sins."

Quinn mentally reached out for Lily. Nothing. He couldn't sense her, couldn't hear any thoughts. She was gone.

Quinn had lived many years without loving someone. When Lily came along, everything changed. Now his worst fear had come true—too soon. "I'll kill you for this." He rushed her, fangs out, ready to rip out her throat.

She cackled and jumped out of his way. He almost crashed into Dimitri. Behind him Faye, in wolf form, growled. She leaped, swiping at Gabby, claws catching against her torso. Gabby screamed and lashed out, her bare hands grabbing at Faye. Faye swiped at her again. This time she connected with Gabby's face. The witch screamed as chunks of flesh dangled from her cheek.

I'm here, Quinn. I'm okay. Finish the bitch! Lily's voice suddenly rang in Quinn's head. Was she alive after all?

As Faye made to attack again, Quinn stood up and lunged at Gabby as she tried to dodge. Quinn pummelled into her, knocking her down. Dimitri came up beside them, hauled Gabby up, held her arms behind her, and bit into her throat. Gabby screamed as Dimitri tore away another piece of flesh. Blood gushed from the wound. Quinn snarled and attacked, helping to hold Gabby down and tear into her. He heard her screaming, but didn't care. Finally, he lifted his head. Gabby's eyes were fading. She gasped for breath. He threw her onto the floor.

"I need to finish her," Quinn said.

"No," Dimitri snarled. "Let her last moments be agonizing. Let her suffer."

"What? Stand here and watch?" Faye asked. She was back in human form, but naked, and covered in blood.

"Look at her. It's not like you'll have to wait long," Dimitri replied.

Quinn felt his knees buckle, and he almost fell to the floor. *Lily.* Was she really alive, or did he imagine her voice?

I have to go see her.

The portal began to glow. A faint chanting filled the air.

"What's happening?" Dimitri demanded.

~ *Flashpoint* ~

They turned and looked at Gabby. One blood-stained hand wrapped around an amulet that hung from her neck. Her eyes rolled back in her head.

Before any of them could react, a demon burst forth from the portal. Ten feet tall, with skin like rock and veins like flames, its wings popped open as it gathered Gabby into its arms. The creature folded its massive wings around the witch in a tight cocoon. Then it disappeared back the way it came. The portal closed.

All was still again.

"What the fuck was that?" Quinn asked, looking to Faye for answers.

She was pale, her eyes wide. "I have no clue. I've never seen or heard of anything like that. Do you think she's dead?"

"I haven't the slightest. But she won't last long if she isn't. We tore her apart. Nobody could survive that," Quinn said, as he turned to leave the house.

Lily gasped and coughed. Her lungs hurt and her mouth was dry. She opened her eyes and tried to focus. She clutched her comforter between her hands.

Is Gabby dead?

She tried to sit up, but it felt like she was crawling out of a fog. *A dream,* she told herself. *It was only a dream. A killing dream, spun by a witch.* She lay back down just as she heard the front door open. Fear washed over her, but she knew she was too weak to defend herself.

Quinn! Where are you?

The footsteps hurried.

"I'm here."

Tears welled up and poured down her cheeks. She looked past Quinn. Dimitri and Faye stood behind him. Both were smeared with blood, and Faye was wrapped in a blanket.

"I thought you were dead," Quinn told her as he knelt down and kissed her.

"I guess it took a moment after I tossed the feather for your bond to be reconnected," Faye mused.

"Did you hear me, Quinn? I could feel you. I remember telling you I was okay," Lily said.

~ Flashpoint ~

He smiled at her. His eyes shimmered with tears as he nodded his head and said, "I heard you."

"Am I still dreaming?" she asked, her voice hoarse.

He smiled. "No, Lily. You're awake. Awake and alive."

Kerry Anne Fudge lives in Cape Breton with her fiancé and two furbabies. When she's not writing, she can be found with her nose stuck in a book or feeding her Pinterest addiction. Her short stories "Awake and Alive," "Airborne," and "Harvest" can be found in the Speculative Elements Series anthologies from Third Person Press.

Hair Trigger

Liesel Cormack cut through the fighter hangar on her way to a briefing and caught her mechanics whaling on Alexa with a sledgehammer.

Alexa was parked in the middle of the hangar with her five buddies, who belonged to Liesel's squadmates in 'A' Flight of the 35th United Nations Lunar Defense Force Close Air Support Squadron (the Reapers). Metal clashed on metal as the other planes received the same treatment from their heartless and obviously insane mechanics, but Liesel only had eyes for Alexa.

Liesel let out an incoherent screech that made Alexa's two mechanics drop their tools to cover their ears—her callsign wasn't "Banshee" for nothing—and flung herself at Flynn, the lanky Irishman.

Liesel, a tiny freckled blonde from Canada—possibly the world's least aggressive country—didn't generally pose a threat outside the cockpit. But they'd never messed with her fighter before. A pilot's fighter was like her baby, and these bastards were knocking dents in the hull, spray painting graffiti on the wings, and scratching the cockpit glass with claw hammers. Grime coated Alexa's deadly needle nose, forward-swept wings, and gold-tinted canopy. And the worst part—they'd spray painted over the portrait that commemorated Liesel's sister Alexa, who had been killed five months ago on a scouting mission.

Everyone yelled at once as Liesel twisted the fingers of one hand into Flynn's curly black hair, pulling his head back so she could wrap her other arm around his throat and squeeze. Her feet flew through the air as Flynn tried to fling her off. She felt strong hands clamp around her ankles. Losing her grip, she flew backwards and landed in a heap on top of Saf, Flynn's partner. Saf's dusky skin flushed dark as he shoved her off and scrambled to his feet.

For a moment Liesel just lay there trying to get her breath back. Silence rang in the hangar. Everyone stared at her.

"What the hell, Liesel?" Saf yelled. He stood between her and Flynn, a pipe wrench ready to swing in case she came at them again.

"You didn't go to the briefing, did you?" Flynn asked in a raspy whisper, massaging his throat. It was studded with purple imprints from Liesel's fingers.

"No," Liesel snarled, eyeing the pipe wrench and wondering if she should go for Saf's knees or his groin.

"Just go to the briefing. It'll all make sense," Flynn rasped.

"And while you're at it, take an anger management class," Saf growled, "before you kill somebody."

He turned his back on her and extended a hand to help Flynn up. The other mechanics had all stopped their work. They watched with undisguised curiosity.

Liesel got up and stomped off without an apology. She needed to put some distance between them so she could cool down. Part of her still wanted to scratch until she saw blood. The old Liesel would never have jumped them like that. Saf and Flynn were her friends. She'd stood for them at their wedding, for Christ's sake. But these days her anger was just too close to the surface to control. The whole squadron—pilots, mechanics, admin staff—knew how she felt about Alexa, both the person and the fighter. When she found out who was responsible for the damage, she wouldn't be responsible for what happened to them.

At least, that's what she told herself.

The briefing room wasn't one she'd ever been to before. Buried deep in the bowels of the base, it probably lay under the lunar surface, but she couldn't tell because there weren't any windows. The further she went from the places she knew, the more apprehensive she got, to the point where she had almost— *almost*—forgotten about Alexa's mistreatment.

The corridors were dingy and dark, like they hadn't been used in ages, much less cleaned. She was starting to think she'd gotten the directions wrong when she came around a corner and found a metal door with the right number on it. Not so much a door as a hatch, the wheel broken and hanging off. It didn't even open by itself—Liesel had to stick a hand into the crack and shove. It came away from the frame with a screech.

She ducked inside and found that the rest of A Flight was already there, draped carelessly over battered metal chairs. As Flight Commander she really should have been there first, so she tried not to call attention to herself as she slid into a seat next to her Second, Dexter—X to everyone but his mother.

"What'd I miss?" Liesel whispered as she looked around, taking in the stacks of old metal furniture that had been moved aside in favour of piles of caving and climbing gear. Ropes of various colours and thicknesses, carabiners, heavy rubberized hiking boots, gear belts, knee pads, harnesses, helmets, headlamps, backpacks, and the like, all designed to fit on or over a pressure suit. Maps of the lunar surface—specifically those craters known to have natural caves, climbable fissures, and old mining tunnels—and diagrams of various types of nuclear bombs covered the walls.

"You know as much as I do," X said, following her gaze. The room was so dim and X was so dark that Liesel could only properly see his eyes and teeth as he spoke.

Liesel caught sight of one of the printed posters that had been stuck up all over the common areas of every base Liesel had visited for the past two months. JOIN THE CAVE DIVERS! it read in a bold font sure to appeal to extreme sports enthusiasts and people with short attention spans. A guy in full climbing regalia rappelled down a cliff wall inside a cave, below a comm channel to ping if you were interested.

"Don't tell me we're supposed to join those loonies," Liesel groaned. Their Squadron Commander had given them some pretty odd assignments over the years, but this topped them all. It also didn't explain why she'd caught Flynn and Saf mutilating Alexa.

"Not loonies," a quiet voice said from behind them. "That's just a cover."

Liesel and her squadmates turned in their chairs as one. Behind them stood a thin Hispanic man about Liesel's age—mid-twenties—with dark, serious eyes and jet black hair that came just shy of hanging over his eyes. He wore heavy canvas cargo pants, the same sturdy boots that occupied the gear piles, and a synthetic long-sleeved shirt under a red pullover. He had filled out since the last time Liesel saw him, particularly in the face, but she recognized him. Adam Cunningham, the work camp escapee Liesel had picked up nearly five months ago after Alexa's scouting op went south. Adam hadn't seen her—she'd had her helmet on—but she'd definitely seen him. He'd been nothing but skin and bones. She'd felt sorry for him until she found out Alexa had been killed saving him. Since then, she'd avoided him like the plague. Deep down, she couldn't believe he'd been worth Alexa's life.

She quickly turned around in her chair, giving him her back before he could read the accusation on her face, trying to focus on his words rather than the fact that she'd like to pound on him for a little while. Liesel let her eyes rest on something safe: a bomb cross section that depicted a shiny metal bowl at the end of a long tube like a gun barrel, the other end of which was loaded with a fat bullet.

"For those of you who don't know me, my name is Adam Cunningham," Adam began, still in that maddeningly calm voice. He had moved around to the front of the room. All eyes but Liesel's followed him, riveted now because of course they'd all heard about Adam Cunningham.

Adam was the one person rescued alive from the Lunar Resistance Army's work camp in the old ice mines. Non-white prisoners snatched from the streets of the major lunar cities had been forced to dig for uranium there, without any protection so the LRA could (presumably) start building their own nukes. With nukes, they'd go from a thorn in the side of the U.N. police and military units tasked with protecting the moon to a credible threat. They hadn't found a bomb yet. By the time Adam had been picked up and a strike/rescue team dispatched, the LRA had killed all the prisoners and abandoned their operation, taking their plans with them.

"After the uranium mine incident," Adam explained, "it became clear to me and the powers that be at the U.N. that they really had no one who was trained to properly scout that far underground without being detected. After I was released from hospital—"

~ Flashpoint ~

Liesel remembered hearing that Adam had spent more than three months in the infirmary recovering from his injuries: malnutrition, radiation poisoning, several badly healed breaks, and a bullet wound in his arm.

"—the U.N. gave me permission to form the Cave Divers, a small group of highly trained scouts who could explore the ice mines unarmed and undercover."

Yeah, that seems less dangerous than sending armed soldiers, Liesel thought.

"Disguised as an adventure sports tour group, my Cave Divers can clandestinely scout and map the natural and long-forgotten man-made tunnels under the lunar surface. Our goal is to discover and disable the nuclear bomb we fear the LRA have made from the material dug out of the ice mines. The problem is that many of the spots we want to infiltrate are inaccessible to civilian transports, which is why I asked for you. With your small, highly maneuverable fighters, you can get us where we need to be. We'll have a test mission this afternoon at 13:00, but I'm confident we'll work very well together."

X shot a glance at Liesel, still buttoned up tight, and asked: "But won't that blow your cover? Having military fighters drop you off for your little adventures?"

"No, because you—and your fighters—will also be in disguise, as sport pilots in military surplus hardware."

"What he failed to mention," Liesel burst out, unable to contain herself any longer, "is that this 'disguise' our fighters are wearing involves beating the shit out of them with sledgehammers and smearing them with spray paint and artificial rust."

X and the other pilots, who had been lounging in their seats a second ago, shot up straight with a chorus of angry protests.

"*My* fighter!?"

"You can't—"

"—ruin the—"

"—top of the line—"

"—she's *mine* goddammit—"

"—keep your hands off him or I'll—"

Adam held up his hands, palms out, as if to ward off the onslaught. "Whoa, whoa, if I'd known you guys felt so strongly

~ Flashpoint~

about it, I'd have requisitioned some decommissioned equipment. As it was, I thought you'd perform better in your own planes. I'm sorry."

Dead silence fell over the room.

"Yeah, that means exactly what you think it means," Liesel said caustically. "They've already done it."

The horrified faces of the Reapers turned toward her.

"Max?" X asked, referring to his own fighter.

Liesel nodded.

"*Alexa*?" X asked, aghast.

Liesel nodded, keeping her arms tightly crossed and her anger up lest she burst into tears in front of everyone.

"Jesus Christ," X groaned, rubbing his stubbled head with both hands. "Jesus Christ."

Adam's gaze sharpened and turned on X. "Alexa? Did you say Alexa?"

Liesel turned her angry gaze on him. "Yeah, Alexa. She's my fighter. She was special, and you ruined her. You sad fucking sack," she growled through her teeth. She tried to shut up then. She really did. But it came out anyway. "It should have been you."

She spun and fled the room before any tears escaped.

Liesel had control of herself by the time 13:00 hours rolled around, but she still didn't want to report for duty. Since she'd skipped out on the rest of the briefing, X had emailed the details of their op to her tablet. She'd expected a reprimand from the Squadron Commander for her outburst, but it never came. Maybe the Reapers had convinced Adam not to report her.

Their fighters had been transferred to a disused hangar in nearby Peary City. Their uniforms were binned in favor of a pile of gaudy civilian clothes collected from second hand shops; colourful t-shirts, canvas cargo pants, jeans, sweatshirts with logos on them, pocket vests designed for photographers, sneakers, hiking boots, and a pile of battered hats. Nothing matched. No rank insignia. Wearing them felt all wrong. Liesel kept having to pull up her cargo pants as they slipped over her hips. The pressure suits were even worse. They were at least six models out of date and they smelled like old sweat. The only things they'd been allowed to keep were their pressure suit gloves, which were specially designed for manipulating fighter controls. She jammed a black tuque down over her ears and boarded a public shuttle for the short flight to the transit hub attached to their new hangar.

Peary City was medium sized—a few eight storey buildings in the center of town but mostly low rises, clustered underneath a faintly gold-tinted dome capping the crater the city was built in. Its transport hub was a series of semi-circular lumps branching off a central tube jutting from the edge of the dome at ground level. In one of those lumps she would find her squadron's new hangar.

The shuttle pulled into the airlock at the outer end of the tube and dropped its ramp, disgorging Liesel and a handful of other base personnel on their way to furloughs in the city. She trotted down the hall behind them, their conversation washing over her but not sinking in, until she found the Cave Divers' hangar and stopped.

She stared at the pressure hatch as the others disappeared down the corridor. How could she face Flynn and Saf after this morning? Or Adam? What she'd said to him was awful, and it sounded racist. How could she explain that the only reason she hated him was because he wasn't her sister? Would that even be better?

She took a few deep breaths. She had a job to do.

When she finally waved the hatch open and walked into the hangar, everyone was already there, kitted out in their ridiculous new clothes and getting the now unrecognizable fighters ready for launch. Adam and his five cave divers were off to the side checking each other's spelunking equipment, which was clipped and tied to hardpoints on their pressure suits. *That's twice I've arrived last.* X glanced over at her from beneath the brim of his tan bucket hat. Their eyes connected and Liesel nodded once to indicate that she had her head on straight. X swiped the sleeve of his orange Hawaiian shirt across his forehead in comically exaggerated relief.

In subdued silence, Liesel ran through the preflight checks on Alexa, noting that Flynn and Saf had been careful to make sure all the damage was superficial. None of the control surfaces, thrusters, or sensors had been touched. She stopped by

~ Flashpoint ~

the flip-down ladder leading up to the cockpit. Adam stood next to it, waiting for her. It made sense—leader paired with leader—but it didn't make it any easier to face him.

He should have been angry; she still was. Every time she saw him she wanted to yell, scream, scratch—something. But Adam just stared at her, like he was trying to peer through her eyes and read her brain. She looked away, and gestured curtly for him to climb up. Adam frowned but obeyed, his climbing gear clanking like a pocket full of change.

He sat in the rear seat and stowed his pack behind the cargo hatch as she climbed up and took her seat in the front. They didn't speak as she ran through her final checks. The silence lay between them like a dead thing. When airlock doors rolled open, Liesel jammed the throttles forward and blasted outside ahead of the rest. This was one area in which she would never fall down on duty. First out, last in. Always.

Liesel kept her fighter low and close, skimming the ground like a skilled fighter pilot—or a reckless sport pilot. Luckily the two were indistinguishable to the untrained eye. She felt better with the stick in her hand, the pedals at her feet, feeling Alexa respond through the controls. The terrain-following map on her instrument panel maintained a steady green arrow at the top, indicating which way to go. They'd head for the pole today and deposit the Cave Divers in the neighbourhood of the old ice mines. It was just one fissure over from where Adam had been rescued and Alexa had died. Liesel tried not to think about that, putting all her focus into keeping on course.

The other pilots and Cave Divers chatted aimlessly over the comms, exchanging funny stories and fictional anecdotes of other adventure trips, trying to sound like just another group of yahoos out for a jaunt. Liesel and Adam should have joined in, but they stayed silent. Every passing second seemed to suck more air out of the cockpit. The computer chime announcing the drop point came as a relief. She signalled Adam to get his helmet on, then slowed down, rolled over, and popped the canopy. He unbuckled and slid slowly down the inside of the canopy, landing on the rocky surface with low-G bounciness.

He shouldered his pack, looked up at her hanging above him through his helmet faceplate, and said, "See you at 17:30?" Like he was worried she might just leave him out here to rot,

~ Flashpoint ~

which gave Liesel an unwelcome pang of guilt.

She nodded curtly. "See you." Then she sealed the canopy, shutting him out.

Five and a half hours was a lot of time to kill. In keeping with their new image as sport pilots, X and the others dug out a soccer ball and gently kicked it around, loping after it with long, graceless strides. Moon football didn't focus so much on scoring goals as keeping the ball from accidentally sailing out of the gravity well. Liesel didn't play. She was still wound up so tight she found it hard to breathe, though that could have been because there was a leak somewhere in her crappy second-hand pressure suit.

She lounged on Alexa's wing and looked out over the pockmarked landscape. It was so grey and ugly that Liesel wondered why anyone stayed here. Why not go back to Earth, where there was grass and blue skies? Wouldn't a little overpopulation be worth putting up with if it meant having colours back? But that was just Liesel's bad mood talking. Her parents lived on Earth, and three days into her visits she always longed to escape the suffocating crowds. At least here she could be alone with her feelings if she wanted.

It was Liesel who first spotted the Cave Divers on their way back. They were clipped to the same ropes they had rappelled down before, finding footholds and handholds in the craggy vertical wall of the fissure. One by one they reached the top, laughing and high-fiving each other, just like real sports nuts. She could hear their chatter through her comm. One... two...three...four...five Cave Divers gathered their gear and wandered over to where the other pilots sat playing poker on a flat case of rations. Someone was missing.

X seemed to have the same thought. He looked up from game and scanned the cliff. "Where's Adam?"

Craig, a burly guy who had been a shuttle mechanic before he transferred to the Cave Divers, shrugged. "He was right behind us when we started up. He's probably just taking it easy. Sometimes his injuries act up."

Liesel sighed. She'd be perfectly within mission parameters if she just sat there on her ass until Adam showed up. The other Cave Divers certainly didn't seem worried. But she had a bad feeling—the same feeling she had during Alexa's last mission. She knew better than to ignore it.

"I'm going up to take a look," Liesel told X. She slid over the rim of the cockpit and into her seat.

"Want me to watch your back?" he asked.

"Naw, I'll be back in a minute."

She sealed the canopy and lifted off, diving down into the wide fissure. She reached the bottom and leveled off, hovering. Adam's rope hung down the cliff, but he was nowhere to be seen. Carefully applying positioning thrusters, she pivoted her fighter around its center, rotating in a circle as she inspected the walls.

It was wide here but narrowed quickly, tapering into a crack barely wider than her wingspan. *There!* On the wall opposite, Adam free-climbed at top speed, using the low gravity to fling himself up several meters at a time. Below him Liesel saw a fat guy in an old brown pressure suit. He had his back to her, but there was no mistaking the rifle on his shoulder. The rifle kicked and rocked him back on his spiked boots as he took a potshot at Adam. A Bubba. Had to be. The LRA had earned that nickname by doing exactly this—acting like redneck assholes.

Liesel's finger twitched on her deactivated trigger. One shell and the Bubba's asshole face would be pink mist. It was one thing to shoot at somebody in a war and another to shoot at an unarmed man who was running away. But, other than a dinky little Swiss Army knife on her belt, she was unarmed.

Except for one thing.

Liesel eased her fighter into the narrow fissure. In the vacuum, he couldn't hear her. Alexa's shadow fell over him, and he whirled around in surprise. She rolled sharply and smacked him with the starboard wing. His body slammed into the wall and slumped to the ground. His broken helmet vented its air into the void. He never even saw her coming. Liesel refused to feel bad about it.

Liesel looked up and saw Adam staring down at her. He dangled by one arm about fifteen feet above her cockpit. His other arm leaked air and blood through a hole in his pressure suit.

Adam let go. He landed on his three good limbs on the port wing. He clambered toward the cockpit as Liesel opened the canopy to let him in. He dropped into the seat behind her like a sack of bricks. The cockpit had barely repressurized before Adam had his helmet and gloves off. He rolled up his sleeve, hissing as the stiff fabric scraped the seeping wound on his forearm.

Liesel handed him a square of gauze from the first aid kit and watched as he wiped off the blood. Underneath, there was a fairly superficial gash, likely caused by a rock chip knocked loose by a ricochet... and a tattoo. Five letters, done in bold black ink. ALEXA.

Liesel's gaze darted to his face, but he wouldn't meet her eyes. She pulled off her helmet.

"Why do you have my sister's name tattooed on your arm?"

His gaze flicked to hers. He shrugged. "She died to save my life. Most of the time I don't feel like it was a good trade, either."

Now Liesel felt like a piece of shit. "I shouldn't have said that. I was angry."

Adam shrugged again.

She wanted to hit him with more questions, but her instrument panel beeped. She checked the boards, switching over from terrain mapping to radar.

"What is it?" Adam asked.

"Company," Liesel managed to say through her constricted throat.

Three big splotches, probably armed troop transports of the type she and her friends had nicknamed Bubba Boats—bore down on them. Three Bubba Boats meant at least thirty people, more if they were overloaded, and they usually were.

"Strap in and seal everything back up. We're out of here."

"No! We can't. If we run, we'll blow our cover. We're just here for fun, right? We don't even have radar. Why would we run?" Adam argued as he struggled to duct tape the hole in his pressure suit one-handed.

"Um, maybe because I just killed one of their guys and his body is lying right underneath us?" Liesel asked caustically, carefully inverting so they could run nose-first from the canyon.

"Maybe it was an accident?" Adam suggested.

"Either way, you' re a 'darkie' " Liesel reminded him, using sarcastic air quotes. "What are the odds they'll let you go?"

Even through their faceplates, Liesel could see his fear.

~ Flashpoint ~

Adam swallowed. "I'm willing to take the risk."

"Yeah? I'm not. My sister didn't get herself killed saving you just so you could end up in another ice mine. Now get on the radio and tell our friends to beat it."

She rammed the throttles forward, putting all her concentration into not grazing the walls as they rocketed toward the point where the fissure opened up. Adam switched channels to the civilian band and called the others.

They had almost made it out when Liesel felt a huge jolt shudder through the fighter. Everything on her instrument panel went red. Her suit switched to internal pressure as they lost the atmo in the cockpit. She looked back and saw that the entire tail section was a ragged hole. Liesel expected to see a Bubba Boat behind them but the hole framed one guy, a Bubba with a shoulder-mounted rocket launcher. He stood on top of an old electric military surplus truck with his boots strapped to the roof so the rocket wouldn't launch him instead of the other way around.

"Holy shit!" Adam exclaimed. "Where'd they get that?"

"What the hell did you stumble into?" Liesel yelled, ramming the throttles past their stops and feeling absolutely nothing happen in response. The engines were dead. They were coasting on inertia. And the Bubba with the rocket launcher was reloading. She couldn't see his face through his helmet, but she'd bet he was smiling. Asshole.

She swore continuously and creatively, racking her brain for a way out of this mess. The others had already scarpered like she'd told them to, and anyway, without their guns they couldn't have helped. Liesel pointed the nose down and used the maneuvering thrusters on the fighter's belly to push them along. It wasn't much, but it would buy them some time.

"Get your feet together," Liesel snapped. "Hands in your lap."

"What for?" Adam asked, obeying.

"I'm sorry, Alexa," Liesel said. She took the escape axe and smashed up the instrument panel, destroying the radar, radio, and anything else that gave the fighter away as not-exactly-decommissioned.

"Liesel! What the hell!?" Adam exclaimed, as the tiny cockpit filled with smoke and flying chips of instrument glass.

~ Flashpoint~

Liesel dropped the axe and pulled the yellow and black lever beside her seat. With a flash of explosives, the canopy shot away. A split second later, a roar vibrated up from beneath Liesel's seat as the ejection system fired, propelling their seats out of the fighter and toward the rim of the fissure. For a second, Liesel actually thought they were going to make it. And Adam did. He sailed over the edge and out of sight. But the last thing Liesel saw before everything went dark was a wall of grey rock rushing at her.

An undetermined amount of time later, something happened that Liesel hadn't expected. She woke up. Her vision was a bit swimmy and her entire body felt like it had been dragged behind a truck for a few hours, stomped into the ground, and then boiled. She tried to rub her eyes but her hands were tied behind her back. She blinked away the blurriness and discovered that she lay on her side on a floor of rough-hewn rock without a pressure suit.

The room was small, the air thin and the rock walls jagged and uneven like they'd been hacked at by guys with pick-axes. A worklight set up on a metal tripod cast sinister shadows on the wooden beam she was tied to and the mangled metal service door set crookedly into the wall in front of her.

Three men crouched over her. All Caucasian, dressed in mismatched surplus combats, and carrying assault rifles. Bubbas. The one with the buzzed hair and the beer gut seemed to be the leader.

"Rise and shine, girly," Beer Gut said. He splashed water onto her head from a battered metal canteen. She sputtered and blinked it away. The three men grinned. The second one, Beardo, looked like a top contender in the Ugliest Mountain Man pageant. The third guy was a sallow, sniffly fellow Liesel decided to call Needs-A-Snot-Rag.

"Now you're gonna tell us what you're doin' down here, or there's gonna be trouble," Beer Gut demanded.

Liesel almost told him to go fuck himself, but then remembered that she was supposed to be a sports nut, not a military pilot. She snuffled and cowered away from them.

"W-who are you? What's going on?" Liesel whined.

~ Flashpoint ~

"What are you doing here?" Beardo growled, enunciating clearly and sticking his smelly face in hers.

"I—I was just messing around," Liesel said in a tiny voice. She killed the only Bubba who'd seen Adam, so it was probably a good idea to keep the Cave Divers out of it for now.

"You tellin' the truth?" Beardo asked.

"Y—yes! I—"

Beardo slapped her—hard—across the face. Liesel's ears rang and she tasted blood. She wanted nothing more than to throw herself on Beardo and claw his filthy eyes out. But she had to keep her cool. If they found out who she really was they'd kill her in a second. Just like Alexa.

So she forced herself to stay loose, to whimper, to hang her head, to cower. She even managed to drum up a few tears, though they were mostly born of frustration at being so helpless.

"My friend said the fissures out here were really dangerous and he bet me I couldn't fly them 'cause I'm a girl," Liesel sobbed. "I just wanted to prove him wrong. I didn't know you were here, honest. Please let me go."

Beardo and Beer Gut exchanged glances, then the three of them retired into the next room to talk privately. Unfortunately for them, they forgot about their crappy door-fitting job.

"Well?" Beer Gut demanded.

"She's just some dumb broad," Beardo told him.

"Good. Go finish loading up. We're outta here in ten."

"What about her?" asked Needs-A-Snot-Rag.

"Leave her here. We'll take her to the new mine once we get back," Beer Gut told him. "She's nice and docile. Make a good worker."

"But how come we need the mine still? Don't we got enough?" Snot-Rag whined.

There was a smacking sound. "Won't have no more after today, ijut."

"Oh yeah, right."

What the hell were they talking about? What did they need more of that they could get in the ice mines? Uranium, Liesel realized. They were still mining uranium, because after today they'd be out. Which meant…*holy shit*.

They were going to set off a nuke.

~ *Flashpoint* ~

The UN had specially trained technicians to disarm nuclear bombs. Adam was one. Liesel was not. But Liesel was here and Adam wasn't. She had to get free. She had to stop them—or at least call in. Liesel listened to them clank around in the other room as she struggled against the ropes. She felt around the knots with her fingers. One of the Bubbas must've been a sailor in a past life, because they were impenetrable.

Then she remembered the knife. Just a crappy little camping tool—something to help sell her cover—but still sharp enough to do some damage. She was so tiny and pathetic that they hadn't even taken it from its little pouch on her belt. Liesel curled up as tightly as she could, scraping her cheek raw against the floor. She strained to get her mouth close enough to her belt pouch to pop the snap. Her neck screamed with the pain and her shoulders threatened to pop out of their sockets. She crunched her stomach muscles viciously and in one last jerk, she grabbed the flap with her teeth. The snap popped. She lifted her hips painfully. Inch by inch, the knife slid onto the floor. She flopped and scraped around the column, maneuvering the knife behind her so she could grab it. She wedged the handle into her back and rubbed her wrists over the blade. She grimaced as it sliced through flesh as well as the ropes that bound her.

Liesel froze when she heard the hinges squeal. She closed her eyes again and pretended to sob quietly. She hoped whoever had come to check on her wouldn't notice the blood.

She smelled Beardo's hideous body odor—a combination of sweaty feet and rancid breath—as he approached, his breathing heavy. He crept toward her quietly, looking back over his shoulder. He shut the door behind him and looked for a lock, but there wasn't one, not on this side. It was obvious, from the way he was looking at her, what he meant to do.

Is this what you did to Alexa before you killed her? She shook with anger, hoping Beardo would think it was fear.

If he touches me, I cannot be responsible for what will happen. He was bigger than her—by a lot. But she was unbound and had a knife. She also had five months of pent up rage boiling in her veins. She held still and waited for him to come within striking distance. *Watch the eyes. Don't let him see your eyes. Then he'll know.*

~ *Flashpoint* ~

Beardo reached for his belt buckle. Liesel tensed to strike. And the door burst open. Beardo spun around, letting go of his belt as if he'd been burned. Beer Gut stood in the doorway.

"Let's go," Beer Gut told Beardo coldy. "You can have your fun when we get back."

With a scowl, Beardo followed Beer Gut outside and slammed the door.

Liesel waited a few minutes to makes sure they were really gone. She breathed deeply, forcing back the rage and the fear of what had almost happened. She needed to be clearheaded to stop this. Finally, she stood up, massaging feeling back into her numb hands.

She'd cut herself pretty badly, so she took off her tuque, cut it in half, and tied the halves tightly over each wrist. Then she got down low and peered under the door. The room on the other side was bigger and brighter than the one she was in. She saw a couple of battered table legs but no boots.

Gripping the knife, Liesel kicked open the door and ducked inside. The room was unoccupied but filled with an assortment of old tables, most of them strewn with gun cleaning equipment or ammo. An old cafeteria, converted into a staging area. Maps of different sectors of the moon covered one wall. Straight red lines connected the domes. On the map for their sector, the Peary dome was also connected to an unnamed base. The Bubbas might as well have labeled it "you are here." From the pattern of the lines, they could only be in one place – the disused controlling station for the solar generators in the Peaks of Eternal Light. She grabbed the map off the wall and stuffed it in her pocket, knowing Adam and his Cave Divers would find it very interesting indeed—provided she could get it to them.

Liesel ducked through an archway into a cavernous, jagged room that looked like it had been blasted out with explosives. It was also unoccupied. Toolboxes, trucks and a ladder leading upward lined one wall. On the other was a massive airlock next to a long row of at least sixty hooks. Only a few on the end held old brown pressure suits.

She snatched the smallest of the remaining pressure suits and checked the seals. They looked good, but the suit was miles too big. It would be hard to move around in. Liesel didn't have a lot of options at that point, so she slipped it on. She clumsily folded her knife and slipped it into an outside pocket.

Liesel stepped into the airlock and jabbed the button that would cycle it through. As the air hissed out and the far door rolled open, she was surprised to discover it didn't open to the outside. Instead, she stood in a rough-hewn rock tunnel big enough for a vehicle. Near the top a multitude of brightly-coloured cables ran past, riveted to the wall in neat parallel lines, following the downward slope of the tunnel. The wall behind the cables was oddly smooth. The power tunnels. The Bubbas had widened them to accommodate their trucks.

No wonder they always seemed to be popping up out of nowhere.

Through the soles of her boots she felt the faint tremor of the Bubbas' truck. She ran down the slope, hoping they weren't far ahead.

The moon's low gravity made running harder rather than easier. She had to keep up a steady, reaching stride with as little spring as possible or she'd spend too much time drifting slowly up and down in lazy parabolic arcs. Despite all the workouts pilots went through to stay in shape, she was out of breath after only a few K. Crashing headlong into a wall probably had something to do with that. She had to ease off whenever black spots crowded into the edges of her vision. This slowed her down, but it ended up saving her.

During one of those dizzy spells, Liesel rounded a curve and saw twenty Bubbas clustered together in the bed of their truck, manhandling a huge nuke-shaped metal cylinder into a chain-link sling.

She dived out of sight and watched. The chains looped around the top rung of the ladder and back down to the ground, where another cluster of Bubbas stood ready to pull. One of the figures in the truck gestured 'up' and the others heaved on the chain. The nuke rose jerkily into the air.

Liesel flipped the comm switch on the back of her helmet and tried to breathe quietly. Any sound she made would be transmitted over their net.

"—steady Buck! Jesus. You want it goin' off on us?"

"No. Sorry. It's heavy!"

Nukes were designed to be dropped from space without going off unless they were armed, so either it was already armed or theirs was a fly-by-night job with no safety features. Either way, this was not a good place to be right now. But Liesel didn't move. How long would she have to get help before it went off? She needed to know.

The Bubba at the top of the ladder reached up to activate the small, iris-shaped airlock set into the ceiling.

"Naw don't do that, Jerry," said Beer Gut's voice. "I ain't givin' them a chance to find it. We'll just leave it right here."

"Whatever you say, boss."

The Bubbas tied the chain off to a spike set into the rock. When they were done, the nuke hung in a cradle just underneath the airlock.

"All set. Let's get out of here."

They headed back to the truck.

"How much time we got, Boss?" asked one of them, looking anxiously at the nuke.

"Twenty minutes," Beer gut answered. "We'll get clear, don't worry."

They hopped in the truck, Beer Gut and his cronies in the cab, the others piling into the truck bed, and started it up. Liesel realized that in addition to being in a tunnel with a live nuke, she had another problem: the Bubbas were heading home. And to do that they'd have to go right past her. She frantically looked around for somewhere to hide but there were no crevices or overhangs.

Beer Gut started the engine and rumbled down the tunnel toward her. As the truck rounded the curve, Liesel stuck to the outside and willed her brown suit to blend into the rock. She flicked off her comm so they wouldn't hear her panicked breathing. The driver's eyes would follow the curve and miss her, but the truck wouldn't. It would scrape her off the wall like a dead insect. Unless...

As the truck bore down on her, Liesel threw herself under the front fender—or tried to—she forgot how much bulk the suit added to her body. She scraped the back of her helmet on the fender and the valve on top of her oxygen tanks got caught. She hung from the fender, her legs dragging painfully over the rocks as she tried to wiggle free. The huge engine block hid her from the Bubbas, but if she stuck around any longer the friction would shred her suit. She grabbed the undercarriage and shoved backward with all her strength. The valve came unhooked and she fell to the ground. She lay as flat as she could and hoped the wheels would miss her.

The rumble of the truck's passing shook the world. Liesel closed her eyes and waited to be crushed. But after a minute, the rumble receded and the truck left her behind. She lay there panting, feeling her suit to make sure it wasn't torn. The old material was tougher than it looked.

When she was sure the Bubbas weren't going to come back, she got up and ran for the ladder. If her calculations were right, the airlock would lead her into Peary City. From there she could call in Adam and his team. They were based right outside of town. If they hurried, they could make it. She pounded on the control pad for the ancient airlock but got only a red light in response to every access code she knew. *Shit.* The thing was so old, it would probably only respond to codes that were fifty years out of date.

She glanced back at the nuke, hanging innocently in its harness, its timer ticking down past fifteen minutes. *There's no help coming. If anyone's going to stop it, it has to be me.*

Liesel gingerly wedged herself in place on the ladder and leaned out over the nuke. Its outer shell was welded together with scrap bits of metal stamped with a variety of company logos. Near the middle, a digital readout salvaged from an alarm clock ticked down the seconds. Thirteen minutes, thirty eight seconds. A red wire ran from the digital readout into the seam of a small access panel that had been screwed most of the way back down. *Should I cut it? What if it's attached to something on the inside, some kind of trap that sets the thing off?* It seemed unlikely, since the Bubbas didn't expect anyone to find it, but that wasn't something you left to chance.

I have time to look. I have to look.

She fumbled her knife from her pocket and picked at the attachments, wishing for her precision piloting gloves. With the thick, outdated suit material, it was like trying to work a zipper with oven mitts on. Eventually she got the flat-head screwdriver out and got to work, but the edge kept slipping out of the groove. Liesel wanted to explode with frustrated energy, but she forced herself to tamp it down. As the clock ticked down past ten minutes, Liesel started to sweat. The sweat plus the blood still leaking from her lacerated wrists made the inside of her pressure suit smell like a locker room crossed with a butcher shop.

Liesel finally pulled out the last screw and levered open the panel. Only five minutes left, and she'd never seen so many wires and circuits in her life. She'd never taken any courses in bomb disposal. The closest she'd ever come to anything like this was opening the maintenance access on her fighter to jiggle a loose wire in the cabin heater. She pawed through the wires, becoming more and more frantic as their function failed to become clear.

Why did she have to deal with this? She was a fighter pilot, not a bomb technician. The whole reason Adam and his unit existed was to find this thing, so— *Where the hell are they?* Liesel screamed her frustration and grabbed the nuke, wanting to shake it, to hit it.

She froze, horrified. If she gave in to these urges, the nuke would probably go off, killing her and everyone in Peary City. Saf's words came back to haunt her. *Take an anger management class, before you kill somebody.* He was right. He was completely right. She couldn't go on like this or somebody really would get killed. A lot of somebodies almost did.

Liesel took a few deep breaths and forced herself to release her grip on the nuke. Adam wasn't here. The Cave Divers weren't here. She was. She had to handle things on her own.

What would they do? She thought back to earlier, staring at the poster on the wall in the Cave Divers' ready room so she wouldn't have to look at Adam. It had been a diagram of a nuke, instructions on how to disarm it. *But what did it say?*

She closed her eyes and pictured it. The nuke on the poster was nicer—shinier, smoother—but only on the outside. On the inside it was the same mess of wires. They surrounded a tube with a bowl of metal at one end and a bullet at the other. The bowl was the important part. That much she remembered. If the bullet hit it, the whole thing went 'BANG.'

She poked through the tangle of wires. They came in all colours. Blue, red, orange, black, pink, and yellow. She tunneled into the nest with her gloved fingers until she hit something. Brushing the other wires out of the way, she saw the tube. She followed it to the metal bowl at the end. *All I have to do is take it out.*

~ Flashpoint~

Liesel was about to jam her knife in there and start prying, but then she stopped. Could she set it off by touching it? She glanced at the timer and realized she couldn't afford to wait any longer. She squeezed her eyes closed and stuck her knife in.

Nothing happened. Liesel pulled the bowl out, grinning like an idiot. She'd just defused a nuclear weapon! Her awkward, sitting-on-a-ladder victory dance came to an abrupt halt when she noticed that the digital readout was still counting down. From *fifteen seconds.*

Liesel nearly had an adrenalin-induced heart attack. She launched herself off the ladder, trying to get away from the thing. It was a reflex. Thirty feet one way or the other wasn't going to make a hell of a difference. Her boot caught in one of the chains and she spun in midair, almost smashing her face against the nuke. She wound up hanging upside-down from the nuke's harness, digital readout in her face, as the clock ticked from one second to zero seconds.

Liesel didn't see her life flash before her eyes. Time didn't slow down. She had no time to think anything other than s*hit!* She squeezed her eyes shut and felt a horrible jolt. Then—nothing.

For the second time that day, Liesel Cormack woke up after expecting never to do so again. This time, she lay at the base of a ladder in a tunnel made of rock. She tried to recall how she'd gotten there and remembered the nuke. She looked up. It was still there. The digital readout flashed zeros but the nuke was intact, apart from a fist-sized hole in the nose, right around where she'd found the shiny bowl. A correspondingly-sized bullet had lodged in the wall about halfway up the ladder.

The jolt she'd felt wasn't the nuke going off, but her head hitting the ground after she flailed herself loose from the chain. She felt like an idiot. Of course the readout wouldn't change. She hadn't done anything to it. The part she'd cut out was something different—the bowl. It now lay on the ground in front of her nose.

Liesel grabbed the first ladder rung to haul herself up and felt the faint rumbling of a truck. She'd been out for half an hour. The Bubbas must have noticed the lack of a big flash and bang and had finally worked up the nerve to come back and reset their piece of junk bomb. Taking off down the tunnel wasn't the best option. There was no cover. But it was her only option, so she stuffed the shiny bowl into her suit pocket and ran as fast as the low gravity would allow. She reached back to flip on her comms, hoping to hear their plans, but found that the entire comms unit had been ripped off by her encounter with the truck.

Her breath sounded ridiculously loud, reverberating through the helmet, completely fogging up her faceplate. She tried to work her arm out of the suit sleeve to wipe off the inside, but before she could do much more than get her elbow stuck in the armpit, the tunnel suddenly ended. Her foot came down on empty air and then she toppled forward. She fell for ten panicky, flailing seconds, then landed on her trapped arm. Thanks to the low gravity, the only thing wounded was her pride.

She yanked her arm out of the sleeve and smeared the condensation across the inside of her helmet. She was outside again, several hundred feet down in the bottom of another canyon She shoved herself to her feet and ran for cover. The tunnel mouth was directly above her about halfway up. Any second now several dozen Bubbas in a truck armed with rockets were going to come barreling down the ramp that switchbacked down the wall. She didn't want to be here when they did.

The low gravity made her bounce crazily. She careened into the canyon walls—a parabolic fish in a barrel. She needed somewhere to duck out of sight until she could make her way back to the base. She hoped she was running toward it, but all these frigging canyons looked the same—a deep V of jagged grey rock. She rounded a jog in the canyon and saw another opening, this one at ground level. Liesel ran for it, intending to hide inside, but before she could get there a half dozen Bubbas strolled out, armed with rifles. She skidded, flinging herself back around the jog before they looked her way, but on the other side the Bubbas' truck was making its way down the ramp. It wasn't facing her yet, but in a minute they would turn around and see her. She was trapped.

She wedged herself back into a fissure in the wall that was barely wide enough to fit a piece of paper, hoping her dirty pressure suit would offer some camouflage. She dug into her pocket for the knife and flipped the blade open. This was it then. The end. She took deep breaths and readied herself to strike.

~ Flashpoint ~

Something dropped on her from above. She'd been expecting to be caught, but not from that direction. She and her captor went down in a tangle of arms and legs. Anger shot through her as she flailed and kicked, trying to stab and slice her way out.

A helmet touched hers from behind. "Liesel! Liesel! Stop!" a voice said, sporting a hint of panic as it reverberated dimly through her helmet. "You'll cut my suit!"

The use of her name shocked her still for a second. Then she spun around and saw Adam. He had his arms out, one of them wrapped in duct tape. He kept his distance, warily eyeing the knife that could depressurize his suit and kill him. Liesel was so glad to see him that she threw down the knife and hugged him.

"Now!" Adam said, presumably talking to someone on his helmet comm, and they shot into the air toward the rim of the canyon. Below, the two groups of Bubbas came together. Suited Bubbas climbed out of the truck, consulting with the ones on foot over whether or not they'd seen her. No one looked up. They eventually split up to search in opposite directions.

When Liesel and Adam reached the edge, four pairs of gloved hands helped them over. Liesel lay on the ground, panting, still entangled with Adam, and looked up into the faces of four concerned pilots. She saw X in the cockpit of the fighter that they had used as a winch to pull her and Adam out of the canyon.

Once they assured themselves that Liesel was okay, the other pilots ran to their fighters to provide backup for the Cave Divers, who were creeping around the edges of the canyon, tracking the Bubbas down below. Adam taped a mike to the faceplate of her helmet so they could talk to each other.

"How did you know it was me?" Liesel asked. She was, after all, wearing an enemy suit.

Adam grinned. "No Bubbas are that tiny. Plus, you were running like hell away from them."

She smiled as she heard the voices of the Cave Divers reporting the locations of the Bubbas's tunnel entrances.

"Where the hell have you been all day?" Adam asked. "We've been looking for you everywhere."

"Long story," Liesel told him. "Here's the end." She fished

~ Flashpoint ~

around in her pocket and held out the metal bowl she'd taken from inside the nuke.

Adam looked horrified when he saw what it was. He took it from her gingerly. "Do you know what that is?"

"Not a clue."

"It's the uranium core. I take it you found the nuke."

Liesel nodded, suddenly glad pressure suits were designed to block cosmic radiation.

Instead of looking happy, Adam was angry. "And you couldn't have waited for me? Jesus, Liesel, you're just like her. Jumping in with both feet, not even thinking about what could happen. You could have been killed!"

Liesel looked up at him, waiting for her hair trigger temper to ignite, but it didn't. Adam had just said what she'd been trying not to think for five months—that part of what happened to Alexa was Alexa's own fault. She was impulsive and she always thought she could handle things by herself. She had gone in without backup, without even much of a plan.

Deep down, Liesel was mad at her for it, and she'd been taking it out on everyone else. That left her feeling mostly just... sad. Sad and tired. All the blame and anger in the world weren't going to bring Alexa back. But maybe...just maybe...she hadn't died for nothing.

"I was wrong about you, you know," she told Adam. "Alexa was right. As always. You are worth it. I just wish...I just wish it didn't have to be one of you or the other, you know?"

Liesel choked the last words out past the sudden blockage in her throat. She couldn't cry, not now, not here, maybe not ever. But then Adam hugged her, fiercely, like he'd been wanting to for ages, and she couldn't stop. She was bowled over by grief at the thought that she'd never see her sister again. It was the first time she'd felt anything other than anger at her death.

After a minute, they sat back, this time without the awful tension that had so far plagued their every meeting.

"So what now?" Adam asked.

"Now the Bubbas better watch their asses, because you and me? We're coming for them."

Liesel tossed the map of the Bubba's tunnel network into his lap.

~ Flashpoint ~

Katrina Nicholson is a former Air Cadet pilot with a degree in history and a diploma in writing for film and television. She has twelve published short stories, two produced short films, and several contest wins. You can read more of her work in the anthologies *Futuredaze, Tesseracts Fifteen, Future Embodied, Kisses by Clockwork,* and the other volumes of the *Speculative Elements* series, or visit her online at www.katrinanicholson.com.

Burning Fear

An old metal fan murmured softly, the only sound within the dimly lit room. The whisper-quiet hum would never escape this room, even if it had been thunderous. Thick books and tomes insulated the walls, shelves, and floor. Every available space was covered, save one. A large mahogany desk, neat and orderly, was spared the heavy burden of books.

Dr. Stanton sat in his black leather Victorian high-backed chair. After forty-two years of patient care he was happy to be teaching now, no longer a clinical psychiatrist. Now there were only a few patients or cases that he continued to handle. They were special projects to him. The more challenging, or disturbed patients, that might mentally chew up and spit out a different psychiatrist.

These special patients encompassed both his greatest accomplishments and his greatest failures. He felt a deep sorrow when he thought about some of them, having to remind himself that he could not help everyone.

He glanced down at one of his recent files simply titled "Vivian and Janet." That one had taken a toll on him. Dr. Stanton took a deep breath and softly closed his eyes.

When a panicky chime chirped out of his old rotary phone, the noise was like a splash of cold water to his face. Dr. Stanton felt his heart hasten. A dark thought crossed his mind, and he foolishly wondered how many tranquil interruptions by phone resulted in a heart attack.

He snapped up the phone mid-ring, pressing the receiver snugly to his ear as he grabbed a pen and held it, hovering over a pad of paper.

"Hello, Dr. Stanton speaking. How may I help you?" Smiling, the professor laid his pen down and leaned back in his chair. "Ah yes, well, I am quite happy to hear from you. You sound very excited."

Dr. Stanton crossed one leg over the other and listened momentarily. "Excellent, excellent. And you no longer fear lighting a match to the stove, or starting a fire in the great room fireplace?"

He absently scratched his raised foot through his argyle sock. "Wonderful. Well, yes, you are quite welcome. Of course you know I was just doing my job. So it seems you have no more need of me, but please send a post card at Christmas. And don't forget, the world is a beautiful place. So get out there and enjoy it. Yes, thank you, goodbye."

Dr. Stanton placed the pearl-handled phone back into its assembly. He straightened up his disheveled sock and sunk deeper into his chair, feeling somehow lighter. A rare moment of pure joy. Not every complex patient of his was an accomplishment of this level.

He picked up his pen, turning it over in his hand, considering the title of his new book. As he did so, he let flow the memories of his patient Vivian. The long months of working with her had been arduous. He was dealt so many setbacks that he nearly gave up on her. Again he closed his eyes and allowed himself to mentally travel back to the day when he finally made a break-through and reached her.

"Vivian, please come into the living room. Please come, sit with me and talk."

Vivian was in the next room, the kitchen. Dr. Stanton knew she spent as much time as she could there; she'd told him many times that it was where she felt most comfortable. He'd made efforts to build trust with her and thought his efforts were beginning to pay off. Vivian seemed to like consistency, so he always dressed formally, with a plaid sweater vest over his dress shirts. Always the same vest, in soothing tones of green, grey, and gold.

Vivian entered the living room, giving him a sad smile.

~ Flashpoint ~

"Doctor, you keep coming, but I am afraid you cannot help me. You know I have always been scared to leave this house, but it is so much worse ever since..." Her voice trailed off.

He nodded. Her agoraphobia was overpowering. He spoke softly. "I know it's difficult for you, and those memories pain you." He stopped speaking as he noticed that her lips were still moving slowly. He leaned forward to hear the barely audible whisper.

"...and the fire was so fast and merciless" Her head slumped forward as she began to reveal the story she had attempted to tell the Doctor so many times before. As she described the events, Dr. Stanton almost held his breath, scribbling quickly in his notebook, capturing her words precisely as they finally revealed her story.

The smell of smoke rolled over me like a billowy blanket as I lay on the couch in my pink nightgown. I coughed myself awake and fell to the floor. The room was choked with black and grey smoke. I instinctively moved toward the wavering yellow light and stumbled and coughed my way into the kitchen.

How could I have fallen asleep? I had been heating some breakfast on the stove, and had only sat down to wait for it to be ready. I must have dozed off.

In the kitchen, fire engulfed the stove. My lovely curtains and wallpaper were covered in bright orange ravenous flames, which crawled and ate as they moved. I stood helplessly in the centre of my kitchen, feet rooted to the floor as the fire consumed everything around me. Unable to look away, I watched as the clock melted to the wall, and the photos on my fridge oozed downward into puddles of colour. My favorite, a picture of me and Charlie laughing, sagged and then melded our faces into one before plopping onto the floor. It was that, I think, that made me move. I screamed to Charlie, sleeping somewhere above the clouds of smoke in the upstairs bedroom. "Charlie! Charlie, we have to get out!"

The fire roared like an animal at my back, pressing me forward, its hot breath blowing my hair across my eyes. I was trapped! Flickering flames circled around between me and the door to the outside. The door wasn't far away, but the horrible feelings that had kept me from leaving the house for six long years gripped my chest. The flames, waving rhythmically back and forth, suddenly stood taller, mocking me, as though they knew I couldn't leave. My legs moved unconsciously, inching closer to the door, my lungs searing with each breath. Just a short hallway between me and freedom. The firetruck's siren wailed nearby. They would come for me, they would rescue me and Charlie, but only a few feet of unburned floor lay around me now. I could not wait.

My will to survive finally overcame my fear, and I ran forward, my short legs pumping as they hadn't in years. I jumped through the wall of flames and scrambled towards the door. The fire embraced my frantic body as I fell hard into the black smoke and onto the floor. The door was close. My hands stretched toward it. Ignoring the pain, I fought with all my will.

Outside, everything felt surreal. I had not seen the exterior of my house for many years; Charlie's garden was so different since last I had seen it that I actually stopped and stared. That moment was all the time I had to admire it before my eyes darted back to the house. I looked on in horror as my home was half-consumed by flames.

I knew then that Charlie would never get out alive.

Four firetrucks filled the driveway, water spewing, brave men charging into my house. The world spun. So many people. The lights. The noise. I was safe, but I desperately wanted back into the house. I wanted the nightmare to be over. I knew with certainty I would go back in as soon as the fire was gone. I would go back inside and keep the world, and the evil flames, out.

The disaster took half my house, and my husband. I stayed in the salvaged, smokey side while the repairs were done. The following months were miserable for me—so many people coming and going from my house. I was so happy when they finally left for good.

"Vivian, it's Dr. Stanton. I lost you for a while, are you okay?" He watched her closely, as she trembled in the emotional aftermath of revisiting the worst day of her life.

"I'm sorry, Doctor. The memory takes me sometimes. I miss Charlie so much. It's hard." Vivian sat in her rocking chair, swaying back and forth.

~ Flashpoint ~

"Yes, of course, and again I am sorry for your loss. I know you feel guilt about surviving the fire." Dr Stanton paused. He knew by now how much he could push her emotionally.

They sat in silence for a while before the doctor spoke again. "Vivian, may I ask you some questions?" She did not respond. Sensing he might be losing her he offered, "I will keep the questions easy, if that's better?" Again, he paused. She broke the silence. "Doctor, I'm an old lady. I forget things. You confuse and trick me with your questions."

Dr. Stanton leaned slowly forward. "Please, Viv, it's very important that we finish our talk. I want to help you conquer your fear of the outside world. Will you try?"

Vivian's lips trembled, but she answered with a soft "Yes." The Doctor shifted into interview mode. Now it was time to challenge her, gently and carefully. "All right Vivian, I want you to close your eyes and relax while we talk." He paused. "Can you tell me what you had for breakfast today?"

"I always have the same thing for breakfast, one soft boiled egg with some tea and toast."

"Ah, yes I remember. Good. Now, I would like you to tell me what it tasted like."

"I don't understand; you know what eggs taste like! You're trying to make me say something." Her sinewy fingers clenched tight.

"Please, Vivian, don't get upset." He moved on with another question. "I would like you to describe the chair you are sitting on now. How does it feel against your skin?"

"Well, it's an old wooden rocking chair. It has a green cushion and—"

Dr. Stanton cut her off. "Vivian, you're describing what it looks like." He put his pen and notebook down, and looked into her tearful eyes. "Okay, close your eyes again. I want you to go back to the day of the fire. You remember the fire trucks and the noise. You remember being outside and watching your house burn. Tell me, Vivian, when you saw all these things...were you looking down?"

Vivian looked panicked as she whispered. "Yes. You're right...I was looking down. How could I not..." She ran her hand along the arm of the chair. "And I don't feel this chair...it's as

~ Flashpoint ~

if...as if I only *remember* feeling it..."

Dr. Stanton stood and walked to the door, "Vivian, it's time for you to leave this house. You have been here for too many years, afraid to leave. You feel guilty about the fire, but you must leave this house." His eyes shone with feeling. "Vivian, it was an accident." He opened the door and sunlight spilled into the room.

Relief flooded over Vivian's face as she rose from the chair, her last tether unbound. Unencumbered, she flowed past the doctor to the entryway. Her pink gown, charred around the edges, showed some of her burned flesh below, the skin black and mottled. As the sun caressed her, her skin lightened and the gown shimmered a vibrant pink, the burned flesh transforming into something whole and healed. She floated out the door, her eyes fixed on the foreign light.

She half turned her head to the doctor, her gaze to the light never relenting. She whispered as she slowly faded, "Thank you, Doctor."

The doctor glanced at the cradled receiver. The things most people take for granted—those were the things Dr. Stanton could restore on a successful case. Janet had been effusive in her thanks, and no wonder. Poor woman, she'd gotten much more than she expected when she purchased Vivian's house. She'd found out the hard way why the price was so low. No real estate agent ever tells you about ghosts.

"I can light the gas stove and there are no screams or flying objects," Janet told him. "I just had to call to thank you again. God bless you."

Janet and her family had certainly felt tormented, but then, Vivian had been, too.

There was more for him to do, he thought. So much more. Dr. Stanton sat a moment and reflected, staring at the blank page of his notebook. Then he wrote the title of his new book: *Spirit Healing—A Psychiatrist's Guide.*

~ Flashpoint ~

Steven Fraser MacLean was born and raised in Cape Breton. He currently serves in the Canadian Armed Forces as a Warrant Officer and Physician Assistant in Kingston, Ontario. This is his first published short story. He enjoys travelling and entertaining at his cottage.

Spark

Zleen glided down the corridor toward the command center, enjoying the hum, buzz and pulse of the transport. The harmonious blending of energies thrumming through the vessel always felt particularly invigorating when one came fresh from a stasis pod, regenerated and ready to face a new cycle.

Zleen fought off the childish urge to extend a few tentacles and slip them into one of the silvery blue energy fields, to let them trail, bobbing in the stream. It was so pleasurable to let the pulses tingle through the entire body.

I am the commanding officer of this vessel. Zleen resumed forward momentum, but the urge remained, tantalizingly strong. The Commander sighed and halted again, tentacles outstretched. *I also have a terrible weakness for stimulation.*

The three extended tentacles recoiled as the streams of energy darkened, pulsed erratically and took on a high-pitched whine.

All six tentacles wrapped around Zleen's delicate ear flaps. The officer fought to send thoughts down into the mind of the Chief Engineer over the excruciating noise.

Minnin, Minnin, allow me entrance to your thoughts. What is happening?

Minnin communicated back a number of disjointed thoughts and images, and whether this was done deliberately or out of panic, one thing was clear: Minnin was hiding something from the Commander.

Zleen raced up the corridor.

The engine room was in utter chaos. Acrid chemical-laced smoke assaulted the Commander upon entrance. Zleen sucked in delicate nose frills to block it out and extended three tentacles, relying on them to guide the way.

~ Flashpoint ~

Recoiling from the densest concentrations of harmful toxins and extending into the freshest paths, Zleen's tentacles found the safest route through.

In a clear patch of the room, two assistant engineers lay, clearly dead. Two others worked to finish a force-field covering a jagged hole in the hull of the vessel, empty space looming beyond.

Minnin stood next to another team who toiled frantically to repair the propulsion system. Through the force-field around the system, Zleen observed dozens of Blikkets zipping through the air in panicked loops. Unable to perform their primary function, the tiny energy beings swarmed in a mass of frenetic movement.

Are they all contained? Zleen barked into Minnin's mind.

Minnin's tentacles curled and unfurled in agitation as the Chief Engineer rotated to face the Commander.

Two large Blikkets zipped in front of Zleen's face, answering the question before Minnin could. Zleen's nose frills furled out in anger and the stench seeped in again. The Commander sucked them back inside and fought for composure.

The Blikkets surged from light blue to deep purple as they battled the urge to combust.

Don't, warned Zleen. The two Blikkets were not among those that served Zleen directly, but, bonded as they were with the other officers, they obeyed the chain of command.

Reverberating with the effort, they calmed to a cool blue.

Good, communicated Zleen in what the Commander hoped was a reassuring tone.

A junior engineer slid forward with a canister and the two Blikkets zipped obediently inside.

Zleen turned to the quivering Minnin. *Report.*

Dozens of Blikkets had died, due to the deaths of the officers to which they were bonded. With so few Blikkets remaining, the ship was at reduced propulsion. A very young officer, now among the dead, had inserted the wrong canister of Blikkets into the propulsion system. Meaning to insert a canister of regenerated Blikkets fresh from stasis, the officer had inserted a canister of Blikkets preparing to give birth. The stress of giving birth while other Blikkets exploded around them had killed the parents and left the offspring, without guidance, volatile and explosive. The far

~ Flashpoint ~

more dire news was that those juvenile Blikkets had escaped into space.

Blake climbed the staircase to the second story of the house and walked across what was left of the ruined hallway. The acrid odors left by ravenous flames lingered, although a welcome blast of fall air billowed in from the shattered second floor windows. Most of the firefighters had left the scene long ago, and, not for the first time in his new capacity as fire chief, he envied them. What they saw was bad enough, but often, he had to dig deeper. He stepped through a splintered doorway into one of the bedrooms, obviously a nursery, and tried not to disturb the hunched form of his wife as she worked. It was impossible to crunch through the debris quietly though, so he stilled and hovered to allow her to collect whatever evidence she so painstakingly gathered.

After a moment Angie sighed. "Even if you didn't walk like a bull, you still breathe like one. It's very distracting."

Blake rolled his eyes. "Yeah, sorry for breathing, babe, but you are pretty much out of time and you know I'm not allowed to leave you here unsupervised." Almost everyone else had packed it in and had started loading the vehicles out front. It was his bad luck that his supervisor had climbed down from his ivory tower and decided to oversee Blake's team on this one. The dead couple must have been politically connected or otherwise of interest.

"Ang?"

There was no response. When Blake leaned to the side, he could see her eyes were distant and staring at an ash-laden stuffed lamb. It was strange how some things remained almost intact while everything else was consumed around them. The rest of what had been the crib and its bedding had melted into a twisted heap of liquefied plastic, embedded with remnants of charred fibers all clinging to the heat-warped metal frame.

"Ang?" Blake fought to keep impatience out of his tone.

"The baby's not here."

Blake looked around dubiously. "You can't know that, just because there isn't any evidence in or around the crib. She may have crawled out, toddled into another section of the house. According to the information we were given she is a toddler, so mobile." Her parents hadn't even made it out of their beds, so the odds were, well, bleak to say the least.

His wife shook her head as she gathered up her kit. "No, I've checked this place top to bottom. I can't find her anywhere."

Blake groaned inwardly. "She's tiny, Angie. The remains will turn up later, after the investigation. Once we gut this place, we'll find the—" he stopped himself from saying "remains" again at his wife's sharp look, "her...we'll find her." He had to, in his job as chief, distance himself from the victims, think of them as remains, but he knew Angie couldn't. In her job as an insurance investigator it was better that she didn't; it gave her the passion to sift through mounds of evidence.

"You know, if the baby isn't here, that's a matter for the police, not either of us."

His wife had picked up the lamb, even her delicate handling sending plumes of particles into the air. She dropped it at his words.

"No. But it might suggest a deliberately set fire. Not a tragic accident. Deliberate. And that," she dusted particles from her fingertips, "is exactly a matter for you and the fire department, but even more so for me and All-World Insurance."

"Blake!" The voice of his boss boomed up the stairwell from the ground floor. "Blake, that's it! Everyone out. We have to secure this place for the night. All personnel have three minutes to gather their shit and get out...and that goes double for insurance investigators!"

Blake gave Angie an imploring look as he answered, "Wrapping up, sir."

Angie pursed her lips and grabbed her last few things, sparing him an answer or one of her searing glares.

He grabbed her bags, grateful for small blessings.

Outside he tried to help her load her gear, but she waved him off in irritation. "Just go," she tossed her head at the heavily barred door, "it's not like I can get back in, and your pal is getting antsy."

It was true. All the other vehicles were gone except his own where, inside, another firefighter, Sam Forrest, tapped his fingers on the dash.

"Sorry, babe, I do have to go. We have three fires to finish the paperwork on. It's going to be a long night. I don't know what the hell is going on the last couple of days...a full moon or something."

"I get it. Go," she softened her tone a little, "and please don't call me 'babe' when I'm working, okay?"

He was tempted to lean in for a quick kiss, but decided not to push his luck. Instead he just slapped the top of her car in farewell. "See you at home in a few hours."

As he and Sam drove up the long, well-treed driveway toward the main road he sank into dark thoughts. Is this what privacy bought you? By the time the neighbours had noticed the smoke, it had been far, far too late. He eased the vehicle up the last steep portion onto the main road when the radio went crazy.

Sam covered his face with ash-streaked hands. "Oh, no, not another one."

It was indeed going to be a long, long night.

Zleen excreted additional mucous in order to allow for a back and forth, back and forth glide. The pacing was an effort to release some building tension, but it was a short glide as the Commander's girth was considerable and the distance between the pilot's controls and the back of the shuttle craft was not. The confines of the minuscule shuttle-craft increased the stress Zleen felt with crushing intensity.

The tiny craft shuddered to a halt.

Zleen's communications officer moved toward the rear of the ship and fussed with an elaborate piece of equipment that could provide salvation from this horrible situation.

Before leaving the main ship, Zleen had received a further update from Minnin. *Commander, we followed the trail as far as we could, but we dare not get any closer to that blue planet.*

Zleen had understood. They had just managed to calm down all of the Blikkets, but were having trouble keeping them distracted without the excitement of full propulsion to entertain them. Providing Blikkets with the perfect environment and stimulus for them to combust was what kept them content and complacent. That, and the mental bond with Zleen's people, which they had never experienced until the two species met.

The more mature Blikkets had helped convince the agitated, young ones to go into a canister for stasis. During that process Zleen had received the only good news since the incident. A mature Blikket had communicated that one like it—in fact one of those bonded to Zleen—had raced in pursuit of the escapees.

Zleen, recovering from the shock of such an act of independence and intelligence from a Blikket, had begun to hold out hope that the elder could keep the young ones from causing too much havoc. And that nearby blue planet was ominously a likely fascination for the fugitives. They had to keep the rest of the Blikkets at a safe distance from the enticing, energy-rich globe.

Commander? The communication officer, Sarran, held out the headpiece of the complex device. *It is ready.*

Zleen fought to control a surge of fear, knowing that a pulse of violet energy had already betrayed the flicker of emotion.

Sarran politely fussed with the headset and pretended not to notice. *Commander, they are sentient beings, and quite high functioning judging by the technology I have detected. However, not so evolved to notice the landing of your module.*

That wasn't what Zleen was afraid of, but the Commander took the headset and secured it with affected confidence.

As Sarran adjusted the fit and began the process, Zleen thought about the real danger: not finding the Blikkets before they did something horrible.

As the chemicals induced the trance-like state necessary for the process of transferring Zleen's consciousness, the Commander thought about the other unpleasant element of the task ahead. *Bipedals. Ugh, they just look so ungainly, awkward and unbalanced. Why don't they tip over? They were strange, so foreign...*Zleen's consciousness tugged from the confines of cells, tissues, viscous fluids, and cartilage and sought the sanctuary of the traveling module.

An energy beam streaked from the device and into a minuscule glowing module that bobbed at the ready. The module, an oblong, purplish-white crystal, trailed spines that looked like tentacles from the stern end. It, in fact, resembled the ancient form of the cephalopods from which Zleen and Sarran's people had evolved.

Sarran tenderly placed the little module into the launch chute, mindful of the delicate crystalline spines. *Good luck, Commander.*

~ *Flashpoint* ~

Dwayne walked along the street feeling like he was exploding with power. *I'm like fucking Superman...no, he's a fucking pussy. Like that kid who could set shit on fire...Pyro, yeah, like fucking Pyro.* He felt drunk—better than drunk—more alive than he'd ever felt in his life. Even the ecstasy of watching one of his fires devour everything it touched didn't compare. This was different. He didn't have to use his tools, or plan, or be careful. He just had to *want* something to be on fire and it was. *Un-fucking-believable.*

He watched an elderly couple setting up some wares under the awning outside their little Mom-n-Pop shop. Curling his lip at the happily striped awning flapping in the breeze, he willed the flames to appear—and they did. The material crackled as the flames hungrily consumed it.

Smiling and nodding at the couple he walked past, inhaling the first tendrils of smoke deeply into his lungs.

A moment later, their cries of dismay made him turn and walk jauntily backward so that he could watch them scramble in confusion.

The woman ran inside, but the old man—*damn him*—snatched up a hose that he used to spray the vegetables and extinguished the fire before it could spread. He saturated the outside of his store for good measure, peering around to see if anything else smoked.

Dwayne's smile faded and curled back into a sneer. *Whatever.*

As he walked past an alley, he paused long enough to will a dumpster into flames. It was quite full so the flames were soon up the wall of the building and had leapt to a stack of garbage bags alongside a door. His good mood returned.

Dwayne was whistling and a block away when he heard the sirens and grinned. *Perfect, that'll keep them busy, so that I can go spend some quality time with my girl.* Well, his ex-girl, that lying, sneaking bitch. He couldn't wait to see her again. He walked faster.

Blake stood in front of his wife's car, his niggling worry—the one that had been chewing at his ribcage—erupting into a burst of panic. It was parked in the exact spot where he'd left her yesterday in front of the burned out home. He'd been so dirty, tired and hungry upon arriving home after working all night that he hadn't immediately noticed her car missing. Once he did, he assumed that she'd already left earlier that morning.

The fire at the shopping center had raged all night, the firefighters unable to go to work until the last couple of propane tanks in the gated area next to the building stopped exploding. How they had ever started to explode was still a mystery. How several had rocketed across the regulated set-back distance to impale into the side of the shopping center and ignite into a conflagration was an even bigger mystery. It denied all logic. Clearly an accelerant was involved, but what could do that? He was so sick of not having answers to give his boss, he felt like puking.

Blake was out of the shower, dressed and deciding between sleep or sandwich when he realized their bed hadn't been slept in. Angie never made the bed. She was many wonderful things, but a keen housekeeper wasn't one of them. He had made it before they left.

Unanswered texts, calls and empty results with friends and co-workers sent his mind spiraling. He thought of her fascination with finding the baby at the house and shook his head. As tenacious as his wife was, she wouldn't risk his career by entering a scene under investigation without a member of his team present. Unless...unless she was pretty sure she could get away with it.

Now, standing in front of her car—the trunk closed, one bag of her kit still on the ground not put away, and no sign of her nearby—he was no longer thinking about his career.

He ran to the front steps, but it was clearly still solidly barred. He jogged around the outside of the house until he saw a pile of debris carefully stacked to allow entrance to one of the windows, now devoid of glass except for a few shards remaining in the frame. One of them glistened with blood.

Scrambling to the top of the pile, he shrugged off his hoodie, used it to pick the frame clean of all glass, and left it draped over the bottom in case he had to carry his wife back through. Stepping gingerly inside, he waited for his eyes to

~ Flashpoint ~

adjust, watching for holes in the floorboards or whatever other danger his wife had encountered. A dark form slumped on the far side of the room.

"Angie!" He reached her and checked her for injury before rolling her over. She was breathing, but unconscious. Chiding himself for touching her before checking the site around her like he would normally do, he did so now. Nothing seemed dangerous, but a huge floor safe gaped open a couple of feet away. It was empty.

Angie groaned and stirred. An angry welt on her forehead, crusted with dried blood, had split, dark bruising already blossoming out across her brow. A gaping slash across her palm had stained her wrist and forearm with blood before clotting.

"Easy, Ang."

She sat up. "Where's the baby?"

"What? Look, Ang, you've had a blow to the head," he glanced around, "I'm not sure on what, but let's get out of here."

Her eyebrows knotted in confusion. She let him help her to her feet. When she noticed the open floor safe, she gasped. "In there. She was in there. I opened it and took her out."

How bad was her head injury? "Ang, there is clearly no baby here. Look around. If there had been a baby inside that metal safe during this fire, she would have..." he trailed off, hesitant to say it.

"Cooked," she said it for him. "She would have cooked." She shook her head. "A dream, a hallucination, maybe?"

"Maybe. Babe, wait until I climb out first."

Once they were back on the ground she grabbed his arm.

"This is where I hit my head." She touched it gingerly. "I remember. I was ticked at you and after you left I decided that even if I couldn't go back in the house, there was nothing stopping me from looking around the outside for evidence. And then...I felt a wave of dizziness...and I pitched forward." She looked around, "and must have corked my head on those cinder blocks, I guess. I can't remember."

Blake didn't know what to say, so he took her uninjured hand and tried to lead her to his car.

She yanked her hand back. "Then...then it's like a dream, but I remember. I remember somehow getting in the house, finding the baby in the safe...she was glowing blue, and..." She

~ *Flashpoint* ~

stopped talking as though the story now sounded ridiculous to her, too.

When Blake re-took her hand she followed without protest. Her grip tightened when she glanced toward the trees.

"What?" Blake turned to see that she was fearfully staring at a dark blue bungalow just visible on the other side of the treeline.

"What's wrong?"

"That house. That guy is a terrible man. He's the one...the bastard that did this. I remember!"

"He's the one who hit you?" The police had already tried to talk to him, but he hadn't been home. Apparently there had been a complaint by the deceased couple about their neighbour. But Angie couldn't know that, and he wasn't allowed to tell her. It was all a part of the official investigation, provided to him by the police liaison.

"No, no! I mean he's the bastard who started the fire. I went inside his house. It's filled with accelerants, incendiary devices...you name it. He's a Pyro!"

"You broke into *his* house, too?" Blake gaped at the woman he thought he knew.

"Well, in the dream...no, it wasn't a dream. Listen to me. It was like I was in a trance or something, but I remember what I found in there. And then I realized I didn't have my car keys, that I must have dropped them, so I was re-tracing my steps—I cut my hand that time because I was rushing—and found them on the floor by the safe. But I felt dizzy again...and then you were here."

Blake covered his face with his hands for a minute. Her head injury could explain almost everything she said, but break and enter? If she had, indeed, done it at the other home too, how would he get her out of this?

Lowering his hands, he stared grimly at his wife. Angie had that stubborn set to her chin, the one that meant she was just about to do something he wouldn't like.

She aimed the fob of her car key at her trunk and pressed the button, which beeped obligingly.

When her trunk popped open, everything Blake thought he knew to be a fundamental truth burned from his brain.

Inside the trunk lay a small girl, asleep or unconscious.

~ Flashpoint ~

She wore kiddie pajamas with the little foot coverings built in and...a pulsing blue glow limned her little body.

Zleen rested, overwhelmed. It had been going well. The Commander had arrived at the planet and followed the trail left by the Blikkets in an exhausting pattern all over the planet. They seemed to have paused momentarily over numerous intense energy sources until they, uncharacteristically, sought a quiet and remote place to land.

What motivated them—fatigue, the influence of the Blikket elder, or something else entirely, Zleen could only speculate. Then, while investigating a nearby site that reeked of Blikket presence, Zleen moved to a much more practical vessel, initial revulsion aside.   This one was far better suited to the investigation than the tiny module which the Commander left bobbing nearby with an energy field to mask its presence.

The new vessel, a bipedal inhabitant of the area, greatly enhanced Zleen's mobility and access. The Commander had discovered much, including that bipedals were engineered quite efficiently and did not have a tendency to tip forward. However, occupying the vessel was confusing, tiring and intense, even for a stimulation glutton like Zleen. Currently, the Commander was aware of what was happening outside the bipedal, but was too overwhelmed to resume control. So, for now, Zleen observed.

Seeing the tiny child lying in the trunk like a discarded piece of luggage was so awful to Blake that it overcame the fear he had of touching the pulsing blue light. Wiping suddenly sweaty palms on his pants, he leaned in to pick her up. *It isn't harming her and it didn't harm Angie, so it shouldn't harm me,* Blake reasoned.

"Stop! Don't!" Angie grabbed the back of his shirt.

Blake pulled his hands back in alarm. "Why? You obviously lifted her into the trunk and you're fine. And why, exactly, didn't you put her in the backseat? Or, better yet, call 9-1-1?"

Angie's face struggled with confusion as though trying to

remember. "Put her in the trunk...yes, I remember doing it, but I don't remember deciding to do it or why...I can't explain it." Angie massaged her temples. "Okay, I'm carrying her out to the car and putting her in the trunk, but the light around her when she is in my arms is pulsing white, not blue. White is safe to touch and blue is not. I have no idea how I know this, but I do." She lowered her arms and looked at the child. "Right now it does not want us to touch her."

"It?"

She shrugged hopelessly. "I know, I'm sorry..."
Suddenly Angie stared straight ahead, her eyes appeared unfocused and she began to sway.

Blake caught her, landing on the rim of the open trunk in a seated position. The vehicle rocked downward with his weight and the trunk swung down to rap him on the head. Ignoring the pain, he thrust the trunk back open. He jockeyed Angie's body into a more comfortable position in his lap, touched the side of her face gently and said her name.

Her eyes opened and blinked at him in surprise. "Interesting," she said, reaching a shaky hand to touch the one he had against her face. "Mmmm," she closed her eyes and breathed deeply. "Amazing sensation. The skin against skin..." Angie shivered.

Shocked, Blake forcefully brought them both to their feet. "Ang, you're not making sense. I need to take you and the little girl to the hospital."

Angie stared blankly for a moment before beginning to shake her head from side to side. "No, I cannot allow you to do this. Your mate was right about the one from the next dwelling. We must find that one...that male? It is male, correct?" Angie cocked her head to one side as though deep in thought. "He—he is male. You refer to males as 'he' and females as 'she'." Angie shook her head. "The division into genders is confusing. I'm sorry. But we are wasting too much time. I'll lose track of them soon."

Blake couldn't speak or move, just stood with his mouth open at his wife's nonsensical babble.

Angie regarded him quizzically. "Do you still not understand? My consciousness is inhabiting the vessel of your mate—"

~ Flashpoint ~

Blake's face went from shock, to confusion, then landed on anger.

Angie raised her hands. "Wait, don't do anything violent. You will only hurt your mate!"

Hurt Ang? Blake didn't want to believe this was anything outside of the side effects of a blow to the head, but he'd witnessed the effects of concussions before and this was...this was...not right. He glanced at the baby in the trunk—even more bizarre. Looking back at Angie, his gaze locked onto her hands held up defensively against him.

Rage flushed Blake's face with heat. "I would never hurt you, uh, her...I would never hurt Angie!" He tore at his hair in frustration. "Okay, you're telling me that you're some other 'being.' And you're inside my wife's body?"

"Correct, and I'm glad you understand that you cannot hurt me without hurting her, because—"

"You will get the hell out of her right now," Blake yelled. He glanced at the baby, "And if you are responsible for that, let the kid go!"

Angie dropped her hands, her voice heavy with frustration. "Well, no, that is not me. I should be able to do something about it, but I can't for some reason. It should be obeying me, but it is not."

"What should be obeying you?" Blake could not prevent the exasperation from flooding into his words.

Angie looked flustered. "Can I explain on the way?" She backed toward the driver's seat and seemed to think better of it, tossing him the keys. "Maybe you should drive."

Blake put his hands on his hips. "I am *not* driving anywhere with a baby in the trunk!"

Angie did the weird head tilt to the side thing again. "Oh, I see. Yes, normally, that would be very dangerous in a vehicle like this."

Driving down the highway, Blake angled the mirror so that he could see the backseat and the compromise they'd reached.

Angie, or rather the being occupying Angie, had negotiated with the "energy creature" surrounding the baby. It was apparently called a Blikket. The Blikket relented and allowed

~ Flashpoint ~

Angie to put the baby in the backseat. The Angie-being insisted that Angie's bags be positioned around the baby and a blanket draped, tent-like, over the whole section so that neither the baby nor the pulsing blue light could be seen. Blake had protested and argued about the need for an infant carrier until the Angie-being explained that the force-field protected her better than any carrier could.

As Blake rounded a corner, one of Angie's cases slid toward the baby. The air filled with an electric buzzing. The bag bounced away, then inexplicably, with a low hum, the bag righted itself and slid back into position.

"Uhh...!"

Angie's voice snapped him out of his fascination with what was happening in the back seat.

The car was drifting toward the guard rail.

"Oh, shit!" Blake centered the car and returned his focus to the road. "Sorry." Then ticked at himself for apologizing to the thing that had high-jacked his wife's body, he snapped. "You're supposed to be explaining!"

"My name is Zleen."

"That's nice. Not an explanation though."

Zleen sighed. "Yes, your wife's mind, aware of me now, is demanding the same thing."

"Huh, yeah, well you should consider yourself lucky that she's inside and not outside. Trust me."

Zleen shifted uncomfortably. "Yes, it, sorry, she, has already made some threats of violence against me which are impossible, but still frightening to contemplate."

Blake chuckled. "That's my girl. She doesn't even like me telling her what to do, never mind some 'thing' that has taken over her body and mind."

"If you would both allow me to explain..." Once it was quiet inside the car and inside Angie's mind, Zleen explained.

Dwayne stood outside his ex-girlfriend's building and leaned against a parking meter to pull out a smoke. His favorite part: thinking about the shit he was about to do.

He put the cigarette in his mouth and thought about it lighting itself. One of the little blue guys appeared and whizzed in to do his bidding. After the smoke was lit, the little blue ball zipped annoyingly around his head.

The door to the building opened and a man stepped out.

Dwayne slapped at the blue ball in agitation and growled, "Stay out of sight, you stupid fuck!" The little ball disappeared, although Dwayne could still see the vague distortions in the air that the three invisible balls made.

He grunted his approval, and nodded amiably at the man who had exited the building as he went by.

The man stared at him, stopped, blinked rapidly and then rubbed his eyes.

Dwayne willed the little balls to move behind his back.

When the man looked back up at Dwayne, he smiled and gave a little shrug. "New contacts."

Dwayne took a drag of his cigarette as the man walked away.

At least these three obeyed him. He wasn't sure what had happened to the fourth, the fucked-up one. When he'd burned that snotty couple, three of the fire balls were eager to help. But the fourth one had disappeared. He'd found the safe, emptied it and then had that amazing idea. He'd grabbed the kid, who fit perfectly in the safe, and stuck her inside, wanting to see what she'd look like after he burned the place down. Then the fourth ball went ape-shit and made some kind of buzzing, blue ball around the baby and wouldn't let him even touch her. So he'd slammed the safe closed, slid the armchair back over it and torched the place.

The neighbourhood had gone all 9-1-1 on him after that so he'd split, but the kid was definitely baked to shit after that kick-ass fire. He'd check it out later.

Flicking the butt into the shadows, he breathed the remaining smoke out through his nostrils like a demon. Smiling at that thought, he walked toward the apartment building.

Blake struggled to wrap his mind around everything Zleen told him. "So, you're tracking this pyromaniac, Dwayne Reynolds, right now."

Zleen pointed. "Turn left onto this street, please." After peering down the street intently, Zleen replied, "Not the man, no, the young Blikkets that have bonded with it, uh, him. I can sense and follow them. Turn left again, please."

They passed a large restaurant awash in flames. Blake watched the first responders scrambling into their gear outside and felt the pull to join them. No doubt the department was wondering where he was. He had turned off his radio and phone. Setting his jaw, he drove past the chaos, following the directions of the alien.

"There! There!" Zleen pointed at a heavy-set man in a grey hoodie who bounded up the steps of an apartment building. Zleen slapped the door in agitation. "Stop the vehicle! Let me out."

He pulled up to the curb, but as Zleen reached for the handle, Blake engaged the locks and grabbed his wife's arm. "Wait! You are not taking my wife in there with that nut. I'll take care of this."

Zleen glared at the hand on Angie's arm. "Release me now. Others may be harmed if I do not retrieve the Blikkets quickly."

"You are going to stay here, or maybe I start yelling at a few bystanders to come check out the blue-glowing kid in my backseat."

Zleen glared back. "I am in command. I am responsible to ensure the Blikkets are returned with as little damage to innocents as possible. If you do not allow me to achieve my objective, I will communicate with my Blikket protecting the child that you are a threat to the little one. That would be very bad for you."

Blake tightened his mouth. "Angie might get burned too. What will happen to you then?"

"The Blikket knows my intentions. Their kind will not harm my kind unless they or their bonded one are threatened."

Blake glared at his wife. He sighed. *The thing that occupies my wife,* he reminded himself. He wasn't fighting with Ang. He closed his eyes and his shoulders sagged in defeat. As he climbed out of the car, the irony—that many of his arguments with Angie ended up the same way—was not lost on him.

Dwayne waited outside his girlfriend's apartment door with a smug smile on his face.

~ *Flashpoint* ~

The peep hole darkened briefly and a muffled gasp sounded on the other side of the door.

"Open up, sugar. I'm back."

He chuckled as he heard frantic movements and noises inside. Concentrating, he sighed with pleasure as flames began licking up the face of the door. He willed them to focus on key places and not to burn anything else. Yet.

Blake struggled into his firefighting gear while trying to balance the phone on his ear. "Yeah, I know, Jim. Just check it out for me, please. Does he have any connection to this building?"

Jim, a hockey-buddy who was the appointed liaison between the departments, had shared the information about Dwayne Reynolds earlier in the investigation.

Waiting for Jim to check the computer file, Blake locked up the car, leaving the windows down a bit, and then followed the frantic Zleen into the apartment building. He slipped his helmet on—so he'd have one hand to pull the main door open—and stepped into the foyer.

"A restraining order? What's her apartment number?" He turned to tell Zleen it was on the third floor, but Angie was already bounding up the filthy, worn staircase.

"Okay, Jim, he's definitely violating the order. I have good reason to believe he did the fire at his neighbour's place, that he's a pyro and that he's going to pull the same thing here. Do a full 9-1-1 on this location. I'm going to start evacuating the building." He hung up on Jim's loud reply, pocketed the phone, and ran full tilt after his wife.

Angie had already climbed in through the wreckage that had been the apartment door and was out of sight when Blake arrived. Grabbing the top railing, he fought to catch his breath, yanking free a fire axe he'd tucked into his belt.

Gripping the axe tightly, he gritted his teeth to keep from shouting out to Angie, worried he'd alert Dwayne to their approach.

A sudden burst of laughter and a blood-curdling scream made him freeze.

A door opened further up the hall and a man stuck his head out.

~ Flashpoint ~

Before ducking in the doorway after Angie, Blake pointed to the staircase with the axe. "Get everyone in your apartment out. And pull the fire alarm on your way."

If the sight of a fireman fully geared up hadn't been convincing enough, the screams and the charred doorway were. The man exploded into action even as Blake ducked inside.

Dwayne, confused and freaked out, stared at the woman in front of him. "Who're you, bitch?"

He had just finished off Lauren and was setting fire to the kitchen when he noticed the woman. At the sight of the tiny brunette, he willed the balls to ignite her clothing. The tiny orbs ceased their consumption of the kitchen cabinetry and zipped toward the newcomer, but then stopped dead. They hovered around her now, three zig-zagging glowing globes, seemingly as confused as he felt.

What the fuck? Burn her, burn her!

Dwayne then realized the flames in the kitchen were crawling across the cabinetry and up the wall toward the foyer. They'd soon be between him and the only way out. *This bitch has to move.*

He took a step toward her, hands outstretched, but then hesitated. *What if she's like me? Maybe she can control the flames too. Is she better at it? Can she hurt me?* Uncertainty and rage battled within him.

He backed into the living room as she walked toward him saying, "I can help you."

Dwayne watched smoke billow from the kitchen and twisted the front of his hoodie in frustration. "Why aren't you on fire?"

She eyed him up and down. "The Blikkets will not harm me. They recognize me for what I am."

A man's voice came from the hall and there was a flash of movement outside. Dwayne closed in on the woman who flailed as he encircled her throat in a crushing chokehold. He yanked her into the living room, out of sight of the doorway. Peeking around, he saw a fireman in full gear rush into the apartment. He pulled the woman further along the wall, tightening his grip to silence her.

~ Flashpoint ~

Blake saw the charred body in the kitchenette and, for one heart-stopping moment, thought it was Angie.

He grabbed the small fire extinguisher from the kitchen wall and began dousing the flames around the body and on the cupboards, screaming Angie's name. He registered the intense tone of her voice in the next room, as well as that of a man.

A second later he could hear nothing but the building's fire alarm. He stooped to pick up the axe with his free hand and walked into the living room cautiously, axe ready.

A man had his arm around Angie's throat while three balls of flame zipped in agitation around both of their heads.

As Blake stepped into the room, the man screamed, "Burn him!"

The balls of flame hit Blake with enough force that he staggered and slammed into the wall. His suit, coated in fire retardant, blackened but did not ignite. Blake groaned at the pain of the impact.

The fiery balls flailed about, nipping at his suit. Blake swatted at them with his axe. One of the Blikkets furiously drilled at one spot on Blake's abdomen and his suit began to smolder. Reflexively, Blake shot a stream of chemical from the fire extinguisher at the ball of flame.

With a high-pitched whine, it changed from orange to bright blue and zipped in retreat to hover around Dwayne's head.

"Yeah, didn't like that did you, you little bastard!" growled Blake, his voice muffled under his helmet. He struggled to stand up. The sight of him hitting the wall had appeared to reanimate Angie who'd been frozen, glassy-eyed with fear. Now she wriggled against big man's crushing grip.

Dwayne edged around him toward the door, the three Blikkets forming a line between them and charging at Blake's helmet each time he moved toward Dwayne.

Dwayne laughed and moved closer to the exit. "We're leaving and you're going to burn, big guy." His voice was barely audible over the wailing smoke alarm.

Blake tried to shoot a stream of chemical at the Blikkets, but, wise to the danger, they zipped quickly out of the path.

Dwayne shuffled toward the door, laughing, but his

~ Flashpoint ~

laughter was cut short by a sudden gasp of pain.

Angie caught him in the ribs with a violent backward elbow and followed that by crushing the top of his sneakered foot with the heavy, block heel of her boot.

She broke free of his grasp. "Okay," she rasped, clutching her throat, "go ahead, Zleen, talk!"

She stood erect and Zleen retook control, eyes widened at the horror of what was happening, one hand tremulously at Angie's throbbing throat. "The violence..." Zleen's whisper faded.

Groaning, the man who had attacked them hobbled closer.

At his approach, Zleen shook off the onslaught of unfamiliar emotions, "Wait!" the Commander called out shakily, stepping back. "I said I could help you. We are..." Angie's head tilted as Zleen sought her help, "...at a stand-off here, but if you let me take the Blikkets back, I can give you a far more powerful weapon."

The man—*what had the one named Blake called him? Dwayne, that was it*—snarled, "I'm powerful enough already, bitch, and I'm going to burn your pal!"

The Blikkets had set patches of fire around Blake, who was cornered and frantically spraying the erupting flames with the extinguisher. There couldn't be much left in it. He looked up and met Zleen's eyes.

Drowning in a flood of chemicals coursing through Angie's body, Zleen was nearly paralyzed by her emotions. The heady rush of hormones, the infusion of chemicals into the brain, adrenal glands pumping, cardiovascular system responding, how did these beings function and maintain a grip on logic? Zleen became aware of Angie's urgent plea to slow down her breathing.

Zleen took a deep breath and let it out slowly. *I am a commanding officer. It is my duty and my responsibility to get control of this situation, of this body.*

Zleen managed to smile at Dwayne, pointing out the window. "Look, here it is now."

A small crystalline craft hovered outside the window of the apartment.

Zleen commanded, "Remove the glass."

The ship shot a beam of light which splayed down the

surface of the glass. Once it was done, the glass was gone, as if it never existed.

"Enter."

The craft whizzed inside, startling the Blikkets tormenting Blake. They zipped over to form a line between Dwayne and the bobbing object.

"See?" Zleen said eagerly, circling toward Blake. "They are afraid, as they know it is a superior weapon."

Dwayne looked concerned. "I...I don't want it. I like fire. Get it out of here!" His voice took on a panicked edge as the craft moved closer to him.

The module shot out a beam of light and the Blikkets raised a protective field around Dwayne, who screamed. The air in the room thrummed as the two energy fields buzzed angrily.

Zleen pushed Blake toward the smoking doorway. As they ran, Zleen shouted, "Complete self-destruct sequence now!"

Outside of the apartment, they bolted toward the stairs.

The thrum of energy intensified at the same time as it became deadly quiet. The pressure was so intense, Blake dropped his axe and the extinguisher to cup his ears in agony, falling to his knees and nearly toppling down the staircase.

Zleen writhed nearby.

And then, release. Waves of energy washed over them, each pulse weakening until finally dissipating.

Zleen looked up to see Blake's face hovering above. His helmet had fallen off. His mouth moved, but no sound came out. Zleen felt Blake scooping Angie's body toward him. Zleen raised one hand to touch Blake's face gently, and Blake lowered his mouth to Angie's in a tender kiss of relief. Zleen's consciousness reeled. Angie's body reacted to the kiss with a flush of intense hormonal response.

Mmmmm, incredible...

Blake ended the kiss abruptly. When Zleen looked into Blake's eyes he saw them narrow and then widen.

Muffled sounds of booted feet on the stairs let Zleen know that Angie's hearing was recovering from the blast.

Blake helped Zleen down the stairs, past the firemen and out into the fresh air.

Zleen sat against the hood of Blake's car, shivering from cold and shock until a kind fireman wrapped a blanket around

~ Flashpoint ~

the Commander. No, on closer inspection, this one appeared to have the attributes of the female gender, though Zleen felt uncertain about the assessment, as the distinctions were subtle.

As they drove away from the scene, Blake still did not speak to or directly look at Zleen.

After an uncomfortable silence, Zleen said, "Did all of the people get out of the building?"

"Yes."

After another long silence, Zleen spoke again. "You need not worry about the Blikkets. They died with their bonding host."

In response, Blake slammed the rearview mirror to an angle that showed the baby in the back seat, still glowing blue.

Zleen nodded. *Yes, there is still that.*

After a few minutes, Blake said, "When do I get my wife back?"

"You must take me back to the child's home. Before setting the self-destruct on my vessel, I requested another craft to rendezvous at the original landing site."

Blake took the next off-ramp to head back to the fire-ravaged home.

"I believe it was a chemical imbalance in the man's brain that allowed him to control the Blikkets. His passionate desire to burn things was likely an intoxicant to them. It was a one-way communication though, as he had no telepathic ability."

Blake's mouth tightened at these revelations and he made a small sound in his throat.

Zleen didn't say anything further, as it was unclear what could be added at this point. Angie remained strangely quiet inside her mind. Frustration gnawed at Zleen as the inadequacy of verbal communication hit home, not for the first time. Zleen wished there was a way to reach into Blake's mind.

Angie reacted. *Trust me, you are better off not going there right now.*

They'd collected the transport module and gone to Blake and Angie's house. The baby, on a blanket on the floor, played with

~ Flashpoint ~

her feet and giggled as a tiny blue light hovered in circles above her head. A larger blue light bobbed nearby.

Blake paced, glancing every now and then at Zleen, who remained in Angie's body. "So, what do we do now?"

Zleen didn't know what to tell him. The new transport module hovered outside, waiting to take the Commander's consciousness back to the shuttle craft and Sarran.

The Blikket refused to leave the baby.

Zleen didn't understand until it revealed the whole truth. It had divided, or given birth, while Reynolds had been terrorizing the couple in their home. Its immature offspring had bonded with the baby.

The tiny Blikket playfully danced in the air.

Zleen faced terrible choices. Kill the baby, and the immature Blikket would die. The parent Blikket—hovering nearby—would either extinguish itself in grief or acquiesce. Either way, the mission was over. As long as the child's body was destroyed, no humans other than Angie and Blake even knew she had survived the fire. Destroying the Blikkets without killing the baby was out of the question—Zleen didn't have the resources here. Even a self-destruct of the new module wouldn't kill the young Blikket, unless it killed the baby.

Back to that unpleasant choice.

Zleen had a sworn duty not to allow the Blikkets to roam free. Using them to enhance the propulsion system was already an unpopular idea on the home world, but nothing more efficient had yet developed. Perhaps this Blikket was mature enough, intelligent enough to understand that either choice would end the baby's life and would help its offspring voluntarily break the bond. Sometimes they survived.

While Zleen thought this through, Angie remained strangely silent.

Zleen looked out the window, up into the night sky, as though trying to see the distant waiting ship. "I could take the child and the Blikkets back with me. Only the two of you know she lives..." Zleen winced as though enduring a headache. "Angie does not think the child would be happy. But I'm not sure that's the most important thing here." The truth was, Zleen thought it unlikely the child could even be provided an environment where she could comfortably survive on their ship or their world.

~ Flashpoint ~

Angie surfaced in control of her body with a gasp. "Blake!"

"Ang?"

She winced. "Yes, me, but maybe not for long..." She rushed through the terrible choices Zleen had been toying with inside her mind.

"My God, Ang, what can we do?"

She held her head and rocked. "I don't know. I can't keep control much longer. Maybe knock me out and take the baby and make a run for it. I think the Blikket knows the Commander is a threat to them."

Blake shook his head. "Ang, I can't. What if I hit you too hard? I could kill you."

"We have to do something. I don't have much time." Blake grabbed her hand. "You've been in his head as long as he's been in yours. You must know something you can use against him. Fight him somehow."

Angie shook her head. "The Commander isn't a 'he,' Blake, or a 'she'." She struggled to think. Looking down at Blake's hand on hers, she drew her eyebrows together. "Zleen does have a weakness..." She gave Blake a wry smile. "It might work. The Commander's not evil, just driven by duty. Zleen doesn't want to hurt the baby, or even the Blikkets really...and with the right incentive..."

Angie released Blake's hand and went still.

"Ang?"

"No."

Zleen stared out the window again. Blake saw several expressions wash over his wife's face in rapid succession. He watched the parade of emotions for a long tortured minute and then, shaking his head, turned his attention back to the baby.

Finally Blake heard Zleen say, "Okay. I agree." He looked up to see Zleen nodding. The large Blikket hovered in front of the Commander. "So, you also agree? Are you sure? It could be dangerous for you and your young one."

~ Flashpoint ~

Blake held his hands in front of him, palms up. "What? What did you agree to? What the hell is going on?"

Zleen looked at Blake as though just remembering he was there. "Oh, sorry. Your mate will explain. Thank you for your assistance, Blake. I apologize for...well, I apologize for some of the things that happened. And that any of it had to happen at all."

With that, Angie sat heavily on the bed as a beam of light shot from her to the awaiting module.

The module zipped into the night sky.

"Ang?" Blake squatted down near his wife.

She stared at her own hands, clenching and unclenching them. She closed her eyes, drew in a deep breath and let it out slowly. Opening her eyes, she smiled. "It's me. Zleen's gone."

Moving to hug her, Blake froze, eyes narrowed. "Are you sure?"

She grinned. "Yes. No more hijacker, I swear."

They held each other a long time, watching the baby babbling at the lights.

Later Angie told Blake the deal. Zleen would be monitoring them. Every few years, the Commander would ensure he was close enough to "check in" on them.

The Blikket had made promises as well.

"It promises to teach the young one not to reveal itself, and to keep it secret from the world, other than us." She explained that the parent Blikket would imprint upon each of its offspring to only bond with members of Blake and Angie's family. The elder Blikket could reproduce at will at least two more times before expending all of its life energy.

"We can't bond with them or communicate telepathically. We are too old to have our brains 'modified,' but it appears that children's minds, when still developing, can be 'enhanced' to allow the bond and the telepathic communication," explained Angie. "Our children, and their children, can bond."

Blake shook his head. "This...whatever this is, we're committing all of our future generations to this? Ang, why did you agree?" They both sat, holding hands, thinking of the dizzying implications, fantastic possibilities and terrible dangers they faced.

Angie looked at him closely. "You were right. I was aware of Zleen's thoughts too, once I realized what was happening to me. I chose this to protect our family. And we, the three of us, are a family, don't you think?"

Blake looked at the tiny girl, now sitting up, trying to catch the Blikkets. She gave him a grin when he caught her eye, but quickly went back to trying to snatch the lights.

The constriction of his own heart at the thought of anyone taking the baby from them told him a lot about his own hopes.

"Yes, she needs us, and I think we need her." Blake said quietly.

Angie squeezed his hand. "Zleen is hiding this from most of his, uh, its people too. The Commander is also taking risks. Keeping secrets in a telepathic community is, as we can only imagine, pretty tough."

Blake shook his head as the larger Blikket drifted closer to them. "How are we supposed to communicate with these things, if our brains are too 'old'?"

Angie smiled. "Zleen taught it just a handful of words for us and suggested to me how to build on that." She got up and opened the drawer of the nightstand, drawing out a tiny LED penlight. Pointing it at the wall she said very loudly to the large pulsing light, "No!"

Angie flashed the light on the wall in one long flash. Then she said, "Yes!" and flashed the light in two short bursts of light.

Angie rotated the light into a circle and turned to the Blikket. "Understand?"

The Blikket pulsed twice and then went back to hovering over the baby.

"Pretty understands, but is apparently very busy right now. Maybe after the little ones go to sleep, we can convince it to try some more."

"Pretty?"

"That's its name. The baby calls it 'Pretty' and it likes that. I suggested to Zleen that I wanted to call it 'Spark', but Pretty decided that was a good name for the baby Blikket." Angie shrugged. "Zleen said that as the baby's language skills develop, the Blikkets' understanding of what we say will as well."

Blake smiled. "Pretty and Spark. Okay. Now we just have to come up with a new name for the baby." His smile faded. "Wait a minute, what deal did you have to make? What does Zleen get out of all this?"

~ Flashpoint ~

Angie gave a wicked smile. "Well, Zleen is a sucker for physical sensation. There will be regular visits…"

Blake leapt off the bed. "No! No way, uh-uh. I am not going to worry every time I kiss my wife that it's actually some perverted, thrill-seeking alien! Forget it, babe, forget it!"

Actually, Zleen had felt bad about making Blake uncomfortable and had promised Angie never do that again. There were plenty of other things the Commander wanted to experience. Angie told Blake all of this, as soon as she was able to catch her breath and stop laughing.

On the mattress, the baby clapped her hands and laughed with Angie as two pulsing blue lights, one large and one small, circled her head like orbiting moons.

Julie A. Serroul writes in various genres under the umbrella of Speculative Fiction, and although she's often drawn to the supernatural or paranormal, she's not afraid to venture into science fiction when the mood strikes. Her short stories have appeared in magazines, anthologies, and online, and she holds down the position of one of the Persons of Third Person Press. Julie lives with her husband, children and yellow lab in a log home overlooking the Bras d'Or Lake, and spends a considerable amount of time fending off the pressures of her co-editors to write more stories. She is currently revising her first novel.

Flame Out

Zeus sat back and grinned. Things were finally going to plan. He hadn't made any progress at all for the first few thousand years, but things had ramped up over the last century to the point where an old score would soon be settled.

"Revenge," he murmured, borrowing a popular quote from the mortals, "is a dish best served cold." And cold is exactly what the mortals would be, very cold indeed. The grin spread until his brilliant teeth gleamed and flashed. His wit set him laughing, a roaring that reverberated and rumbled across the heavens.

"Was that *thunder*?" Lucy asked, frowning.

"Sure looks like rain to me," Rory dead-panned, leaning back to stare up into a sky as blue as lapis lazuli. He looked over at Lucy and nodded. "Yep. Any second now, I'd say."

Lucy scrunched up her face and tossed him a scowl. Rory puckered his lips and smacked a kiss right back at her.

"Stop *worryin'*, Luce darlin'. The weather is perfect, not a cloud in the sky. The forecast says sunny all day and clear tonight. This is gonna be our best Labour Day barbeque ever."

Lucy stared off to the west where a string of cotton-ball cumulus clouds chugged along the horizon. Otherwise the sky was clear.

"I'm sure I heard thunder. And I think I saw something flash."

"There you go. You heard a jet and it flashed in the sun. Now come on, sweetheart, give me a hand moving this picnic table over. The boys'll be here in an hour."

~ Flashpoint ~

"Here's to Lucy and Rory!" yelled Dougie, lifting his bottle of Keith's high in the air. The group echoed his shout as brown bottles clinked with cans and ice rattled in glasses. "You two sure know how to throw a party. I swear, if I ate one more sparerib I'd bust wide open."

"You already did, buddy. Your buttons are after busting off your shirt," Mike said, pointing.

Dougie looked down at his bulging belly as laughter rippled around the circle of friends.

Rory and the weatherman had been right. The afternoon had stayed sunny and warm. The ribs, steaks, potato salad and roasted corn had been wolfed down, and now six of their closest friends remained, gathered around the firepit. The temperature had dropped along with the sun and the partiers were grateful for the warmth from the blaze.

Rory picked up a gnarly piece of spruce from the pile beside the picnic table and tossed it onto the fire, releasing a cascade of sparks and embers into the chill evening air. Lucy, snuggled beside him on the picnic-table bench, leaned back and looked up. It was a clear night but she could see only a handful of stars through the orange city haze. Light pollution.

We should fit in one last camping trip before winter. Get out into the deep woods, where you can still see a zillion stars.

Laughter brought her attention back to the circle of friends. Eyes sparkled and skin glowed golden in the light from the fire. All eyes were on Dougie, waiting for a story. Rory turned to Lucy, rolling his eyes and feigning an expression of dread. Lucy giggled and squeezed his hand. *This is what it's all about. Good food, a few drinks and friends sitting around a fire telling stories.* She leaned into Rory and listened as Dougie launched into the infamous tale of Malky's truck.

"There was just nutt'in we could do to get that Jesus car started. So Rory says, 'Why don't we just take Malky's truck? He's so passed out from the rum he'll be dead to the world 'til mornin'.' So we go over to Malky's place and—"

"Hello there!" a commanding voice called from over the side gate.

Everyone turned as two men entered the yard.

"You're welcome to join the party as long as you brought

beer," Rory called out.

The group exhaled a collective groan as the newcomers stepped out of the shadows.

"Police," the taller of the two said. "We received a complaint about your party."

Lucy stared, confused. She bolted up from the bench and walked towards the pair of uniformed officers.

"Are we being too noisy?" she asked. It was only a little after eight on a Saturday night. "Because we can keep it down a bit..."

"No Ma'am. There was no noise complaint. We were informed that you have an open fire back here. That's not permitted under Bylaw 666."

She looked back at the firepit. Seven faces stared back, skin still gilded by firelight, but glowing smiles vanquished.

"So who called you?" she asked, frowning.

Rory strode over and stood beside her. "What's the problem, officers?" he asked. "I mean, look at this pit. There's cement all around it. There's no fire hazard whatsoever."

"Sir, it's not about the fire hazard," the taller officer began.

"Backyard fires cause smoke pollution," his shorter companion added.

Even Lucy, a relatively law-abiding citizen, couldn't resist a snort at that.

"Pollution? From this little firepit that we use maybe half a dozen times a year? You've got to be kidding! What about all those cars and trucks jamming the streets and parking lots and drive-thrus? *That's* pollution."

"Now Lucy, don't be talkin' that way about cars," Dougie said.

But Lucy was on a roll.

"If you're worried about pollution why not have a bylaw limiting the use of automobiles? But I suppose people wouldn't be very happy about *that*, would they?" She looked up at the tall policeman, feeling rather feisty after, perhaps, a few too many beers.

"Ma'am, we don't make the laws. But we do enforce them. You have to extinguish your fire."

"We'll let it go out, officer," she said, smiling her cutest smile. "Not another stick of wood. We promise."

"Put it out *now* please, Ma'am."

~ Flashpoint ~

So much for cute.

"All right then. Fine." Lucy turned away from the cops, walked over to the side of the house and began unfurling the hose where it was curled up like a basking snake. She turned on the tap and walked back to the fire. Everyone was standing now, faces reflecting frustration and dismay.

"Stand back!" she said, and they stepped away, pulling lawn chairs out of the line of fire. Lucy adjusted the nozzle to its most powerful stream. She stood opposite the cops and was pleased to see them jump back when she aimed at the pit and fired. There was a powerful hissing screech, as though she had mortally wounded a fire-breathing dragon. Belching clouds of smoke roiled through the air as the beast writhed in its death throes. Everyone began coughing and turned away to escape the punishing billows of smoke. Lucy turned to the police. She smiled sweetly, hose aimed like a weapon.

"There. No more pollution. Satisfied?"

"They have no right!" Rory ranted. "They can't take away fire. Humans have a right to fire! It's a fundamental element. Like air. And water. And beer." He paced the kitchen. At the utterance of the word 'beer' he pulled open the fridge door, leaned in and pulled out a pair of cold ones. He flipped both the tops and handed one to Lucy.

"What I want to know is who called the cops," said Lucy. "What kind of miserable, twisted person would resent a few friends enjoying themselves around a fire on a Saturday evening?"

Rory tipped back the beer and guzzled half of it.

"Who cares?" he said. "My point is that *no* one should be able to turn us in, because having a goddam fire in my own goddam firepit my own goddam back yard should not be a goddam crime! It should be a human right! Am I right?"

"I think it must have been the McSweens," Lucy said. "They hate the idea of people having fun. Makes the miserable buggers jealous. They've probably never had fun in their lives." She sipped her beer. But the liquid that had tasted like the nectar of the gods around the fire now just tasted like...beer.

"Think about it, Luce. We've been sitting around fires since we were cavemen—and cavewomen—and now all of a sudden some arsehole on town council decides he's got a right to tell me I can't have a fire? Who the hell is *he*? It's my ancestral right! As a human being!"

Lucy leaned back against the counter and gazed upward at the kitchen light. The curly bulb's harsh white fluorescence dazzled her eyes. She blinked and looked away.

"I bet it *was* Mrs. McSween," she said. "That old bat ruined my party! I have a mind to go over there tomorrow and just ask her point blank if she complained to the cops."

It was only a little after nine, but the others had already gone home. The hose had, all too literally, put a damper on the party. It was too chilly to sit outside without a fire, so the party had been forced indoors. Now a kitchen party during the cold winter months was all kinds of fun, but to be forced inside on a lovely September evening by a pair of bylaw-toting cops? To have warmth and conviviality doused with cold water? The magic had gone out of the night along with the fire, and there had been no way to rekindle the mood that had bathed them all in its golden glow.

Rory and Lucy were left with a smoking mess of charcoal and wet wood, a pile of dirty dishes, and a pink ticket sitting on the kitchen table. Lucy stared at the ticket. Had she detected a soupçon of satisfaction on the tall cop's lips as he made out the citation, skipping past the 'warning' box and ticking off the '$250 fine' box? That was what happened when you sassed the law—the law won.

Lucy took another sip of beer but it tasted bitter. Their third Labour Day Barbeque, which had begun with so much promise, had ended in a big washout just as she had feared. She heard a distant rumble and turned to the window. Was it going to storm after all? She pulled open the patio doors, stepped outside into the chill of the evening, and looked up into the sky. Still clear, with those same faint stars against the over-lit urban sky. But thunder rumbled again, as if, somewhere up there, a god was laughing at her.

Zeus leaned back against his throne, threw his head back and bellowed. It was so easy! For millennia, ever since Prometheus

~ Flashpoint ~

had stolen flame from Olympus and brought it to Earth, humans had valued their precious fire above all things. Generation upon generation huddled around its blaze, warming themselves, cooking and talking and dancing and chanting and drumming and all manner of mortal nonsense. Their puny little lives revolved around the hearth. And now, in less than a human lifetime, they had all but forgotten the very existence of fire.

And now the mortals themselves had begun to forbid the use of the gift of the gods by outlawing fire. Soon they would forget all about the power and magic in an element they never should have possessed in the first place. Zeus snorted like a bull in rut. Cows lowed nervously down on earth.

Oh yes, his scheme had been a brilliant success so far, thanks to a bit of help from that scrumptious little lightning-rod goddess, Astrape. Of course his wife Hera, goddess of the Hearth, was not pleased to be abandoned by the mortals. He chuckled. Little did she know her own husband and one of his handmaidens had conspired to turn the humans away from her beloved hearth. Well, she deserved a little comeuppance. She never should have thwarted his will by urging Heracles to rescue Prometheus from his torment.

Poor, pathetic Prometheus. He must be weeping rivers to see the mortals shun his precious gift. You could say the humans were adding insult to injury—injury inflicted by a certain liver-munching eagle. Zeus grinned and let loose a god-sized guffaw.

It was no joke! There was *nothing* funny about that damned eagle. How he'd dreaded the sight of it, a speck soaring high above the rock to which he was chained, then circling downward, ever larger, until the nasty scavenger perched on his rocky prison and began pecking. It wasn't getting his liver eaten night after night for thousands of years that was the worst. Luckily Zeus was no whiz at biology, and, when dreaming up his sadistic punishment, had failed to realize that the liver has no nerve cells and feels no pain. But that wicked beak piercing through flesh and muscle every single day—*that* was torture. And, since he was immortal, every night the liver regenerated and the flesh healed and he had to go through it all again.

All that agony, just to bring humanity fire. And now, not

long after Heracles had rescued him from his horrific torment, the fools were giving up the flames for which he had paid such a terrible, terrible price.

Like little children, the humans had been so easily distracted by their shiny electronic toys—all blinky lights and buttons and bells—that they hadn't even noticed the godly gift vanishing from their lives. Mere mortals? Mere morons!

Well, to Hades with them. If they were such fools as to allow Zeus to steal their fire, won at such a high cost, he was damned if *he* was going to retrieve it and spend thousands more years getting his liver gnawed on by some gussied-up buzzard.

"You're on your own this time, ingrates," Prometheus said as he downed his wine and poured himself another hefty goblet. He had been drinking rather a lot of wine since the end of his ordeal. From now on, if his liver was going to be destroyed, he was damn well going to enjoy the process.

"It's me, Grammy. Lucy. Your granddaughter."

"Oh, hello dear. Thank you for coming." There was no sign of recognition in her pale, rheumy eyes. Lucy glanced over at Rory, who had plopped himself onto a chair in a corner of the room. Grammy Morag was lucid less and less often.

Lucy pulled up a chair alongside the bed and took her grandmother's bony hand in her own. Knobby knees and stick legs poked up beneath the thin white blanket. A woman who had always been so strong, healthy and independent was reduced to this, a patient in a nursing home, spending most of her days propped up in bed. "Do you know my mother?" Grammy asked, her voice high and tentative, like a little girl's. Lucy smiled and nodded. "She might be outside, hanging out the laundry," the old woman continued. "You can wait for her here."

"Yes," Lucy said, "I'll wait here with you, Morag." Her grandmother had been time-travelling more and more often, back to her girlhood and forward to the present, back to when she had first arrived at the nursing home two years earlier and then back to the time when she was a wife and mother, working long, hard hours at the farm in Cobh Dhu.

"I have the sight, you know," she said after a while of silence. "And my grandmother before me. It skips a generation, some say. My granddaughter may have it too."

"I *am* your granddaughter, Grammy," Lucy said, but the old woman went on as though she hadn't spoken. *Where in time is she now?*

"We didn't have the hydro then, you know. We used oil lamps. Father had to take the horses and get firewood for the winter. In the woods behind the house. The men would go and cut wood for winter."

"It was a hard life."

"Yes, we worked hard. But it was a good life too. I saw him, you know."

"Who?"

"My brother. I was out feeding the hens and I saw him walking up the hill into the woods. I told my mother and she said that it couldn't be Angus because he was out fishing with my uncle. But I knew it was him because he turned to wave at me."

All Lucy knew about her great-uncle Angus was that he had been killed in a tree-cutting accident when he was only sixteen. She looked into her grandmother's eyes and knew that Morag was seeing beyond the nursing home walls to her long lost brother.

"Three weeks later I really did see my brother walking up the hill to the woods. He turned to wave at me, exactly like before. He was killed that very day. Later I understood that when I saw him the first time it was a forerunner."

A forerunner? Lucy had never heard that part of the story.

"Back then, some of us would see things before they happened. But then the forerunners stopped."

"When did they stop, Grammy?" Lucy had a funny feeling she knew what Morag was going to say.

"When the hydro came. Oh, it was good to get the power, you know. I liked all those bright lights and the refrigerator and the hot water. The house wasn't so cold in the winter. But the electricity scared off the forerunners."

"How did you feel about that?"

"Oh, I didn't mind so much. It's not like the forerunners changed anything. You saw things before they happened, but you couldn't always tell what they meant. I like the lights."

Morag turned to Lucy as if suddenly noticing her.

"Hello. Have you come to see my mother? I think she's outside, hanging out the laundry. But you can wait for her here."

~ Flashpoint ~

Lucy tried not to let the tears come, but just caressed the fragile hand and sent love and warmth to the woman whose strong arms had held her when she was small.

"Did you hear what she said?" she asked Rory as they walked back to the car.

"About what?"

"About the forerunners. How they stopped after the power came in. As if electricity killed the magic."

Rory raised his brows in mock horror. "Do not think for one moment, love of my life, that I am giving up my big-screen TV so we can sit around freezing in the dark while you have visions of death."

"They didn't freeze in the dark back then, Rory. They had this nifty little thing called 'fire'."

"Fine," said Rory. "*You* go sit in the bedroom and stare at a candle while I sit in the living room and watch hockey. But if you get a vision of my imminent demise, my dear? Do me a favour and keep it to yourself."

Lucy reached out a finger and poked him.

Astrape reached out a finger and zapped a tree. The goddess of lightning was annoyed. She zapped a golfer and a cow and then another tree.

"Cut it out!" Zeus yelled from one the back peaks of Olympus. "That tree you zapped just fell over and knocked out a big chunk of the Macedonian power grid!"

Astrape shrugged and zapped a few more transformers for good measure. She was annoyed with Zeus, but afraid to confront him. His powers had waned considerably since the glory days of the Greek empire, but he was still formidable. Get the old sadist angry, and you could spend eternity doing some miserable, fruitless task. Just look at what had happened to Sisyphus, forever pushing his boulder uphill. Or worse yet, poor Prometheus. She shuddered at the thought of having her liver shredded by a big hungry bird. She hefted a boomerang bolt, flung it out over the Aegean Sea, and caught it expertly as it bounced back at the speed of light.

It wasn't all nectar and roses being a handmaiden to Zeus. Certainly she had been thrilled, a few millennia back, when he gave her the power of lightning in exchange for a few...well, favours. But after that he pretty much ignored her until just over a century ago when he approached her with his proposition. She was pleased to be noticed again and had been naïvely eager to help. Not to mention glad of chance to annoy that jealous old harridan Hera.

"Listen, Astrape," Zeus had said, "humans don't even *believe* in you anymore. They think that lightning is just a discharge of electricity from high voltage to low voltage."

"It is," she said, honest and simple still.

Zeus' hairy eyebrows wiggled like caterpillars.

"Yes, Astrape, it is. But what they don't know is that, thanks to me, you *create* that voltage potential, with your great artistry. Don't you think you should get the credit? Some nice marble statues, a feast day with honorary sacrifices, a temple or two? Perhaps a fountain in Rome. Look at how much attention Athena and Aphrodite get, even from the moderns. Why should you be left out? Wouldn't you like people to stand around and admire a statue of *you*?"

Astrape had fallen for it like Eros falling for Psyche. She had let Zeus persuade her to give mortals the power of lightning. And for what? Where were the temples, the feast days and sacrifices, the fountains? Not one lousy statue even. Not a single adoring worshipper. The mortals continued to goggle at paintings of Aphrodite (a sea shell? a *sea* shell?) and moon over marbled Athena (the stuck-up old cow) but they still ignored Astrape. She'd given away her power for nothing.

She should have known that Zeus never did anything that wasn't in his own best interests. Now that she was a little older and a whole lot more cynical, she finally understood why Zeus had persuaded her to give lightning to the mortals. He had just been using her to get back at Prometheus!

Like an overgrown petulant child, Zeus was still mad at the Titan for stealing Olympian fire and giving it to the mortals so long ago. And so he had used her in his scheme to steal it back. Annoyed just thinking about it, Astrape moulded some lightning into a ball and hurled it along the deck of a cruise ship. *That* would wake up those snoozy cruiser losers.

Ungrateful mortals! They had taken her gift of lightning and then, instead of worshipping her, had enslaved her power for

~ Flashpoint ~

trivial pursuits. All that beautiful pulsing electricity, imprisoned within hideous wires and ugly insulated cables! Electrons shuffling back and forth like zombie commuters, endlessly stopping and starting at the careless flick of a switch. Astrape fumed just thinking about currents snaking through conduits instead of dancing free in the air, putting on extravagant light shows that could be seen for miles. Shows so brilliant that the goddess Bronte's booms of applause thundered across the heavens and caused all creation to tremble.

What sacrilege! Angry Astrape filled both hands with jagged bolts and began to make them dance over the Himalayas, laughing as mountain climbers scrambled for safety. Puny, stupid mortals!

She'd had enough. She was sick of being used by Zeus and by the humans. She would set her precious power free. On the other hand, when dealing with touchy gods, it paid to be discreet, and she had already upset Zeus once this morning. Astrape strode across the heavens to the edge of a faraway continent and flicked her fingers. The goddess of lightning giggled as transformers erupted like volcanoes and fountains of sparks leapt free into the sky.

"What was that?" Lucy cried. The lights had gone out with a pop. She stood in the kitchen in the darkness.

"Damn!" Rory yelled from the living room. "I don't believe it! The Leafs were on the power play!" He stumbled into the kitchen. "What the hell's going on?"

"The power went out."

"Uh, thanks, Luce. I actually figured that out all by myself. But why?"

They stumbled through the kitchen and stepped out into the back yard. Into a world of dark. No lights as far as they could see. No streetlamps, no lights in houses, just inky black.

Lucy looked up.

"Oh my god. Look!" The black sky pulsed with stars. The Milky Way was a cosmic stream of celestial cream spilling from Hera's immortal breast. Orion the hunter strode towards the Highlands with Sirius the Dog Star at his heels. Pegasus galloped over the western horizon while Andromeda hung on for dear life.

~ Flashpoint ~

Cassiopeia sat regal upon her northern throne.

"Well, it wasn't a lightning strike," Rory said, scanning the night sky. "Not a cloud anywhere. It's totally calm. Not to mention totally cold."

"We better check the news," Lucy said. Power outages happened now and then, but for some reason, this one made her feel distinctly uneasy.

"Yeah," said Rory, "you go do that. Good luck turning on the radio or the TV."

"There must be some batteries for that old ghetto blaster. It has a radio."

"You know where they are?"

"No. You?"

"No. Don't we have a flashlight somewhere?"

"Yup."

"So where is it?"

"Haven't a clue."

They listened to the radio in the car. Transformers were blowing up all over the Maritimes. Given the extent of the damage, it could take days for crews to restore power.

"We should go to Grammy's old house," Lucy said, cranking up the car heater to warm her frosty feet.

"Why?" Rory asked, scanning radio stations for the game.

"Just until the lights come back on. Everything we'd need to live without power is still there from the old days."

"Hey, look what I found." Rory pulled a flashlight out of the glove compartment. To their surprise, it worked. "Let's go back inside."

Without the furnace running the house cooled off rapidly. Lucy and Rory went to bed early and cuddled under the blankets for warmth.

"I'm still cold," said Lucy.

"I think I might be able to do something about that."

"Warm enough?" Rory asked.

"Totally toasty," Lucy said. "Isn't this wonderful?"

They were cuddled up once again, but this time on the couch in front of Grammy Morag's wood stove. They had arrived that morning with a cooler of food (now chilling out on the back porch), a bundle of warm clothes, and a bottle of red wine (now open and breathing on the table in front of them).

"So whaddya think? Am I an awesome lumberjack or what?"

"You certainly look the part," Lucy said, stroking the sleeve of Rory's red flannel plaid shirt.

"Look the part? I'd say I'm pretty darned handy with that axe."

After they arrived at the farmhouse, Rory had chopped sticks from the big wood pile beside the house. Lucy's father had cut a winter's supply just before Morag had the stroke that had forced her into the nursing home. The seasoned hardwood burned hot and bright. An old lamp, the kerosene yellowed with age, sat on the table beside the wine, the flame turned low and the light soft and golden.

Just like the olden days.

"We can pretend we're pioneers," Lucy said.

"Yeah, or back-to-the-lander hippies," Rory said

"Totally groovy, man," Lucy said. She stared at the flames dancing behind the glass and began to feel vaguely mesmerized. "Think about all the things this wood stove can do, Rory. It can keep us warm *and* cook our food *and* heat water. Plus it's great entertainment. I just love watching fire."

"Psychedelic, baby."

"Way better than TV."

"Whoa! Now you're going too far, Luce. That's not even funny."

"I'm serious," Lucy said, punching him in the bicep.

"So am I, dear. Never more so. Anyhow, I'm not going to bed at eight o'clock again tonight. What are we going to do all evening?"

"What did people used to do before they had electricity and TV and computers and video games? Visit each other and play cards and tell stories and play music."

"That's it! We'll have a kitchen party. Go on," he said, shoving her gently. "Go call a bunch of your Grammy's friends to come over."

"Don't knock it, wise guy. Maybe people were more connected to each other before they connected to the grid. Beside, wasn't it you ranting and raving when the cops made us put out our fire on Labour Day? About your ancestral right to fire that

~ Flashpoint ~

goes back to caveman days?"

"Well yeah. But Luce, that was a real fire. Like a *bon*fire."

"Rory!" Lucy said, clutching his arm and staring at the flames. "I'm having a vision of the future!"

"Oh Jeez, Luce. Not one of those forerunner things?"

"I don't know," she said, her eyes sparkling in the firelight. "But I can see that you will be very happy before the night is over."

"Now you're talking," Rory said, turning to embrace her.

Lucy pushed him back gently and sat up. "Hold your horses, cowboy."

"Cowboy? I thought I was a lumberjack. But I can be a cowboy if that works better for you."

"What happened to my caveman?" Lucy asked, as she poured wine into a pair of jam jars.

"Caveman works for me," Rory said.

"But first, a toast." Lucy lifted her jar and the fire-lit wine sparkled like rubies.

"To fire," said Lucy.

"To fire, and to my favourite cavewoman," said Rory.

They clinked jars and the flames in the stove flared and crackled as if fuelled by their adulation. The whole room glowed golden. Lucy felt as if some goddess up there somewhere was smiling down on them.

Hera smiled, the rosy glow of her immortal face reflected in the rosy glow of the hearth.

"She who laughs last, laughs best," she murmured. Zeus wasn't the only one who enjoyed mortal turns of phrase. She laughed and the fire in the wood stove flared. She cackled and the flames crackled. A final snort produced a spray of sparks. Oh, Hera knew all about her conniving spouse's plan to lure humans away from the hearth. *Her* hearth that had sustained mortals ever since Prometheus stole Olympian fire and took it down to Earth. She also knew about his philandering with that little hussy of a handmaiden. But Hera played a long game. The goddess of the hearth lifted her wine goblet and turned toward the vineyard where a certain Titan had taken to lolling about with Dionysus and the satyrs. Her voice echoed across Olympus.

~ Flashpoint ~

"The mortals have proposed a toast, Prometheus! To fire!"

On a southern slope where grapes fit for the gods grew plump and juicy, Prometheus roused himself from his stupor and raised his golden goblet. "To fire—and to those mortals who esteem it!"

Zeus untangled himself from Aphrodite and cocked his ear. Was that Prometheus hollering? Something about fire and mortals? The Greek god flared his nostrils like a raging bull and sniffed. He smelled wood smoke and human contentment. Zeus raised his massive head and roared with fury.

"Was that thunder?" asked Lucy, turning to the window.

"Shush, sweetheart. It was nothing. Nothing at all." Rory gently tipped Lucy's face up towards his and kissed her wine-dewed lips.

Far from the Olympic peaks where the gods squabbled, Eros winked.

Sue McKay Miller was born and bred in Alberta and spent many years in the not-so-hallowed halls of academia as a research geophysicist. Ten years ago she fled the bright city lights and moved to the North Shore of Cape Breton. She spent eight years living off-grid in a yurt and was grateful for the fire burning in her woodstove and oil lamps. Sue writes fiction, essays and articles, some of which find their way into print. She also enjoys trolling forest and shore for bits of wood, bone and stone to use in her mosaic artworks, and watching wild animals from her woodland home.

~ Flashpoint ~

Keeza's Retribution

Coming back was a mistake, but news that my hometown was scheduled for demolition roused in me a curiosity that I confused for sentimental attachment. In the rain, I walked once-familiar streets, sickened by the dangling shutters and grotesque slants of roof, the black-stained fronts and gaping rag-adorned windows.

The government has bought every lot in town to make room for a colossal prison. These rotting houses will be razed and the earth beneath them cemented over. The catacombs will have to be sealed off, too. Almost everyone I used to know is down there, in mud cabinets. Yardley and my parents are buried there. They went quickly, like everybody else, on a wave of lost nails, teeth, and blood. No one in our town survived long after the Spectacle of 2186. Most spectators gasped their last by the end of that year. A few clung on till '87, but by then the catacombs had reached capacity. All remaining bodies had to be floated out to the sharks.

The brain is a vile deluder. It confuses time with distance, trauma with growth, guilt with virtue, irony with fortune. After the Horror, I became known by people in neighbouring villages as that lucky young man. But it was irony, not luck that saved my life. My boss refused—refused in spite of numerous entreaties—to let me have that fateful evening free. I owe my survival that afternoon of Moon 10, day 6, 2186, to cruel and beautiful irony.

The ruinous succession of events began three years before, when Keeza and Dustin, her clammy wisp of a boy, moved to Haybuxtershire, the sleepiest of small towns whose eyes never close. We did not exactly welcome newcomers. They upset the predictability, and often brought purge-resistant parasites with them.

Keeza rode into town in a real, gas-burning truck, which aroused suspicion straightaway. We traveled by government-issue hyperwagon. A very few turbocharge stations still carried gasoline, but gradually they were being snuffed out. Combustion power is anti-survivalist, as we all know.

There were other ways in which Keeza did not meet the unspoken criteria for a Haybuxtershire resident: she had no training for an authorized profession. Most townspeople worked at Yummex, the nutrient factory, but Keeza, different in all ways, hung a blue plaque with the words "Channeller Within" from her porch and stood every weekday at 4:44, quitting time, in the doorway of her bungalow, offering her services to all passersby. For small sums, she arranged audiences with alter-egos, divined forecasts, and cured those suffering from inter-dimensional infatuation (the phenomenon that she blamed for most cases of depression). She did profess a specialty, however, and that was tracking the transmigration of souls from being to being.

The people of Haybuxtershire considered her the worst possible addition to our remote parochial burg, yet Keeza's business thrived. There are always a greater number of desperate and downtrodden individuals among us than we care to recognize, and these became her clients.

Though we weren't that far apart in age I never befriended Dustin. He did not attend the local secondary school but was tutored at home by his mother. According to gossip, Keeza let him study whatever second language he wanted and instead of Mandarin or even French, he was learning Ancient Samodeic, an extinct tongue once spoken near the Ural Mountains.

Their front yard was crowded with bizarre figurines and ornaments. There was a statue of a man with the head of a falcon and another of a four-armed woman standing in a flower. Strung from the eaves of the house were hollow sticks that knocked together in the breeze. They had a queer resonance that made me think of bones. Sometimes I would pass the house and see Dustin lying on a blanket reading one of those cardboard books. He had a puffy face, like a baby's, and limp mousey hair. If he looked up and smiled, I pretended not to see him and kept walking. His blanket frightened me because it clearly hadn't come from a factory and the blue and white squares of it always seemed to be moving, as if mimicking the sky.

~ *Flashpoint* ~

In early summer 2184—two years before the horror that was to come—my younger brother Yardley and I were arguing in the air. He wanted to turn the glider towards home because it was almost 1:11, feasting time, and we had promised not to be late. But on this afternoon, updrafts were unusually good. We could have covered the whole region if we wanted. Of course, our parents had forbidden this. We were only supposed to repeat the same wide worming circles again and again.

At 1:09 I insisted that we skip feasting, but Yardley refused. I jabbed him hard with my elbow, and he punched me in the ear. Soon we were engaged in an all-out leaning, buffeting war that only stopped when the glider pitched down and back up on the wrong side, causing a descent neither of us could agree to. We managed to throw our legs over our heads and flip the wings around just in time to career into a tall elm that stood in back of Keeza's house. My harness caught on a branch, shooting all the air from my lungs. Something in my shoulder tore painfully slack. Yardley's nose and mouth oozed blood and he wouldn't look at me. With my returning breath, I cried out and then noticed Keeza bounding toward us carrying a long wooden rod with a shark hook on one end. I shrieked. She seemed about to tear us down one chunk at a time (the rumours about her were that bad).

She ran across the tall grass in her bright, floral house dress with the hook held high over her head looking up at something I couldn't see. "Keep quiet," she hissed, "or you'll frighten him away!" In retrospect, I could not have known what she meant by this, but I grew silent all the same.

"Where are you going, Ancient One?" she cajoled the empty air. "Your place remains here. Come down. All is well." While she spoke, I managed to pull myself free of my harness and settle dazedly on a thick branch some height from the ground. A comfortable heat spread through me and I watched her wave the hooked pole back and forth. *Ah,* I mused, deep in shock, *she's our friend, just weird.* I suspected that my brother had stopped breathing, but nothing felt real enough by then to care.

With a deep grunt, Keeza let the hook fall to the ground.

"You are too right, Grandfather," she said, smiling, though

~ Flashpoint ~

there was no one else there but Yardley and myself. She lifted the hem of her dress and pulled at the fibres until she had loosed a number of threads and twisted them into a bit of string. "To bind you to your duty, cherished ally," she said, then carefully she looped and tied the string to the shark hook.

Next I knew she was looking up at me. "You're being very good," she said. "But I need to do one more thing before I get you down. Okay?" I nodded, and she started climbing toward us, hoisting herself into the branches where Yardley hung, bloodied, with his chin to his chest. When she reached him, she slid the loop of string to the tip of her big hook and directly onto one of Yardley's limp fingers. His hand lay heavy and lifeless in hers as she tightened the thread, humming a low, rich melody and stroking his black hair as though he were only asleep. I don't know how much time passed. Eventually, his fingers trembled. His eyes fluttered open. With a dry, crepitating whistle his chest rose and fell.

The black back door of Keeza's house opened, and a pale puffy face appeared, looking bewildered. It was Dustin.

"Call an ambulance," Keeza whispered.

Shortly after that, help arrived.

Yardley never recovered. With time he regained his ability to speak, read, and write, but there were other assets that no amount of provocation could bring back. His jesting, jovial side had vanished. He frowned most of the time, but could never tell you why. We continued to share a bedroom, but quickly became strangers.

Our mom had to leave her job teaching chemical husbandry at the local college in order to stay home and amuse him. Otherwise he would sit on the edge of his bed all day, fidgeting with a Rubik's cube that he'd painted completely black.

No one blamed me for crashing the glider into a tree. Nor did they blame my parents for giving us boys such a dangerous toy. No. Local talk simply blamed That Tree. Over a period of months, however, conversation adopted a more suggestive designation, and people started to refer to the culprit more specifically as Keeza's Tree. In the space of less than two years, during which time the dead elm in Keeza's backyard succumbed to a windstorm and was hauled away, residents of Haybuxtershire seemed to forget there had ever been a tree behind her house. Yardley's accident became a boon for the town's unspoken prejudice. Hateful theories circulated in which Keeza had lured our glider from the sky with thaumaturgy then poisoned my brother with some untraceable extract. The crime was carefully rationalized: Dustin's frail build and languid spirit led his mother to envy any youth showing a healthier zest for life. I was lucky to have escaped, everybody kept repeating, and they almost had me convinced. But when I thought about it on my own, I remembered what had really happened: Yardley was all but dead until Keeza, with her hooked staff and her improvised string and her gentle touch, somehow brought him back around.

Occasionally, I wake in the middle of the night with my head full of what-ifs. I wonder: what if the tree had been in a different yard? What if Keeza hadn't tried to save Yardley? What if she let the "ancient one" go—would Haybuxtershire be the ghost town it is now?

I continued to stay away from Keeza. Her bright red hair tightly plaited against her head; the dozens of bronze rings jangling about her ankles, wrists, and neck; the long pole with its shark hook; her fuming truck and pasty, tumid-faced son with his impractical interests, all aroused in me a fascination that threatened to dislodge everything I had been taught about science and the virtues of uniformity. Because of this, I made long detours every day to avoid walking past her house, which stood along the fastest route home from school. Other kids did the opposite. They passed it at every opportunity, flinging eggs, pouches of sour milk, animal dung, sometimes rocks.

Keeza's business slumped. Regular clients cancelled their appointments without rescheduling, and no one new ever dropped by. One night someone wrenched her blue plaque from the porch and left it in pieces on her walkway. The grocer stopped delivering her orders and hateful messages began to arrive in every possible form. People put on croaky, wicked voices and called her day and night, threatening to take justice into their own hands if she didn't leave town.

One sweltering day of Moon 8 the odium took an awful, unwarranted leap. Keeza and her son were foraging along a nearby roadside when an h-wagon swerved onto the shoulder

~ Flashpoint ~

and ran the boy down. I can only assume it happened so quickly and brutally that Keeza couldn't take the same measures that had once helped Yardley. Perhaps she didn't keep a hook in the truck or she was too upset to handle the thread properly. Perhaps Dustin's soul fled too quickly beyond her reach. He was dead before they reached the hospital.

Overnight, the prank calls and vandalism stopped. The grocer found Keeza's past orders and started leaving them on her front step. No one sought her channeling services, but many planned to after a decent interval, during which time all guilt could sink into recesses of memory too remote and all-around bizarre to think on.

We expected life in Haybuxtershire to return to normal. We were idiots.

Keeza did not leave her house for weeks, not even to take her groceries indoors. Untouched crates of Yummex tins baked in the sun outside her door. The strange blossoms in her front garden parched and withered to grey husks that scraped and crackled into neighbours' dreams. The statues took on a sinister aspect, their expressions turning accusative with hard, hateful stares. Since the day she took Dustin to gather wild mushrooms and berries, the windows of her truck had not been closed and soon its cab began to moulder and then to rot.

Moon 10 arrived. Kids returned to school. All the leaves flared red and fell. People tossed their dark recollections of summer along with other rubbish into the bellies of robot composters.

I had passed my exams the previous spring, but was still trying to decide which subject to study at the Academy. Meanwhile, I had taken a job charging wagons at the local turbo station, which also sold basic commodities like dehydrated food, heat-casters, sake, and fishing bait and tackle. Less than fifty kilometres to the south was an ocean restock facility that generated only large predatory fish of the types man came so close to wiping out after the millennium. The waters around Haybuxtershire swarmed with arti-fish and the people of our town gloried in catching them. Even so, I should have questioned the jump in hook sales at the station that fall and the reason everyone gave for buying a new set: theirs had been stolen.

~ Flashpoint ~

I spent most of my time at the station in a far corner playing an incredibly addictive arcade game called Moon Crusade. One night my boss caught me there instead of cleaning the rat-traps as he had asked, and for the sake of my employment file, I agreed to his blatantly opportunistic scheme of punishment. For one full week, he docked my pay and doubled my shifts.

If he were still alive today, I'd kiss his feet in thanks. Instead of going to Haybuxtershire's fiftieth annual firework display—which has since been renamed "The Death Spectacle of '86," "The Haybuxtershire Horror," and "Keeza's Retribution," among other things—I went to work.

None of the actual spectators are still alive. I know only what people gibbered to me afterwards and what could be deciphered from the scattered writings of my mother's last diary entries.

The anniversary ceremony opened with a couple of speeches highlighting particular moments in Haybuxtershire's short history: the founding of its public observatory, the year Émile Wong caught an escaped dodecapus, the success of Yummex. It was a mild clear evening. Buckets full of sand and explosives lined the water's edge. Cups clinked and long-pent squawks of laughter drifted on a lazy breeze. When the speeches ended, fuses were lit and the first round of blossoms split open. Silver peonies and lime green dahlias hit the air, followed with grand golden palms, wistful purple willows, and furnace-red kelp. Mouthy blue fish darted across the sky in schools. Giant leggy spiders hatched and hovered. A ghostly horse reared into stillness. There was a pause. Then another round of hissing rose into the air—the finale.

All of Haybuxtershire waited for a burst of colour and noise—brighter, boomier, and faster than before. But no explosion happened. No embers flashed open. Nothing crackled into view. Friendly boos were passed around, yet the hissing did not die. In fact, it grew steadily louder. Eyes squinted into the darkness. The hissing was dropping down again, back towards the crowd. The main canisters of coloured explosives had yet to burst, but in the coal dark, came the sound of their lit fuses spiralling closer, closer, closer.

~ Flashpoint ~

People jolted to their feet. In another second they started to run. But no one outpaced the great manifold whisper. It grew louder and louder until people fell to the ground, clutching one another or curling into lone terrified balls, convinced they were about to be blown apart.

Then came the burst. An omnipresent clap of doom. A splintering, deafening wrench of air. It elicited thousands of screams, though none could be heard above its mutinous, skull-scouring roar. It opened a black endless void of false excruciation as all spectator-turned-victims imagined their limbs and faces and guts being unmade. In this moment, the souls of an entire town shot from their clay vessels and hovered, disoriented, through the night air—vulnerable.

A body without a soul draws Death immeasurably closer with every breath, sharpening inevitability to ghastly imminence and dim worries to piercing truth, until the whole work surrenders to the cold ground.

No one understood what had happened, but within a few short weeks, the effects became revoltingly clear. All of Haybuxtershire turned moribund. First, people's memories foundered. Then their appetites disappeared. Their mouths parched. Bowels froze. Then bones began to splinter. Medical experts arrived but their treatments could not reverse what Keeza had done.

"Her curse," muttered the dying. "She cursed us—the hag."

I hope never again to look upon the hulk of this ghost town, to hear its sodden groans or smell its decay, and I will rejoice when news reaches me of its demolition. Coming home—as if this place were once the haven of my youth!—has re-etched only those impressions that curse my life. One in particular haunts me most cruelly.

I had been watching the fireworks from outside the turbo-station. The display, I remember, seemed shorter and less spectacular than in years past. The sound of the final explosion did not reach me, which only proves its sinister logic. Sulkily, I was turning to go inside when Keeza's truck cruised past the station, headed for the speedway. There was something scraping

~ Flashpoint ~

the pavement behind it. As she drove beneath our glowing signboard, I glimpsed what that was, and all these years later, I still wake up nights trembling in horror at that monstrous, glimmering retinue of stolen fish hooks and the way she dragged them down the asphalt. As though impaled souls could be made to bleed.

Bridget Sprouls /sprʊəls/ was born in New Jersey but has spent most of her adult life in Eastern Canada. Her poems, stories, and reviews have appeared or are forthcoming in various journals in the US, Canada, Ireland, and the UK, including *The Quarryman, The Belleville Park Pages, Southword, Scrivener Creative Review,* and T*he Rutherford Red Wheelbarrow Anthology.* She is currently pursuing an MA in Creative Writing from University College Cork and working on a secret book project code-named *Gothic Brick.*

Loving After Dark

*"Deep in the forest there's an unexpected clearing that
can be reached only by someone who has lost his way."*
Tomas Tranströmer, "The Clearing"

The words, "I'm sorry, we did all we could," devastated Graham
all to hell, because it came down to one tragic certainty. Lesley
was dead.

It was supposed to have been a routine operation. Routine,
his ass. A massive infection had set in, and he'd heard about the
friggen doctors who don't wash their hands while the goddamn
super bugs free-range around the hospital.

To make it worse, Lesley's parents refused to add Graham
to the family visiting list. He visited anyway. Was there to hear
the news. After being banished from the room in which his dead
girlfriend and the grieving family were congregating, he'd gone
berserko. Major berserko. He loved Lesley. Before shooting out
through the hospital's revolving doors, he'd left a security guard
with a busted nose and several pieces of technical equipment
strewn about.

"Sorry. I did all I could."

He rushed to Lesley's apartment, packed a suitcase, and
hit the road. The mountains and a different province would put
space between him and the siren cars. Like the song says, "All
God's children need travelling shoes."

He drove all night. Listening to loud, eardrum-destroying
music kept him awake. His thick black hair was so uncombed
that when he looked into his rear view mirror he'd swear he was

looking at a knotted spaniel. And boy, did he have lots of time to think. Like about how her family was not going to miss him at the funeral. Because they couldn't stand him. "Homeless Graham." Except when Lesley let him stay with her.

He didn't blame her parents, really. He had a history of selling drugs and more than enough charges of driving under the influence of whatever. They didn't know the half. Bad things happen, but at least he was still alive and hadn't hung himself like his brother. If that was a good thing.

He was a cowboy, driving into the rising sun, leaving no silver bullets behind. Only a dead girlfriend he'd loved like no one else. He slammed his hand down on the steering wheel and swore at the oncoming headlights.

Up ahead he saw a service centre. As he approached the entrance, two grey dots appeared in the sky. They darkened and joined to form a large, blotchy shape which squeezed itself into a dense black hole from which two tiny flames flickered and floated. It was like looking through black fabric and glimpsing a darker dark, barely lit up by the two minuscule flames. It felt like his head had been jammed through a door too small and it scared the bejesus out of him. When this episode ended, he shook all over, his head spinney and hot, his mind scattered and wondering if this was what having a stroke was all about. He was also left with a low grade apprehension that he'd not actually exited the bizarre space he'd entered.

Goddamn weird. Almost mystical.

He filled the truck with gas and paid a frizzy-haired woman at the counter. He sauntered over to a coffee machine. It was a new-fangled piece of shit, and past events having rattled his brain, too complex for his exhausted mind to figure out. What was he supposed to do? Push a button, pump a lever, hit a switch or kick the shit out of it?

She emerged from the useless things aisle, with its stuffed animals, gigantic dangling dice cubes, truck belt buckles and other amazing pieces of dazzling futility. She walked over and poked thin fingers into his arm. Got his attention. This slim, free-spirited looking woman wore a well-used, black leather jacket and her fine black hair partially covered her face. A large silver cross hung around her neck and she had a one-inch scar across her forehead. It looked like a series of deep puncture wounds which had improperly healed. Not something he imagined she would ever want to talk about.

"Want me to show you how to use the coffee machine?" she asked.

"Great," Graham said. She was cute in a tough way. Lots of miles on her pretty face.

Her fingers worked a miracle on the coffee challenge.

"Cream and sugar?"

"I can do that," Graham said. He took the cup from her. Her fingers massaged the lip of the cup. *A message?*

He paid for the coffee. She followed him to his truck, and before Graham knew what smote him, she'd jumped into his truck, he'd found out that her name was Rebecca and she was hitch-hiking to Wolf Back.

They were soon on fire. Romantic spontaneous combustion. They holed up in a tiny, disintegrating motel room, with only one bed, an ancient television and a narrow shower stall which comfortably held one person. But they made do, and their shared longing was consummated in a tight, soapy, lusty ceremony. When they were flaked out on the bed watching a Scooby Doo cartoon, with his grieving heart quieted for the time being, she invited him to come to Wolf Back with her.

There are times in a person's life when the concepts of light and dark, rationality and superstition, balance and delusion, good and evil, are in such turmoil that the only possible action is to drop anchor in the first harbour sighted.

They arrived late in the afternoon at her house on the outskirts of town at the end of a desperate excuse for a road. The house was a one-storey, faded green structure with a saggy, moss-covered roof. The side door dangled from one hinge. The front of the house was half-hidden behind an untidy copse of stunted apple trees. A mountain's ass sat thirty feet from the back patio window.

As Graham got out of the truck he saw the grey dots again. They darkened and formed the same way they'd done over the service centre. This one blanketed the mountain forest. Then the two tiny fires came from its depths and their wee light gained strength and washed away the blackness. Graham's saliva tasted like steel and his stomach rolled over because this time it seemed like he was looking through a window, that he was in the space where all this strange shit was being manufactured. Friggen scary, and when this flashback, seizure, stroke, whatever the hell it was, finally ended, Graham shook like he had the last time with that warm, spinney head. Hell, he hadn't had a flashback in three years. And for sure, none of them had been like this.

The inside of the house was something else. Chaotic. Two fridges in the kitchen. A living room with too much furniture. A bathroom with decaying magazines on the damp floor and a broken piece of soap lying in grungy-looking liquid next to the sink. Her bedroom was in meltdown mode. A rickety old dresser was pushed against the wall. A broken rectangular mirror hung above the dresser and two night tables were upside down at the foot of a rusty metal bed with a saggy mattress and a sleeping bag for a blanket. Crumpled up curtains were piled on the dirty wooden floor. The window had a spiderweb-shaped crack. *Would make a perfect city flophouse.* He and Lesley had known what those were all about. A faint smoky smell permeated the house, and when he tried a light switch, nothing happened.

That evening they sat outside, drank red wine and shared a bag of chips and wieners they'd bought at a grocery store.

"What put you on the road?" Rebecca asked.

She'd built a small fire at the edge of the mountain forest not too far from one of the two fires he'd seen in his episode. Its feeble flames reflected flickering fingers of light onto the silver cross inset with two red ruby-like stones.

"Oh, probably a similar reason to yours," Graham said. Deep sadness lounged around in Rebecca's hazel eyes. A melancholy that looked like it intended to stay for an extended visit.

"So what's your reason?" Rebecca asked. Her hand rested on Graham's upper leg. *A little incentive for him to spill the beans?*

"No job, a dead girlfriend, a bashed up security boy, an incompetent quack and dreams smashed to hell. What's yours?"

"I'm looking for my sister, Molly. She was last seen on the Trans-Canada highway near here."

"Oh. You'll find your sister. I'm sure of that."

Where'd those friggen words come from? He'd been staring at the little fire when the words grabbed his tongue and swung out of his mouth like a wild monkey. Monkey words for sure, 'cause he would never have said them on his own. His strange unproven statement was followed by the humble fire blazing up into a powerful sheet of flames. *Holy shit, I'm becoming a friggen Merlin who can make flames rise and fall.*

"My God, I hope you're right. You know, I won't be hanging around here long. I have to keep looking."

Graham watched thick and miserable fatigue fog up her face. He pulled her head onto his chest. He'd seen the same tired pain on Lesley's face, and Lesley and Rebecca both had similar bruises and needle marks.

Lesley had been so brave. She'd return home after a night shift and still be able to give him a bit of true love and a brave smile. Her greatest gift to him, and maybe proof to herself, that the hours she made herself available for desperate needy men to maul, grope and poke hadn't wiped out her spirit.

"Can I go with you? Wherever you're going?"

"I have to go alone. I don't know why I even asked you to come here tonight. Maybe it was because you looked like you'd seen the darkness. And when you told me I'd find my sister, your voice sounded like my grandfather's. He was a Shaman. He said he healed people by going into the dark behind the dark."

"That's weird shit. I don't even know why I said you'd find your sister. Just did. I normally believe in luck. Good luck, bad luck and me, Mr. No Fuck'n Luck."

"That's what made your words so remarkable. So real."

Clouds hastened the night's darkness. An owl hooted. An owl replied. A coyote howled from somewhere on the mountain. A coyote answered. Rebecca poured two more glasses of wine. Graham slugged his down.

"That's an interesting looking cross."

"A monk gave it to me. Gave one to my sister, too. He just walked out of a Halifax alley. How weird is it having a monk walk out of a city alley? He said one red stone represented me and one represented my sister and that the crosses would keep us together. He even hung them around our necks. It was like some kind of ancient ritual."

Graham touched the red stones. A wee surge—like electricity—rushed through his finger tips.

"Molly had an old second-hand Polaroid camera she'd

picked up at the Salvation Army. She asked the monk to take a picture of us standing on the street. Molly had been feeling guilty and wanted to let our family know we were okay. She put the photo in with a letter she'd written to our mother and mailed it off.

"A few minutes later we hitched a ride with a guy in a white van. It's a dangerous thing to do. 'Specially because it didn't have any windows, but we figured it would be okay because there were two of us."

By the third glass of wine, it was only the fire that kept the night's darkness at bay. Rebecca added a chunk of dried birch to the flames.

"My sister and I ran away and took to the streets when we were in our early teens. Our fuck'n stepfather used us as his personal sex playthings. You know, I got this weird mark on my forehead the night after my stepfather first raped me. My sister said it's like a stigmata. Said my soul went into the dark and brought the mark back. Like the crown of thorns scar left on Christ's head when he was crucified."

After one more glass of wine they went to bed and made love. Removing Rebecca's darkness helped remove his. For surely, if there was anything he was good at, it was recognizing pain. But afterward, when he thought he might have offered her some respite, he felt her darkness returning like an old mouldy blanket covering both of them.

The next morning, Rebecca was gone. While searching outside the house, Graham was surprised to see that the fire still burned brightly, as if tended. *Rebecca must have re-started it before she left.*

He sat on the rickety back porch and waited for her. When she didn't show, he smothered the fire with water and drove to the store. It was a beautiful sunny morning. The sun's heat radiated off the dashboard and warmed Graham's bare arms.

He bought a few groceries and then drove around looking for Rebecca. She was nowhere to be found. Back at the house he made a peanut butter sandwich and poured himself a glass of red wine. He walked to the back porch and was, once again, surprised to see the fire blazing away. Hadn't he given it a good enough soaking? Was Rebecca having fun with him? He doubted that. He sat and waited for her until the mountain began to change into its grey, evening PJs.

Graham went into the kitchen and popped open another bottle of wine. He drank and stared at the almost dead fire. Where the hell was she? He drank until the bottle was empty and he felt drunk enough to face going to bed.

He didn't want to sleep on the saggy old bed. It reminded him of Rebecca and of Lesley. Strange how thinking about Rebecca gave him the same sad and lonely feelings as thinking about Lesley. He chose the couch.

He was almost asleep when he was startled by a creaking sound. He opened his eyes. A figure sat on the large reclining chair in the corner.

He searched for the flashlight on the floor and turned it on. It was a woman. She was plumper than Rebecca, but her features were similar, with the same sad gaze. A cross like Rebecca's hung around her neck.

Then the flashlight's luminance began to struggle to stay alive as it was swallowed by the darkness. Being drunk, he closed his eyes and pretended this hadn't happened. *Lot of strange shit going on, Cap'n...*

The next morning, black clouds cut the heads off the mountains. They clawed the light from Graham's soul, opened up his mental photo album. Lesley dying. Rebecca gone. His aimless, useless life, plus a friggen hangover. Maybe his brother wasn't so stupid after all.

He thought about the woman in the chair. Had he really seen her? Maybe she was a goddamn flashback too. Maybe he needed hospitalization. That would not be a good thing, nor was his habit of losing women. Flashback or no flashback.

He checked the fuzzy, furred chair that he thought he'd seen the woman sitting in. Poking up, just above the cushion, was a cross just like Rebecca's. Two red stones where Christ's hands would have been spiked to the wood. He had a sudden desire to hang the cross around his neck.

When he did, a warm feeling drifted around his forehead and made him feel closer to Rebecca. And more surprisingly, to Lesley and even to Molly. Strange emotion.

He made instant coffee. When he stepped out on the porch the fire was ablaze with hungry flames. It had rained last night. *So how did the fire get so healthy?* The flames died down when he

~ Flashpoint ~

stared at it. *Bizarre.*

He wouldn't stay here. Without Rebecca, the house was a spirit-sucking void. He drove to a service centre and grabbed some breakfast. He still grieved for Lesley, and now was mourning for Rebecca. So confusing. Maybe it was because they were so alike.

Two aboriginal women who'd lived in the same despairing pit, while the cities' tidy-bowl critics experienced the warm fuzzy feelings they got from their shallow apologies. Hypocrites who handed out mandatory sentences while pretending ignorance of history's foul breath.

Darkness had followed Graham around, too. All his life. From when he was first put up for adoption, to his first night in jail. At least he'd dumped the drugs. Not easy when the words he spoke hardly ever jibed with the words spoken down at him.

He bought a newspaper and brought it to his table. He spotted an ad for an attic apartment. Three hundred dollars a month with the option of working in the antique shop to pay off the rent. He phoned the number, but nobody answered. Another customer told him where he could find the only antique shop near Wolf Back.

The shop would have been sitting on the Trans-Canada highway, but for a pinch of grass and a few cups of ditch water. Inside, the shop was dark and packed to the rafters with nostalgia. Felix Campbell, the proprietor—who looked like he was in his seventies or eighties—stood behind a glass counter. He had a shrunken face, but when he smiled his whole antique world smiled with him.

"Do you still have that room for rent?" Graham asked.

"I do. I'll show it to you."

The owner took him up a flight of wobbly stairs, unlocked a knotty oak door and let Graham in. Graham looked it over.

"I'll take it month by month if that's okay with you."

Instead of answering, Felix said, "Where did you get the cross?"

"It was given to me."

Felix took it in his hands, looking at it closely. "I've only seen this kind of Celtic cross once. Come on."

Graham followed him down the stairs. Felix walked to the corner of the store and pulled open purple curtains. A small parlour lay behind the cloth barrier. Across a soft blue carpet, an old piano sat. Above the piano hung a picture.

Graham walked to it and stared at a small photo of Rebecca standing on a street corner with the woman he'd seen last night. They were smiling and wearing the same clothes they'd worn when Graham saw them. The crosses dangled around their necks, shining in the moody sunlight.

"That's Rebecca, the woman I stayed with, and I think I saw the other one on the La-Z-Boy chair last night."

"They disappeared fifty-five years ago," Felix said.

"What the hell? That's not possible," Graham whispered. He threw himself into a wicker rocking chair. "Where'd you get the picture?"

"Where'd you get the cross?"

"I picked up Rebecca in New Brunswick." Graham stood again, walked over to the photo and pointed to her image. "She invited me to stay and when I got up the next morning she'd disappeared. I waited around, but she never came back. Then last night I woke up and saw this other woman. Must be her sister who she was looking for. Rebecca said her name was Molly. This morning, I found the cross on the chair.

"I slept on the couch after Rebecca left because sleeping on the bed made me feel too lonely, even though I'd only been with her for a few days."

It had only been a few days, but how many does it take to get a lover into your heart? A year? A month? Two days?

"These are my sisters you're talking about! Our mother got this picture, with a letter, in the mail. That's the last we ever heard of them." Felix took the picture down off the wall. He rubbed it with his fingers, leaving streaks across the old glass. It looked like he was trying to rub them back to life, like they were genies in a bottle. "I'm getting you a drink," he said, "because I need one."

Felix went into the back and came out with two beers. He was shaking so hard that he spilled some on the carpet.

Graham could feel the man's furious emotions as Felix tried to decide whether Graham had anything to do with his sister's disappearance.

"Cripes man," Graham said, "I can hardly be blamed for something that happened fifty plus years ago. I'm not that old."

~ Flashpoint ~

But Felix needed something more. *What the hell.* Graham told him about his girlfriend dying and all the other reasons he took off for Nova Scotia.

Graham's openness got Felix to talk more about his sisters.

"I was the oldest. Rebecca was next and Molly was the youngest. They took off and disappeared like a lot of abused women do. Our step-dad was a bad one. I was the chicken-livered one. I hung in and took his abuse. God, the shit I watched him do to my mother. He died of a massive heart attack after a drinking binge. There is a god after all. That's what I thought."

He fetched another beer. Graham could feel that he wasn't so suspicious now. The beer had helped to calm both of them.

"Where was the house you were staying at?"

"Other end of Wolf Back."

"Would you show it to me?"

They drove in Felix's car, pulling off the Trans-Canada and entering the dirt road to the house. They got partway up the laneway and Graham felt a searing heat in his head.

They sat and gazed at an abandoned house. The roof covered no more than a pile of wood. Then he noticed that the fire he'd put out was again throwing out a healthy display of flames. Graham started to shake.

Then he spotted a rusted-out white van sitting in a thick overgrown copse of alder bushes, along with a belly-up refrigerator and a decomposed dresser. And there was the fire, power dancing on the fringe of the mountain. Six-foot flames and climbing Jacob's Ladder to who knows where. Maybe to Graham's rubber room.

"Your whole story is damned impossible," Felix said. "But...I believe you anyway. I've always avoided this road. It was so hard for me to drive past the house, but I never knew why. Hell, once passing by, I had to pull over and phone somebody to bring me home. Couldn't friggen drive 'cause I was crying like a baby. I thought it was because of my spending too much time around all the old things that dead people leave behind. That maybe, looking at the old run-down house was setting off some kind of PTSD."

"Do you know who lived here?" Graham asked.

"Some crazy old guy who kept chickens. Probably long

dead by now."

They got out of the car and walked around an old metal bed post. Graham recognized it. The lump in his throat grew. As he approached the fire, the flames dwindled.

"I can't get any closer," Felix said. He plunked himself down on an old stump and watched Graham.

By the time Graham got there, it was out. Dead out. Without knowing why, Graham grabbed a rusty shovel that was nearby. He dug in. The ashes were stone cold. On the fourth shovelful, Graham hit something hard. He placed the tip underneath and lifted up a human leg bone. He felt as cold as the devil's heart right before a searing heat and pressure set in—like it was trying to lift his head off his shoulders.

Three police cars and a forensic van flashed their lights to the world and turned this tiny road into a newsworthy curiosity.

A large constable, with a slight limp, approached Graham and Felix. He introduced himself and asked them how they came onto the bones.

"I'm an antique dealer," Felix said. "My tenant and I came up here to see if we could find some antiques lying around. There's supposed to be an old dump in this area."

"You going to do a DNA on those bones?" Graham asked.

"Standard procedure, sir. They'll try and match it up, if they can."

The man gave Graham a good long look, but then went back to the real action at the fire pit where the forensic unit was poking around.

Graham didn't believe the police around here would know about his previous breaking bad behaviour. And he wasn't crazy enough to mention having spent a night in the house.

From a distance, Felix stood with Graham. They watched the police put more bones into a bag. Graham knew the bones belonged to Rebecca and Molly. Like he knew that Rebecca had found her sister. Like he knew that the intense love he'd felt for Rebecca had been mysteriously fed by his love for Lesley. And, weird as it sounded, Graham believed that Lesley had already met or would soon meet up with the two sisters.

"You going to tell the police that you think they're your

sisters?" Graham asked.

"I'll get them to take my DNA, but does it matter? I know they're my sisters, thanks to you. Don't really have a clue how all this worked out, but it did. Fifty plus years to find them." He hugged Graham.

Graham looked up and saw familiar grey dots form. Vertigo filled his head. Seconds later they turned into two shiny dark clouds which flew over the mountain, absorbed by the accepting sky.

Graham was filled with gratefulness and pride at having helped someone. And hadn't he truly loved two women? Lesley and Rebecca. Both of them had shared a world with him. One for a long time and one for a short time. He might never experience this kind of love again. A love that everyone searched for. The kind that burned the insides of your soul.

Graham removed the cross. "You should take this. They're your sisters. You deserve it."

Felix accepted it and then stood stone still, staring at Graham's neck. "My God."

Graham felt it first and then looked down. Around his neck, lay the other cross.

Bonds can be formed in the tiniest amount of time. Maybe, just this once, he deserved something too.

Larry A. Gibbons a graduate of Queen's University and St. Lawrence College, is a former library clerk, photo technologist, and veterinary technologist. Known as a passionate writer and an enthusiastic hiker, cyclist, hockey player and cross-country skier, he spent years moving back and forth from southern Ontario to Cape Breton, but has now settled permanently in Cape Breton. His short stories have been published in several anthologies. A collection of his stories, titled *White Eyes*, was published in 2011. His story, "Prophets Don't Honk" was selected as one of the 32 titles on the "long list" for the 2013 CBC Short Story Prize. Larry's writing often focuses on the paper-thin veil between the familiar and the unknown. Visit him online at www.larryagibbons.com

~ Flashpoint ~

Nancy S.M. Waldman

Hearth's Glow

Jani stood alone on the observation deck, looking down at planet Hearth. The starship *Hyliah's* orbit had degraded somewhat since she was a kid, but she'd come here often and regularly adjusted the scope's settings so she could see what she wanted.

She glanced at her wristpad. On it was the Colonist Selection Board's response to her application. She hadn't looked at the message yet. She wanted to be here with the view of Hearth she loved most as she read the good news about when she would finally get to emigrate.

She put her eye to the scope and saw the first fiery volcano emerge over Hearth's glowing horizon. The viewer adjusted its position to her programmed coordinates while she watched. One-by-one, twelve erupting peaks showed themselves. She left the scope then and took in the whole scene: pinpoints of vivid orange, some with streamers of lava flowing around them, arrayed in a graceful paisley swirl over the green and blue southern hemisphere of the colony planet.

On-planet she wouldn't be able to see the design they made. Each of them, she'd been told, was huge and very far from one another. Having lived her whole life on-ship, she'd never even seen fire, much less a volcano up close.

But soon...

Jani had worked so hard for this. She wanted it more than anything. She opened the message on her wristpad and read it. An involuntary noise welled up from deep inside her. She read the message again and then one more time to be certain.

Her application had been rejected without explanation.

Tears stung her eyes. Her vision blurred.

Why did I think would this be any different? Every single

time I've tried to better myself, I get rejected. Jani slipped the comm off her wrist. *The only mystery here...*She bashed it against the sill of the viewport...*is why I thought...*Over and over...*this would be different.*

Long before she was born, Jani's grandparents had been on board the starship *Hyliah* when it left the Near Colonies on its mission to seed three separate colony planets. The real leaders left at the first stop. The second attempt, less well-equipped, ran into immediate twin disasters: famine and disease. By the time the *Hyliah* got into a stable orbit around the third planet, Hearth, the leadership and will to mount a proper colony had eroded.

A handful of settlements sustained themselves on-planet, but most of the two thousand or so people on-ship had opted to stay aboard, afraid of the rigours and risks of planet life.

The wristpad lay in minced and mangled bits at her feet.

Seconds or minutes later—time had suspended for her—Jani heard Maj coming up the spiral stairs. Maj was the closest thing she had to family and Jani had asked her to come here to share her good news. As she listened to the *click, click* of Maj's shoes on the metal steps, a plangent rumble rolled from somewhere in the bowels of the *Hyliah* and the ship shuddered.

The clicks stopped.

Jani didn't turn around to face her friend.

"What have you done to your comm?"

Jani sighed. "I'm sorry I asked you to come all this way. I've got no good news after all. They rejected me."

Maj walked over and touched her arm. "For what? Did you apply to be a colonist?"

Jani nodded slowly.

"I wish you'd talked to me first. So...you destroyed your comm device? That's shooting the messenger. Are you nuts? How will you function without it? Shit, girl. You'll pay a high price for a refurb—*if* you can find one."

"My credits are obviously useless for anything I really want in life!" Jani turned, the words spewing out. "Tundé got into pilot training while I was rejected. I couldn't even get hired as a shuttle mechanic—even after all you've taught me! And now this."

Maj grasped Jani by both arms. "I'm sorry. I'm so sorry. It doesn't make sense. They've been begging for colonists—"

~ Flashpoint ~

"All my life! Now that I've grown up and finally earned enough credits, they reject me and don't even give me a reason!"

"If you'd told me about your application," Maj said, slowly, "I would have told you that there's been a sudden uptick in the number of colonists going down."

"Since when?"

"Recently. But, calm down. We'll find a way. You'll...I don't know...reapply."

"I'm not like you, Maj. I can't be content here. I have to get off this hulk. We weren't meant to live all our lives on-ship."

Jani turned back to the view below. The winking orange lights of Hearth that had so recently beckoned, now seemed only to mock her.

Late to her job as a *medica* in the elders wing, she jogged along the glide, her thick ponytail swishing against her shoulders. Most people avoided the moving walkway because periodically and without warning, it jolted to a standstill. She got down it this time without being thrown off her feet and arrived at the cross-ship transit that would take her portside.

Alone in a four-seat compartment, Jani flashed her wrist over the sensor panel, but the high-speed train didn't move.

"Blast me," she whispered, wrapping her fingers around her naked wrist. *There must be another way to start this thing.*

She saw a raised edge on the bottom of the panel, put a finger under it and flicked it open. Two buttons, one red. She pushed the other one and the cab sped off, throwing her back against the molded seat.

Arriving at work, Jani bathed, fed, dressed, undressed, diapered, medicated, transferred, entertained, cajoled and suppressed irritation for dozens of the oldest Hylians over the next eight-plus hours. Finally, she went to visit Ell.

Jani's favourite centenarian was asleep. His head lolled against the high back of his hover recliner, mouth gaping wide. She hated to wake him, but he'd given her strict orders to do so whenever she had time to visit. She touched his thin forearm and he started awake. "Hi."

He shook his head.

"Can't hear me, huh?" She reached into the medibag

strapped to her thigh and brought out a small cylinder of *H-Ear Spritz*. Lifting each large, knobbly ear in turn, she squirted in the drying nanoagent. It took only a few moments for the particles to reach the inner ear, dry it out, and restore functionality to his implants.

Ell stretched his jaw, bobbed his head back and forth a few times and then said, "I see you're still burning the candle at both ends."

"What's a candle?"

He grinned, his teeth still strong. "Wax stick used for on-planet lighting. Fire, you know."

"O-kay. But what does that mean?"

"If it burns from both ends, the candle lasts half as long...or less. Another way of saying: you look tired."

"My appearance probably reflects the bad news I came to tell you about. Plus—*aughh*—it's been a long shift." She sighed and patted her medibag. "I had to use the ConIMm—twice."

He grimaced.

"I know, but—"

He waved his hand. "Stop. I'm not criticizing you. Some of these blighters need to be let out of their misery permanently. Since you can't do that, I'd say immobilizing them temporarily makes a lot of sense."

"Thanks. I hate to use it, but..." She didn't bother finishing.

"How old are you now?" he asked.

"Twenty-six."

"I guess you can take a little hard work at your age. Just don't forget that at one end of the candle should be some kind of fun."

"I visit you."

"Worse than I imagined! So, when are you departing from our illustrious tin can?"

"My application was denied—no reason given."

"No!" He stared at her for a moment. "I can't believe it. You're a perfect candidate. Strong, youthful, hard-working, clever."

"You should have filled out my application."

"What's your theory?"

She rolled her eyes toward the ceiling. "If it didn't sound

so paranoid, I'd say someone in Central Command doesn't like me. Only that really is crazy, because no one there knows me. I guess that's the real reason. I'm a nobody. No family connections. The only reason I got to work here—no offense—is that no one wants this job."

"I should have put in a good word for you with Ledroit."

"No offense again, Ell, but why would that have helped? Commander Ledroit is one nasty piece of work. He isn't going to care about—"

"The opinions of one very old and forgettable man?"

She looked up at him apologetically.

"I'll have you know my whole career was in Central Command. Plus, little known fact: I'm related."

"To the Ledroits?"

He nodded. "I feel bad. Maybe I could have helped. It never occurred to me that you wouldn't be allowed to go. For years they begged people and couldn't get anyone to take the risk!"

"Yeah, like all my life." She paused and then added, "I'm sorry I called your relative 'nasty.' "

He laughed. "No problem. He's not blood. He's married to my granddaughter. Criticize away! He's been a disaster. Hasn't taken care of the ship or built the resources we need. Hell, he hasn't done the one thing that needed to be done: properly colonize Hearth! I've always said that all the talent on this ship left at the first planet...or died on the second."

"My parents included."

"Ah, I wondered. How'd you...?"

"I was an infant, so they left me with my grandmother until they could risk bringing me down. It never happened."

"That's a tough start."

"Well, they saved my life by leaving me here." She raised her hands, palms up. "Grandma died when I was eight. I lived with a neighbour's family until I could take care of myself and then got to know Maj. She's like my older sister."

He patted her knee and said, "I knew your grandparents slightly. That was way back when we first started this journey. I never told you because it was so long ago and I didn't even know if you remembered them." He lay back and looked off into space. "Life is long and unpredictable. Don't give up." He turned back to her, suddenly energized again. "You know, I remember planet life

~ Flashpoint ~

from when I was a small boy. The green. The breezes. Wouldn't mind spending my last days on-planet."

"Why didn't you go down before?"

"My wife wasn't colonist material. I wouldn't have gone without her."

"But..."

He nodded. "Yes. I know. She's dead. But if they won't let someone young like you go down, what would my chances be?" He winked and said, "Maybe we should both stowaway."

"I like the way you think."

And afterwards, that was all she could think about.

The next night after work, Jani sat alone in the huge colony transport vessel—nicknamed The Beast. Unused for decades—since the mass colonization of the previous planet—it sat in the farthest corner of the hangar bay. A mechanic's light, hooked to the fuselage, shone over her shoulder, casting long, looping shadows.

She was waiting for Tundé to return from his run to the planet. Sweat formed on her forehead and under her breasts. The cooling transfers were on the fritz again. That's why Maj wasn't here. She, Lizzy and their whole crew had been working on the problem. The walls sweated with previously unheard-of humidity.

The vast hangar bay with its odors of fuel and lubricants was rarefied air to Jani; she'd spent all of her spare time here since she was a teenager. Maj took her on back then—first teaching her this and that about the maintenance of the smaller transports like the ones Tundé piloted. Later, after Jani had been rejected for pilot training, Maj had the idea to let her practice on The Beast. She didn't ask permission—not even from Hayek, the Lead Pilot. They had secretly worked here in their off hours, refurbishing what they could as a teaching exercise for Jani.

That's why I didn't notice the increase in the number of colonists, Jani thought, wiping the back of her neck before the sweat could trickle down her spine. *I'm always in here with my nose in the drive block or hydraulics.*

Tundé popped his head in. "There you are."

She jumped up and greeted him with a hug. They'd been best friends since childhood.

~ Flashpoint ~

"Did you get my messages?" he asked.

She rubbed her wrist. "Uh, no."

"What happened?"

"I broke it."

"Well, that explains why you haven't answered me. Maj told me the bad news."

"Oh."

"I'm so sorry. But don't give up."

"I'm going to stowaway."

"What? No, Jani. Apply again. They'll let you go eventually."

She shrugged and shook her head. "Pretty much made up my mind, Tundé. I'm going...with or without your help."

"Not on my ship! Do you want me to lose my job?"

"No. But that wouldn't happen because I won't get caught."

He cocked his head forward and peered at her. His brown eyes and skin contrasted nicely against the blue-grey of the worn flight suit. "Calm down. You shouldn't do it and I can't help you. I have responsibilities now. I have to set a good example to the other pilots." Tundé had risen through the ranks fast, recently having been named leader of his cohort.

"It's okay," she said. "I understand." But his words stung and reinforced the simple fact that they were separated now by his position as shuttle pilot. He had moved on and up. She hadn't and wouldn't until she got off the *Hyliah.*

"Jani, please don't do anything stupid."

But, stupid or not, she had already made up her mind. Every few days a waste run carried refuse off the ship. The next time, she would be part of the *Hyliah's* unwanted cargo.

Jani snuck aboard in the wee hours—not that anyone on the hangar deck would have given her a second glance. She knew which shuttle to choose because it was already half-loaded with compressed garbage.

As the time grew near, she settled into a hiding place between two stationary bins in the aft of the passenger section, sitting on her clothes and bedding which she'd formed into a floor seat using cargo tape. It was contoured, cushioned, and not very

~ Flashpoint ~

comfortable. She pushed her rear end and head back and forth to make it fit better. Her knees were bent, feet on the floor.

She hadn't told Maj or Tundé. Only Ell knew. He agreed to contact them once the flight had left. *Sweet Ell.* She hated to leave him behind. Jani still hoped that she could persuade Maj to come once she was on-planet.

Jani didn't know who the pilot would be, and that made her nervous. They gave the waste runs to the less experienced ones. Her heart seemed to flutter instead of beat. She pulled cargo strapping from the wall and secured herself and her makeshift seat. Then she strapped down duffels in front of and over the top of the two bins, completely hiding herself.

Thank god the cooling units are working again. She would have melted if the bay had been as hot as it was a few cycles ago.

Jani's legs and rear end went to sleep. She loosened the straps a little so she could shift around and told herself over and over to be patient because her dream was finally coming true.

The cargo bay on the other side of the bulkhead next to her opened with a *swoosh* and she heard the crew talking while they loaded containers of compressed garbage.

The hatch opened. The pilot boarded.

Jani breathed a quiet sigh of relief when she heard the pilot's voice. It was Aneka; she knew from Maj and Tundé that the woman was a competent pilot. She listened to the preparatory back and forth between the pilot and flight control.

This is really happening.

Then, Aneka's voice changed from normal pilot monotone to inexperienced pilot's stress. "I was told I couldn't carry passengers yet." Pause. "Affirmative. Hold, please." Then she heard Aneka talking to herself. "Passengers. Shit."

This caused a delay.

Aneka deboarded and Jani heard unintelligible voices on the hangar deck. She already needed to pee, but tried not to think about it—or the cramps in her calves.

Finally, the passengers arrived. She distinguished voices of two men and one woman as they spoke loudly, anxiously. They asked multiple questions until Aneka told them firmly that they would have to give her complete silence while she prepared the craft for *space flight.* She stressed the last two words.

Nicely done, Aneka. That shut up these so-called colonists.

~ *Flashpoint* ~

Even if she resented their sanctioned passenger seats, Jani shared their anxiety. Her heart raced. She felt like she might pass out.

A long series of checks and counter-checks with flight control followed. Then the craft moved. Jani knew the routine.

The floor rolled them into the airlock lift. The outer and inner doors locked, the cabin pressurized, the airlock depressurized and the floor rose, lifting them onto the launch pad outside the ship.

"Spark—HS-18. Cleared for launch. Acknowledge."

"Affirmative. HS-18 ready."

Jani held onto the cargo straps. She began to count as a way to tamp down her fear as the shuttle drive ignited, vibrating around and through her, and the ship sprang to life.

She immediately felt the loss of ship-grav as they lifted away from the *Hyliah*. The ends of the cargo straps floated in front of her aimlessly.

Nausea hit her and she cursed herself for not having foreseen this. There were anti-emetics in her medibag stash, but it was packed away. Her stomach roiled uncontrollably as she listened for Aneka's occasional, brief, staccato instructions.

"Relax."

"Don't fight the G's."

"Over soon."

She knew about G's, but her imagination couldn't have come close. At that point, there were no more instructions. No talking. Just hanging on till it was over.

Jani passed out, rousing again sometime after they'd entered Hearth's atmosphere. She felt terrible—overwhelmed by nausea. Her heart thudded against her chest as if trying to escape.

"Sit tight," Aneka said. "At the airfield, security will check our papers."

What? They were supposed to go directly to the landfill. *Security check wasn't part of a waste run...Shit. The last-minute passengers had changed everything.* That meant more waiting, more cramped muscles, a bladder that might not last and a stomach in full revolt.

As Aneka slow-spiraled down, she said, "You'll feel heavy, sluggish. It'll be your new normal soon, but you won't like it at first. Hold on. We're coming in."

"Blazes!" The word spewed out of her involuntarily.

But no one heard because the other passengers were cursing at the same time.

There was a tiny bump and then all went still until those up front exploded into nervous laughter and exclamations.

Jani swallowed repeatedly, fighting down bile.

The air shifted the minute the pilot opened the hatch.

Heat.

Aneka bustled her passengers out. "Security's coming. They'll check your papers and tell you where to go from here. Please hurry. I'm behind schedule."

Between the bags piled around her, peepholes of light pierced so brightly it hurt her eyes. She squeezed them shut and unbuckled the strap around her waist and shoulders, shifting her position slightly. *Gods, I'm going to vomit.*

The passengers exclaimed about their legs not working properly and being shaky and how hot it was. Eventually, they climbed out, their chatter growing fainter.

I'm going to vomit.

She unstrapped herself completely and pushed on the duffel in front of her. It was strapped down. She reached up and found the buckle, but even loose, it was far heavier than it should have been. She could barely lift herself forward.

Gravity.

She got enough space to shift onto her hands and knees, unable to think of anything but the upheaval in her gut. With great effort she moved forward looking for something, anything she could throw up in. She swallowed and swallowed, but involuntary muscle contractions took over. She couldn't stop it. She vomited on the floor of the transport, feeling immediate, blessed relief at having her stomach emptied. She reached with the back of her hand to wipe her mouth, lifting her head up to face the glaring sun and the silhouetted figure of a security guard looking right at her.

Within hours, she was back on the *Hyliah.*

The return journey was as physically traumatic as the first one, but made immensely worse because of her emotional devastation.

They escorted her to Central Command. She could barely sit up. *If they knew how sick I am, they wouldn't need to dish out more punishment.*

After a long wait, a uniformed guard led her into none other than Commander Ledroit's office. *Why would he take the time to see me? Doesn't he have underlings for this kind of infraction?* She had only seen him on monitors and he somehow continued to look unreal even now that he stood a mere metre from her. Except that he was sweating. Profusely. The cooling transfers were obviously on the blink again.

Neither of them sat down.

"You were recently denied permission to emigrate," he said from behind a ridiculously big console.

She nodded.

"Perhaps you could have appealed or applied again later, but since you took illegal steps, we will not be giving you a second chance. Your image has gone out to every person on the *Hyliah.* The pilots have been warned to report you if you come near the transport bay. The pilot who carried you is on probation."

"Aneka did not know I was on board—"

He held up a hand and said, "Your version of events has been noted, but your word is of no value. Do what you are told or face greater deprivations. We will assign you jobs for which you will receive no credits. We will provide a berth and enough food chits. You'll report to security daily as ordered or face incarceration. Dismissed."

"Might I inquire as to why my application was denied?"

"You may not."

"I should know."

"Do you want me to lock you up?"

"No, Commander. I want to work."

"Considering your family, I doubt that."

Her gut tightened. "Sir, with all due respect, my family's record is clean. My parents and grandparents were and always will be upstanding *colonists,* which is what I consider myself to be —if only I could get the opportunity."

"Your family didn't deserve to be colonists any more than you do." He spit out the words.

~ Flashpoint ~

"Deserve? Ah—" Jani said then stopped, his words confusing her. "What— What do you know about them?"

He turned and, in four broad strides, came around the console. This was so unexpected, and happened so fast, that Jani gasped. He came close enough that she could feel heat radiating from his body.

"Your parents were actually lousy colonists, weren't they?" Ledroit said, between clenched teeth. "Good colonists *survive*. Now get out."

Jani couldn't seem to draw another breath. Her vision receded to a pinpoint and she felt herself rock back on her heels. She bent over to keep from fainting as he called for security to remove her.

Jani had almost no free time after that, but she managed to squeeze in a visit with Ell to let him know what had happened.

He nodded slowly. "I heard, Jani. I wish I could have intervened before this happened. Evidently Ledroit sent a picture of you to everyone."

"Oh right, I forgot. He told me that. I haven't seen it." Jani held up her wrist.

"Ledroit took your comm? That's outrageous!"

His sudden fury made her laugh in spite of her permanent overlay of sadness. "No, no. I—very foolishly—destroyed it the day my application was rejected. Pure, personal stupidity."

He clicked his tongue on the top of his palate several times. "That *was* stupid." He thought for a moment and then said, "Take mine."

Jani stared at him.

"I'm serious." He held up his spindly arm. "I don't wear it anymore. I'm too skinny, and have no use for it."

Jani thought about it. It was true that many of the old folks didn't wear their wristpads anymore. "But..." she stammered, "that's not— Just...no."

He rolled onto his side and reached into the table drawer, but couldn't find it. "See? It's been so long since I wore it that it's way back there. Go on. Dig it out."

As Jani looked for it she wondered if this was yet another situation she'd come to regret. She had to start using better

~ Flashpoint ~

judgement. She found it and handed it to him. "Thanks, but no. If anyone finds out, they'll say I stole it. I'm in enough trouble."

His mouth tightened into a thin line. "I'll make sure that doesn't happen." He tilted his head back and looked down at it through his focal implants, fiddling with it, punching and cursing until it showed the settings he wanted.

He held it in front of his mouth. "Recording...I, Ellery Wilgreen, still being of sound mind, if not sound body, do hereby give this wristpad computer to my esteemed companion, Jani Mendes, for her personal use for as long as she may need it. She doesn't want to take it, but I'm insisting. Life's given Jani one bad lump after another, but she's a hard worker and a good person who should have been allowed to be a colonist as we were all supposed to be. This is my voice as anyone who knows me can well attest to and I am affixing my digital seal to this message and expect that my word in this situation be honoured."

She hung her sign—*Cleaning in Progress*—on the wall beside one of the stalls in the Central Command offices staff lounge.

Outwardly, Jani's life hadn't changed all that much. She still worked all day every day—mostly cleaning toilets. But now she worked without hope for anything better. She often thought of Ell saying that she "burned the candle at both ends." She hadn't identified with it before, but now she did. Every day she felt smaller than the day before.

Jani heard someone come into the lounge. She peeked out the doorway into the small room and saw a woman humming as she made tea.

Another woman, who sat at a small table said, "How can you be so cheery with what's happening?"

"Stop. Nothing's going to happen. Too many alarmists on this ship."

"If a coredrive meltdown isn't something to be alarmed about, I don't know what is."

"Well, they're repairing it, aren't they?"

"Why's everyone scrambling to get their families off-ship then?"

"Precautionary. They'll come back when the problem's solved."

~ Flashpoint ~

A meltdown? Blazes. That's why so many people are leaving? If so, this had been going on for weeks. *How serious could it be?*

Jani longed to pop out and just ask, but of course she couldn't. *But...why not? If something so dire is happening, shouldn't everyone know?* She realized then how long it had been since she'd heard any news. Maybe everyone did know.

Later, Jani was on the glide going from a newly-cleaned toilet to the next filthy one when Ell's wristpad buzzed sharply three times. The same buzz came from the comms of a couple of people nearby. They, she noticed, wore Central Command uniforms.

The message started:

—CONFIDENTIAL—
Priority Alert—Personal Evacuation Order

and ended with a terse order for Ellery Wilgreen to present himself and one duffel bag of belongings to the transport bay for permanent emigration to Hearth.

If Ell had been scheduled to go on-planet—permanently— did that mean everyone was getting a transport time? She checked her own message thread. Nothing. But then, she was never going to get one. Ledroit had promised her that. Would he purposely leave people on the ship if it were going to...explode?

She had a full schedule of work ahead of her, but she also had to get this message to Ell. She dithered in the hallway for only a minute. *Contacting Ell is your priority,* she told herself.

While walking, she pinged Tundé. "It's me."

"You okay?"

"A message just came..."

"I know. Did it come to you?"

"No. Ell."

"Everyone here is checking with their families. Some got it. Some didn't. We're in touch with engineering. They've been sworn to secrecy up to now, but it's gotten scary enough that they're talking. They haven't given up, but it's bad news. This thing's not contained."

"Shit. How much time...?"

"They don't know. Maybe weeks. Maybe not."

~ Flashpoint ~

"It's not general knowledge, though?"

"No. I don't know. It's getting out. Maj has been down in engineering most of the day. There've been fires. Arcing from short-circuits, she said. All these temperature swings have wreaked havoc on the wiring. Hey, I gotta go. I'm due for two runs today...maybe more. We drop people off and come back to do it again."

"That can't be safe."

"We sleep when we can. And Jani? Fuck Ledroit. I'm getting you out of here one way or the other." He told her when he was scheduled to be back on-ship, but added, "Any of the pilots will take you."

She stopped by Central Command on the way to Ell's. She was due for her daily check-in. She didn't know how this was all going to play out, but there was no reason to call attention to herself.

The outer office was always open to the corridor. At the back, a long curved console ran in front of private offices. Usually it bustled with people coming in to do their dealings with administrators who stood behind the console, but today there were no staff. A few people wandered around, waiting for someone to show up.

She stood a moment looking at the empty slots where their ship administration should be, thinking *Ell used to work here.* She walked over, slipped behind the console near the office she usually reported to and flashed Ell's wristpad over the security panel. Her eyes widened as the hatch slid open. *I can't believe that worked.*

She held her breath and peeked inside. Empty. Not only was no one there, it looked as if they'd left in a big hurry. Drawers stood open, trash cans were overturned.

Then, from below and aft, a powerful, deep boom sounded and grew, reverberating and lasting so long that Jani—holding onto the sides of the doorway—found herself waiting, waiting, just waiting for the ship to simply explode into tiny pieces. By the time the noise died away, a sheen of sweat coated her skin.

Jani started to ping Tundé and then realized he'd be off-ship already. She called Maj instead.

"Can't hear you. Hold on." Soon she was back. "Chaos! Get over here! Ledroit's on the manifest."

~ *Flashpoint* ~

"They're all leaving? They haven't even told people what's happening?"

"I know. The rats. Get here. Now."

"Maj, the pilots are their life-line, and you keep the transports running. They need you. Don't take orders from them about how often to fly. Keep safe."

"Good point. One more thing," Maj said, "Hayek's agreed to fire up the colony transport."

"Oh! Will it fly?"

"Hell yeah, it should, with all the tender loving care we've given it. But..."

"But there's no way to be sure."

"Right. Talk soon." She clicked off.

Jani couldn't quite believe it. This was it. Once Ledroit was off ship, who could stop her from going too? But what about everyone else? What about the people who didn't know someone in Central Command or engineering or the transport bay? Her mouth filled with a bitter taste. It was obvious Ledroit never had any intention of evacuating this ship properly.

Ell didn't want to come, but she had insisted. Now he was enjoying himself. All through the trip on his hover scooter from the other corner of the *Hyliah*, he had given everyone a kingly wave as they puttered around knots of scared people in the corridors. While they rode cross-ship on the train, the scooter locked into place, Ell smiled at her and said, "You're coming with me, you know."

She shook her head but said, "We'll see." She didn't feel hopeful about any of them getting off safely. A scorched chemical smell filled the increasingly fetid air. The heat hadn't let up for days.

"You're my *medica*," he said. "You have to keep me alive."

She patted the bag strapped to her leg. She planned on giving it to him as he boarded his shuttle. "I guess it's worth a shot, old man."

He grinned at her, but she couldn't work one up for him. *We are all on the verge of being blown up. What is one person's life?* Living life on-planet had never felt so far away.

When they arrived at the hangar bay, the passenger

entrance in the main corridor was clogged with people trying to get in. Ell's sweet smile and encouraging words helped open and smooth Jani's pathway through them to a small side hall that led to the crew entrance.

"Good gods, would you look at this place?" Ell said, when they got in. It overflowed with people and panic. Staff had set up lines to try and corral people, but they were clearly not being honoured.

"It's okay," Jani said. "You have a place on one of these shuttles."

"I am probably the only one here who is *not* worried about my own skin."

She steered the scooter away from the middle of the chaos toward the pilot's breakroom. *Where Maj and I spent so many hours hovering over The Beast's operational database.* They reached the hatchway which—oddly—was closed.

While Jani helped Ell off the scooter, she turned to look at the huge craft off to her right on the other side of the expansive room. It was a little hard to see through the crowd. The Beast still resided in the corner, but—*Has it moved? Yes! They've turned it toward the airlock.* The colony transport was too large to fit in the shuttle airlock; its own huge sliding doors had, all these years, been a static wall behind it.

Good for you, Maj.

Jani felt a surge of hope.

She was about to go check out the manifest to see how long Ell had to wait, when she saw Maj moving quickly along the catwalk over the colony transport ship. Jani pinged her on Ell's wristpad. It took Maj a moment, but Jani saw her wave and then heard her voice.

"Never so glad to see you."

"Is it running?"

"Looks good so far. Lizzy and the crew are working on it. Get over there when you can, okay? You know it better than they do. I'm putting out one fire after another. Sometimes literally. Gotta go down to engineering and help them with...another crisis. Not sure what I can do, but—"

Jani watched her hurry toward the lift down to engineering. Maj entered and the hatch closed behind her, but the wall of the lift was transparent so Jani could still see her as

~ Flashpoint ~

she stood, waiting for it to start down.

"I'll get Ell situated and then help with the transport," she told her.

The elevator moved downward now. Maj raised her arm high and said, "You're on it when it flies, girl. Shit. Gotta go!"

Jani could see only her head now. "Bye," she said, but Maj was gone.

She turned toward the breakroom door to wave her wristpad over the sensor panel, but a boom sounded from below —like a huge piece of heavy equipment falling over. The hangar bay fell silent.

Shouts rang out from engineering, drowned out by a riotous wrenching of metal-on-metal. Then the deep bass of an explosion thundered and rocked the ship. Jani staggered, clutching at Ell to keep him steady.

Another sound, unfamiliar and ominous, made Jani look back. Up through the lift, a roaring pillar of flame flashed, filling the space.

Fire. Jani had always imagined it being useful and beautiful, *but this...this...* The transparent wall held back the orange flames, then turned black. *This horror...*

"Maj!" she screamed, sprinting toward the fire. "No! Maj!"

Hands grabbed her from behind, at first roughly and then more gently.

"Stop!"

"Come back!"

"Don't!"

"You can't—"

The fire triggered long-unused firewalls. They creaked and groaned, and then with sudden finality, slammed down, shutting off engineering from the rest of the ship.

"The goddamned firewalls work?" she screamed. She could never have gotten to Maj anyway, but with everything else on the ship failing, it seemed cruel, and somehow personal, that they had done their job so abruptly. Jani would have crumpled to the floor in rage and grief, but people were holding her up.

Tundé appeared. He touched her cheek, and brought her into his arms, squeezing her. She felt his tears in her ear as they cried.

But there was little time for grief. The bay had gone from

~ Flashpoint ~

controlled chaos to absolute mayhem. People shouted and pushed and shoved toward the small shuttles. Hayek's deep voice thundered over the speakers, trying to regain control, but no one was listening.

Jani's eyes widened as she spotted something over Tundé's shoulder.

"What?" Tundé turned. "What is it?"

She wrenched herself from his arms and, heedless of the people she had to shove out of the way, ran back to the breakroom where Ell still stood by the hatchway, now open. He was talking to a man in civilian clothes. Jani screamed, "LEDROIT!" and plowed into him, bashing him against the wall. "You're not going anywhere!"

He reacted, grabbing her left arm and, when she didn't immediately relent, twisted it backward.

He's stronger than me. He's going to break my arm. She struggled, but his grip didn't yield.

But she had learned some tricks in seven years of working with occasionally-combative old people. She reached down with her free hand, pulled the ConIMm injector out of her medi-bag, and jabbed it into his thigh.

He squealed and looked down, loosening his grip. That gave her a chance to pivot, hook a leg around one of his, and grab him around the waist. The injection acted rapidly. He was already feeling it, knees sagging.

She looked at Ell, who had an odd smile on his face.

"Help?"

"With pleasure."

He guided the scooter toward her and she pushed Ledroit, who was growing heavier by the second, over the back seat.

While most of the crowd in the hangar bay fought to get closer to the shuttles, some watched Jani. But no one moved toward them. No one seemed to know what to do. Whatever security Ledroit usually had around him was gone. *Maybe already off ship? Or maybe just looking out for their own skin, as Ell would say.* Jani didn't have time to think about it. They pushed the scooter into the breakroom, manipulating Ledroit's head and feet through the opening. She closed the hatch.

Tundé, though, followed them in. He arrived just as Ledroit, his face twisted in rage, said to Jani, "I'll have you

~ Flashpoint ~

killed."

ConIMm immobilized only the large peripheral muscles. He could still talk, hear, see, but he couldn't lash out or walk away. Ledroit was her prisoner...for a little while.

Ell cuffed him on the shoulder and said, "Shut up, Bobby."

Jani ignored him, and turned to Tundé. "Help me put him in the chair. Then find me something to tie him up with."

"Jani..."

"Okay, don't. But find someone who will." She took him by the shoulders and shook him. "We've got to get organized or *everyone's* going to die. Do you get it? The main thing is—" she pointed at Ledroit, "—he and I are definitely going to die on this ship unless he calls for an orderly evacuation of every single person." She turned to the Commander and said, "I have quite enough ConIMm to keep you paralysed for cycles, so you'd better start cooperating. Now."

Tundé—wide-eyed and speechless—left, closing the hatch behind him.

Ledroit made a terse general evacuation announcement within the hour. He handed the speaker to Ell who, consulting a long-ago-devised evacuation plan on the Commander's comm, calmly told inhabitants of each section of the ship what to bring and where to gather.

"Once you are in your interim space, we will give you updates on our progress, to let you know how long you may have to wait. Unfortunately, most of the administrative staff of the ship has left us to fend for ourselves, so we expect all citizens of the *Hyliah* to proceed with dignity and respect for others so that the rest of us may follow them safely to our destination."

When Ell finished, Jani said, "You should have been Commander of this ship."

He waved her off with a modest grin, but then said, "I couldn't have done worse, I guess. Speaking of that," he addressed Ledroit, "where's my granddaughter and the rest of my family?"

"They went weeks ago," he said through tight lips.

"Hmm, nice of them to let me know," he said, looking

genuinely hurt.

Ledroit now tied to a chair, turned to Jani and said. "I've done what you asked. Let me go."

"Not a chance. You and I are the last two off. End of discussion. I have to go help out there, but first, I have to know. What did you mean about my family—that day in your office after I'd tried to stowaway? Did you know them?"

Your parents took my place."

"What?"

"They conspired to jump ahead of me in line. I got left on-ship because of them."

Jani and Ell looked at each other.

So, I wasn't paranoid after all. He did have it in for me.

"*If* that is true—which is highly doubtful—it seems like you should be grateful to them, Bobby," Ell said. "You might have died on the second planet. A lot did."

"And a lot didn't. Your parents," he looked at Jani, "got what they deserved."

Jani wasn't even incensed by this statement. She just felt sad. She started to ask him what any of that had to do with her. Why she had been denied what she'd worked hard for because of some long ago dispute with her parents whom she didn't even remember. But it would be wasted breath. The man was who he was. At least now she understood.

Hayek gave a sobering announcement to the mob.

"Attention! We will commence boarding the colony transport. There is room for everyone here, plus many in the corridor. However, since the *Hyliah*'s Command hasn't properly colonized a planet in generations, the transport has not been flown in recent memory. We do not have time for a test run. It may not make it. You may stay here, quietly moving aside to let others on, or you may go to the transport in an orderly fashion. Give your belongings to the ground crew for stowing and take the next seat in order. Anyone who causes a delay will be removed and put at the back of the queue. The plan is to continue transport and shuttle runs until *everyone* is evacuated safely."

The hangar bay buzzed with fear and anxiety, but now hope was in the mix.

~ Flashpoint ~

Hayek would pilot the ship, with the second-most experienced pilot as his first mate. Tundé, Aneka and the rest of the pilots would continue to do shuttle runs, but nothing would move from the bay until the lumbering Beast, holding a thousand souls, left. With the *Hyliah*'s administration gone, they didn't know how many people were still left on the ship, but they thought two transport runs—along with the shuttles—just might get everyone off in time.

She'd given Ledroit another dose of ConIMm so that Ell could relax, but they still waited in the breakroom. Jani, who knew the inner workings of the transport as well as anyone here, had been helping the crew for several hours.

No one spoke of Maj or the others who had been lost, but they all knew, they all felt it.

Hayek told her he was impressed with the maintenance and restoration she and Maj had done.

"Sir," she asked him, "does Hearth have an airfield large enough for The Beast?"

"We've been in contact about that for days, since Maj came to us about the possibility of its flying. There's a dry caldera in the southeastern quadrant that should do nicely. They're setting up a makeshift landing strip as we speak. At this point, I'm just hoping we get that close." He blew out a long, anxious breath. "You coming with us?"

Jani shook her head. "Nope. Gotta stay with Ledroit. We'll come on the last ship out."

He shook her hand and said, "Maj would be proud of you."

It was time.

All passenger seats on the The Beast were filled. The pilots were in place, the cargo doors closed. Hayek engaged the drives. A rising thrum filled the bay as they spun up in preparation for firing the engines.

Jani stood next to Tundé holding her breath.

It seemed to take forever, but eventually, the airlock doors slid open. A cheer went up and Jani could just make out Hayek raising a thumbs-up. Slowly the floor rolled until The Beast sat in the center of the airlock.

Minutes passed. The airlock doors stood open. Nothing

happened.

"Tundé, what's up?"

He was listening in to the pilot's transmissions. He shook his head at her and then, suddenly, everyone knew.

"Inner airlock door's not closing!" Lizzy called out.

Jani and Tundé ran over as the mechanic opened the electrical panel and trained a pin light inside. Lizzy said something to her crew that Jani couldn't hear. Remote controls brought no response. After several minutes, the woman spoke into her comm device and the pilot shut down the drives.

Jani's ears ached at the sudden quiet. She thought of Ell and his implants. *Maybe that's what it's like for him when he can't hear.*

Hayek, face red from frustration and anxiety, strode from the airlock to the control panel.

"It's gotta be this condensation," someone on the crew said. "The temp's been swinging from hot to cold and back again for weeks now."

"Short circuit?" Hayek asked.

"The doors were cranky earlier," one of them said, "but we got it to open several times. Since then the cold air came back on and it seemed to dry things out."

Lizzy pried off the inner panel. "Dried out the ambient air, but it's wet in here."

"Did it spark?"

"I don't think so, but it's going to. Look at the corrosion."

Ell's implants!

"Hayek?"

"Jani, not now."

She stepped back, but thought again of Ell. Not his ears, but his confidence, his zest, his belief in her. Maj had believed in her, too.

Jani felt herself impelled forward as if by Maj's invisible hand. Scooting past Hayek, she went up to Lizzy. She could hear Maj's brash voice saying, "Speak up, kiddo. Don't hide what you know!"

"Maybe this can help." Jani reached in her bag for the small cylinder of *H-Ear Spritz* and handed it to Lizzy. "It's a nanoagent that dries out the inner ear."

"That's not gonna work," a crewman said. "There's a big

difference between complex circuitry and an inner ear."

"You got a better idea?" Lizzy asked.

"It works fast," Jani said.

Lizzy shook it for good measure, peered deeply into the electrical panel and sprayed it multiple times.

Jani could only think about how it was going to feel when this didn't work. Or, when it did.

Hayek told everyone to get out of the way. Without looking back, he went into the airlock and reboarded The Beast.

Soon they heard the thrumming transport drives.

Lizzy took a deep breath and hit the button for the airlock doors.

They creaked, shimmied, and then slid closed.

A cheer went up.

Lizzy beamed at Jani as she said into her comm, "All readings green, Leader Hayek."

From the observation deck, Jani watched through the scope as The Beast landed for the third and final time. By then, the air and ground crews were experienced at this. The on-planet populace had placed bonfires around the rim of the huge caldera to guide their way in. They made beautiful beacons, guiding the colonists toward their new life.

Life on Hearth would be a challenge, but it was a life. A chance at one.

Jani felt weightless at the thought of all the lives saved.

Only a handful of them remained on the *Hyliah*. Ledroit, Lizzy, Ell, who flatly refused to go without her, Tundé—their pilot for this one last shuttle run—and a few other hold-outs, who now seemed to have changed their minds about planet life as the aging colony ship rapidly decomposed around them.

Jani lingered a moment longer, aware that she would never see Hearth from this vantage point again. Then she turned, took the stairs down—thinking of the crisp clicks that Maj's footsteps had made on them—and ran for the last time down the corridor toward the hangar and the shuttle for home.

~ Flashpoint ~

Nancy S.M. Waldman—for the record—would not be happy living on a starship all her life if she had the choice to be on-planet. Nancy writes short stories and novels. She is one of the founders of Third Person Press, a 2013 graduate of the Viable Paradise SF&F Workshop for Writers and a busy submission reader for *Bastion SF Magazine*. Her stories have been published in *The Nashwaak Review*, *Wild Violets Magazine* and *The Men's Breakfast*. They can also be found in all of the anthologies published by Third Person Press. She's @nuanc on Twitter and her author website is at nancysmwaldman.com.

www.ingramcontent.com/pod-product-compliance
Lightning Source LLC
Chambersburg PA
CBHW071829020726
47502CB00004B/1289